THE FORTUNE TELLER

NATASHA BOYDELL

B

Boldwood

First published in Great Britain in 2024 by Boldwood Books Ltd.

Cover Design by Head Design Ltd

Cover Imagery: Shutterstock

A CIP catalogue record for this book is available from the British Library.

Paperback ISBN 978-1-83533-302-0

Large Print ISBN 978-1-83533-298-6

Hardback ISBN 978-1-83533-297-9

Ebook ISBN 978-1-83533-295-5

Kindle ISBN 978-1-83533-296-2

Audio CD ISBN 978-1-83533-303-7

MP3 CD ISBN 978-1-83533-300-6

Digital audio download ISBN 978-1-83533-294-8

Boldwood Books Ltd
23 Bowerdean Street
London SW6 3TN
www.boldwoodbooks.com

PROLOGUE

What would you do if you were given the choice to marry the man of your dreams knowing it will end in tragedy five years later, or to just walk away from him and live a long, healthy life?

You might say that it's better to have loved and lost than never to have loved at all.

You might say it's not worth the sacrifice, that there are plenty of men in the world but you only have one shot in life and it's too precious to risk something that you may never recover from.

But it doesn't really matter, does it? It's a trivial conundrum, a 'what if?' question that might come out at dinner parties or on long, boring car journeys. It's not real. You can consider it for a few brief moments, give your answer and then laugh it off as theoretical nonsense.

That's what I did. I discussed it with my friends and moved on to other topics, immersing myself in the warm, blissful enjoyment of good food, wine and company. I listened, I laughed, I talked, I ate. I was single and carefree, and I had plenty of other things to occupy my mind. I still had the rest of my life to look forward to and the path ahead was full of possibilities.

In truth, I almost forgot about it. *Almost.*

But now I can't forget. It's all I can think about. It haunts me day and night, extinguishing the light, plunging me into a deep, desperate darkness. It is a curse that has consumed me, eating me up from the inside out until I don't know who I am or who I can trust. It has already cost me my happiness, my relationships, my sanity and what scares me most is that I know the worst is still to come. I ignored the signs and now it's too late. I am in the eye of a great storm, facing terrible danger but unsure whether to run or hide from it. The storm is building up around me, I can feel it. It's determined to destroy everything in its path and I don't know who will survive it. Something very bad is about to happen and yet I am powerless to stop it.

Have I created this? Did I bring it upon myself or am I the victim in a game that I did not want to play and which I do not control? I don't know any more. When I think about that person I once was, the younger version of me who laughed and ate and drank with her friends, unaware of what was yet to come, it's hard to believe it was me. I am no longer the person I was and I don't know if I will ever find my way back. All I know is that all storms die out eventually and only then do you truly know the damage they have caused. It started with a choice and I'm about to find out where it ends. It's nearly time for the clock to stop ticking.

It has been four years and eleven months since I faced this choice. And I married him.

PART I

1

FOUR YEARS AND ELEVEN MONTHS EARLIER

We giggled as we stumbled into the tent, four grown women as giddy as children. The sounds of the funfair, the excitement of the evening, the lights and the painted carousel horses fed our imaginations and captured our minds, transporting us back to an innocent time in our lives.

We weren't innocent any more, though. We were in our early thirties and had experienced too much. We had lived hard, we had played harder, taken reckless risks, and now we were slowly moulding into new people again, grown-ups who had responsibilities and mortgages.

But that night we had freed ourselves from the burden of our daily lives and allowed ourselves to morph into excited girls again as we linked arms and strolled through the fairground, dodging overexcited children clinging onto candyfloss sticks and gaggles of teenagers flirting with each other. We had ridden the carousel and taken selfies for our Instagram grids, we had hooked ducks and scoffed toffee apples until our fingers were sticky. By the time dusk started turning into dark, we still weren't ready to leave. There was an unspoken agreement in the air between us that we wanted to stay in this bubble of nostalgia for a little while longer, reliving our youth. We saw the gaudy fair through rose-tinted glasses that night and we didn't want to take them off.

By chance, we had paused outside a small tent, so unassuming among the other attractions that you could easily miss it. I hadn't given it a second glance but my friend, Emily, had leaned forward to read the sign outside and waved me over. *Unlock the secrets of your future with Mystic Maggie*, I read. *£10 a reading.*

Emily had grinned. 'Shall we go and see the fortune teller?'

I had laughed dismissively, but the truth was that my curiosity was piqued. I'd never had my fortune read and it was an unofficial bucket list goal, like bungee jumping or seeing the pyramids of Egypt, something I wanted to experience once just to say I had done it. There was a tiny sliver of hope too, somewhere deep down inside me, like a schoolchild who knows that Santa isn't real but still wants to believe. *What if they really can read my fortune? What if they tell me what's in my future?*

'What a waste of money.' Helen had scrutinised the hand-painted sign, which was slightly peeling at the edges. 'You know it's all a load of nonsense, right?'

I shrugged. 'Ah come on, Hels, it's only a bit of fun.'

The three of us had turned to Shivani, who had been affectionately known as Shiv for as long as I could remember, to cast the deciding vote and I'd held my breath, hoping she said yes.

'Go on,' she'd said, with a mischievous expression.

A rush of anticipation had run through me as we parted the curtain and piled into the dimly lit tent, stopping in front of a small table. A woman was sitting quietly on the other side and she watched us, her expression blank beneath her red and gold headscarf. Her outfit was just like the fortune tellers in storybooks, and she was covered in heavy gold jewellery, her dark eyes thick with eyeliner and her long jet-black hair falling around her like a river of silk. She was younger than I had imagined, mid-twenties perhaps, and I instinctively felt disappointed, as though her youth made her inexperienced in a practice I wasn't sure I believed in anyway.

Her slender hands gently stroked a crystal ball as she studied us, unsmiling. We all shuffled around a bit, suddenly nervous under the intensity of her gaze.

Shiv nudged Emily. 'You go first,' she hissed.

'Your friends can wait outside,' the fortune teller said, in a voice that was both gentle yet authoritative, and we obediently slunk back out of the tent and hovered by the entrance.

'What do you think she'll tell Em?' I asked.

Helen shrugged. 'Probably that she'll meet a tall, dark, handsome stranger.'

'Poor Mark.' I thought of Emily's short, sandy-haired and jovial boyfriend.

'Or that a great fortune awaits her,' Shiv suggested.

'Oh, that would be nice.'

Helen rolled her eyes. 'You don't seriously believe in this crap, do you?'

'Of course not, it's just a giggle, Hels.'

Helen folded her arms across her chest. 'Well, I'm not parting with my hard-earned money just to be told some absolute bull by a girl who doesn't look much older than my niece. I'm out.'

I looked at Shiv. 'What about you? Still up for it?'

She shrugged. 'Why not? I've spent a tenner on worse.'

I grinned, relieved that she was still game. 'Me too.'

We stood about listlessly, waiting for Emily to emerge, which she did a few minutes later.

'Well? What did she say?' I demanded.

'Apparently I'm going to meet a tall, dark, handsome stranger.'

Helen was victorious. 'I told you!'

But I was still curious. 'What else?'

'I'm going to get a new job opportunity. And my current worries will end soon. The usual stuff they teach you in fortune-telling school. Who's up next?'

Shiv and I exchanged glances. 'You go,' I said.

Shiv grinned and headed in, turning back to wink at us before she closed the curtain behind her. Emily and Helen drifted over to a nearby van selling snacks and drinks, but I stayed close by, waiting for my turn, eager to keep my place in the non-existent queue. Time crawled by and I began to grow bored. My stomach rumbled, reminding me that it had been a long time since lunch and the smell of onions frying from a nearby hot-dog stand tempted my hunger. I felt the first drops of rain start to fall, which I hoped was a passing shower, not a full-on downpour, and I put my hood up over my head. Helen and Emily wandered back over, glancing up at the dark and increasingly ominous-looking sky and pulling out their umbrellas.

'Our dinner reservation is in twenty minutes,' Helen warned.

'The restaurant is only across the park, I'll be five minutes,' I insisted.

'Shiv's been in there forever.'

As if on cue, the curtains parted, and Shiv emerged, shaking her head.

'So?' I asked.

'I'm going to live abroad, apparently.'

'Ooh!'

'It's never going to happen.' Shiv and her husband had just bought a new house to accommodate their growing family as well as her parents. A move to sunnier climes seemed unlikely.

'Well, you never know what's around the corner.' I observed Helen and Emily, who were looking fed up now, the rain and the lure of a tasty dinner dampening the magic of the fair. 'Why don't you three head to the restaurant and I'll follow on in a few minutes?'

Helen was relieved. 'Good shout. I'm ready for a drink. Good luck with Mystic Meg.'

'It's Mystic Maggie,' I replied, but they'd already turned away. I watched them disappear into the crowds and then parted the curtains and made my way into the tent, pulling my hood back down and nodding my greeting at the fortune teller who gestured towards a card payment reader on the table and a sign which read, *no fee, no fortune*. Trying not to feel disappointed by the transactional nature of our interaction so far, I tapped the reader with my credit card and sat down opposite her, smiling. Even fortune tellers had a business to run, I supposed.

'Hi.'

'Hello, Simone.'

My eyes widened in shock at the mention of my name. How did she know? Excitement and incredulity surged through me as I considered the possibility that Mystic Maggie really was psychic. Then I glanced down at my credit card, still on the table with my full name printed across it, and felt foolish for thinking that she might possess supernatural powers.

'What would you like to learn today, Simone?'

'Oh I don't know,' I said with a nervous laugh. 'I'm just curious about my future, I guess.'

Mystic Maggie nodded and then closed her eyes, breathing in and out deeply. Feeling a little awkward in the intense silence, almost as if I was intruding on a private moment, I looked around the sparsely decorated tent, the scent of sage tickling the back of my throat. When I turned back to the fortune teller, she was gazing directly into the crystal ball and her eyes were unfocused. I watched her curiously and waited for her to speak.

'You've had a difficult few months,' she eventually said.

'Yes.' It was true. My father had died suddenly in the spring, and we were all still trying to come to terms with it. Then, when I'd returned to work after a couple of weeks' leave, I'd learned that my colleague had been promoted to a job I'd thought would be offered to me. A month later, I'd been informed that my landlord was selling the beautiful garden flat I rented and I'd have to find somewhere else to live. Mum always said that bad things came in threes, so I was hoping that was the end of my run. But I tried not to read too much into Mystic Maggie's words. I knew that this was the fortune teller's trick, a verbal sleight of hand, to make you convince yourself that their generalised statements were specific only to you.

'Things are about to change,' she said. 'The tide is turning.'

'That's good.' *Whatever*, I thought.

'Good things will be coming your way soon, the stars are in your favour. Something you have lost will be found again. And I hear the pitter-patter of tiny feet in the not-too-distant future.'

It was the last one that really extinguished any hope I'd had that I might learn something from the reading. I had polycystic ovary syndrome and I'd been told that I might have difficulty getting pregnant. If Mystic Maggie had alluded to my health condition in any way, if she'd mentioned a struggle to become a mother, or overcoming adversity in my journey to having children, she'd have had me, hook, line and sinker. But her statements were too generic, based on taking my age and gender and assuming that this was what I wanted to hear. It was like fortune telling by numbers. In any event, procreation took two to tango and there wasn't even a hint of a male admirer in my life, nor had there been for some time.

I sighed with disappointment and, as if on cue, my stomach rumbled again. I was bored now and I wanted this to be over so that I could go and join my friends in the restaurant. The rain spattering against the canvas made the tent seem even more oppressive and the incense was starting to irritate my throat. I shuffled in my seat, preparing to stand up and leave.

'Wait!'

The abruptness of her command made me stop. When I looked at her, she was frowning, like something was troubling her, and I couldn't help being drawn back in.

'What is it?' I asked eagerly.

She was staring into the ball, her eyes almost vacant. 'I see something. A dilemma.'

I fidgeted nervously, unsettled by the change in her tone and the shift in her demeanour. Before I had felt that she was simply going through the motions, but now something seemed different.

'You will face a choice soon, Simone, a very important choice. And what you decide will have a profound impact on your future happiness. You must choose wisely.'

'What kind of a choice?'

She seemed annoyed that I had distracted her, but she answered the question. 'Someone is about to come into your life, someone very important. You will be drawn to this person, you will think that they are your future. But you must be careful. The sword is double-edged.'

I was enthralled now, captivated by her words. 'Who is this person? A man?'

She nodded. 'A man. If you choose him, Simone, he will make you happy, happier than you have ever been. But the happiness will not last, it is destined to end. Five years after you marry, a terrible tragedy will befall you. There is nothing you can do to stop it. It is written in the stars.'

My logical personality told me that there was no way she could see all that in a sphere of glass and yet a shiver still ran down my spine. In that moment it was as though we were the only two people in the world and nothing else mattered, nothing existed.

'And if I don't choose him?'

'Then you will live a long, healthy life. When you reach this crossroads, you will choose your path. But you cannot go back. Once the wheels have been put in motion, there is no return.'

I had so many more questions, so much I wanted to ask her, but her eyes had come back into focus again and she looked away from the ball. 'Time is up.'

I stared at her in disbelief. 'Wait, I'll pay for another session.'

But the fortune teller shook her head. 'There is nothing else I can tell you.'

'What kind of tragedy will befall me?'

She was pale, as though exhausted from her efforts. 'I do not know. Look for the signs.'

Signs? What signs? There was still so much I wanted to know and I was about to push further, to insist that she let me have another reading, but there was a finality to her tone which instinctively stopped me. Whatever spell had been cast over us for a few minutes had passed.

I stood up. 'Okay, well, erm, thanks I guess.'

'Goodbye, Simone.' She had pulled out her phone and was looking at the screen, as though I no longer existed in her world. I watched her for a second longer, confused and upset, and then turned and left the tent, pulling my hood back up as I walked through the driving rain.

Outside, the fairground seemed to be wrapping up, the crowds dwindling from the increasingly bleak weather and the late hour, and I hurried towards the exit, craving the warm restaurant and the easy company of my friends. The fortune teller had affected me more than I wanted to admit and I couldn't shake off her words, which followed me through the park and across the road. *You will face a choice. A terrible tragedy will befall you. Look for the signs.* It was so different to everything else she had told me, all the lines she had fed to Emily and Shiv. It had seemed, in some way, personal.

When I entered the restaurant, the others were sitting in a booth towards the back, a bottle of red and four wine glasses on the table in front of them. I slipped in next to Helen, shrugged off my coat and grabbed my wine glass. When I looked up, they were all watching me.

'You look like you've seen a ghost,' Emily remarked, but her tone was jovial. 'Did the fortune teller summon Elvis back from the dead to give you a message or something?'

'Shh,' Shiv hushed her. I assumed that she thought Emily was being insensitive given the recent passing of my father but, in all honesty, I had other things on my mind.

I shook my head. 'No, nothing like that.'

'So what happened?'

Part of me wanted to keep it to myself, to lock it away in a vault, because saying the words out loud made them more real. But a bigger part of me wanted to get their opinions, and as I took another sip of my wine and relayed what had happened, I was aware of how absurd I sounded.

When I was finished, Helen looked furious. 'That's the most ridiculous thing I've ever heard.'

In contrast, Shiv seemed delighted. 'So, let me get this straight. If you marry the man of your dreams, you'll be happy for five years but something awful will happen, and if you don't marry him, you'll be fine? Wow, that's quite the choice.'

'Don't encourage her, Shiv,' Helen said, scowling. 'How dare this woman say something like that to you? She's a con artist, pure and simple. It's one thing to take your money and deliver you a load of bull, but this is out of order. For the love of God, don't tell me you believe a word of it?'

'Of course not,' I said. 'But it was weird. I don't know, it's hard to explain.'

'It's not hard to explain. She hooked you in because she knows that you're impressionable. She's probably laughing to herself right now about how she's messed with your head. I've a good mind to go back there and give her a serious talking to.'

'You think I'm impressionable?' It was the first time I'd heard this.

'Yes, you're impressionable. It's not a bad thing, I'm not having a go. But seriously, Simone, there's no way on earth that this stupid Mystic Meg has any idea what your future holds. Anyway, think about it logically. If she really could read your fortune, and I'm telling you that she can't, then she'd know what decision you made already, so why give you the choice?'

Everything that Helen was saying made sense and I was grateful to her for pulling me back to reality. I took another fortifying sip of wine. 'It's Mystic Maggie but yes, you're right.'

'I can't believe you let her get to you.'

'All right, Helen, leave it out.' Shiv jumped in to defend me. 'Just because you're not a believer it doesn't mean no one else is either.'

I pounced on this. 'So do you believe what she said, Shiv?'

'Of course not, it's all nonsense.'

Helen nodded smugly. I turned to Emily. 'What about you?'

'Of course it's nonsense. But it's an interesting conundrum isn't it. What would you do, if given that choice?'

Helen rolled her eyes. 'I can't believe we're still discussing this.'

'I wouldn't marry him,' Shiv declared with conviction. 'There's plenty of fish in the sea, you'd meet someone else. I don't believe in this soulmate rubbish.'

I laughed. 'I'll be sure to tell your husband that.'

Shiv grinned. 'Avyaan would say the same thing. What about you, Emily?'

'I agree. I mean I love Mark and all that, but if I knew a terrible tragedy was around the corner, it would seriously mess with my head. I'd rather be single and have lots of cats.'

'Oh for God's sake.' Helen was seething. 'If you're all stupid enough to believe that your life is mapped out for you already, then you deserve to be sad and lonely.'

'So you'd plough on, would you, Hels? If you met someone tomorrow?'

'Of course I would, and I wouldn't give it a second thought.'

'Well, best not date anyone for a few months, Simmy, just to be safe.' Shiv was grinning as she said it though.

'I don't think that will be a problem, given the current wasteland that is my love life.' I looked around the restaurant at all the happy couples surrounding us. 'Anyway, I'm starving, let's order.'

As the bottle of wine ran out and was quickly replaced by another, and the food started to arrive, warming my stomach and satisfying my gnawing hunger, I felt myself relaxing, my earlier anxiety ebbing away as I settled into the evening and enjoyed the company of my friends. Occasionally my mind drifted back to what the fortune teller had said but as the night progressed it became easier to push it away again as my thoughts were consumed with everyday life once more; Helen's foray into internet dating, Shiv's house renovation project, Emily's work dramas. I wished I hadn't gone to see the fortune teller at all, but Helen's words kept coming back to me, reminding me that it was all a scam and that none of it was real.

I was tipsy by the time I hugged my friends goodbye, caught the bus home and let myself into the flat, wishing again that I didn't have to find somewhere else to live in a couple of months.

When I had peeled off my clothes, brushed my teeth and flopped into bed, my thoughts were monopolised with contacting letting agents in the morning and scouring the internet for a suitable home. The fair, the fortune teller and everything else that had happened during the course of the evening were already a distant memory, real life pushing to the fore again.

In the morning, I woke up with a heavy, red wine headache and the sinking feeling that something bad had happened the previous evening. But when, as I tossed and turned, I finally remembered what it was, I was grateful that it was nothing serious. In the cold light of day, after a night's sleep, it all seemed even more ridiculous than it had the previous evening. I thought briefly of the fortune teller again, reminded myself of what Helen had said, and then reached for my phone and lost myself in a world of one-bedroom apartment rentals.

2

I had seen some horrific flats over the last few days but this one took the top spot. As I peered into the small bathroom crawling with damp, I wanted to cry. Was this seriously all I could afford? When I'd moved to London ten years ago, I hadn't cared where I lived. House shares, bedsits, it hadn't mattered to me as long as I was in the thick of it, with the bright lights of the capital right on my doorstep. But as I'd eased through my twenties, my priorities had shifted and the idea of a nice home to call my own had steadily gained importance. I couldn't afford to buy but I wanted a decent rental, a place I wouldn't be embarrassed to show my mother, and I'd lucked out when I found my garden flat in North London four years previously.

But it seemed that while I'd been living in rental bliss, the area, and the housing market, had changed significantly and the realisation was dawning on me that I wouldn't be able to afford anything nearly as nice as what I had now. Which meant that I either had to downgrade or move out of the area, and neither were appealing prospects. I loved where I lived, with my friends close by, shops and pubs on my doorstep and an easy commute to work.

As I took in the 'double bedroom' that barely had room to swing a cat, I considered calling my mother and asking for a loan, but I was too embarrassed. At thirty-two, I was old enough to stand on my own two feet and anyway, she was still getting used to life without my dad and I didn't want her stressing about me too. I hadn't even told her I was being evicted yet and I knew that if I did, she'd try to persuade me to move back home to the Midlands, where housing was more reasonable and I could probably even afford to buy somewhere.

There was less and less stopping me from making the move. I was single, I didn't own my own home and my interest in my job was waning after I'd been sidelined for that promotion. But I still wasn't ready to let go of the life I had in London and moving home almost seemed like an admission of defeat, a step back in time. I'd be returning to the place where I had grown up with nothing to show for myself except for a hundred thousand pounds' worth of wasted rent money.

I was staring at the limescale-riddled kitchen sink and trying to ignore the letting agent hovering in the background when my phone rang and I looked down at the screen to see Helen's name.

'We're going out tonight,' she said without preamble when I answered.

'After the morning I've had, I'm definitely in. Any particular reason?'

'Um, nope.'

But I could always tell when Helen was fibbing. 'Tell me.'

'No reason,' she insisted. 'The Usual Place, seven thirty.'

The Usual Place was a gastropub on a quiet road near Finsbury Park. Emily had first discovered it years ago and we'd been meeting there regularly ever since. We were a bit of a motley crew, the four of us. I'd met Shiv at university, and we'd moved in together after we graduated, sharing a townhouse with four other strangers who quickly became friends, because we had little choice when we all lived on top of each other. Helen, a born and bred Londoner, had been one of them and she had introduced us to Emily, a colleague of hers who she often went out for drinks with after work and invited us along. The four of us couldn't have been more different to each other but somehow we had just worked, slotting into place like a pieces of a jigsaw puzzle.

We had started getting together for drinks on the last Friday of the month, meeting somewhere central to accommodate Emily who lived in Wimbledon, and it had become a bit of a ritual that had survived the test of time. Even when Shiv had got married in her mid-twenties and had three children, she had still tried to make the Friday night drinks whenever she could, gratefully leaving her children with her more-than-capable mother and dragging herself into the West End, where she would regale us with the horrors of early motherhood. Helen had moved to Spain for a year but we had continued in her absence, and when she returned she had fitted right back in as though she had never been away. Eventually, when Emily had left Wimbledon and moved to North London with Mark, we'd relocated to Finsbury Park because it was so much easier for Shiv, and that's when we had discovered The Usual Place.

We still made every effort to meet monthly, but we often got together in between too, particularly Helen and I. Shiv was juggling so many responsibilities that she went to ground for weeks on end and Emily was getting married in a few months to Mark, who she'd been with for years. She'd made no secret of the fact that they were already trying for a baby because they didn't see the point in waiting until after the wedding and I expected we'd see even less of her soon. I loved Emily but she was prone to throwing herself into whatever new thing was going on in her life, whether that was a new partner, friend or project, and I could see her diving head first into married life and, hopefully, parenthood too. Helen and I didn't have partners or children and that afforded us more freedom to meet whenever the fancy took us. I wondered if it would soon just be me and Helen left and occasionally it felt like we were edging ever closer to the end of an era.

'Who else is coming?' I asked her now.

'A few work colleagues,' she said. 'You've met a couple of them before.'

'Emily and Shiv?'

'Both busy.'

'Okay, well I'll see you at seven thirty.'

I hung up and turned to the letting agent, too fed up to be polite. 'It's not for me.'

He shrugged, like he didn't care either way. 'Fair enough.'

As I followed him out of the gloomy flat, I took a deep gulp of fresh air, glad to be back out in daylight again. 'If anything else comes up, give me a shout.'

He nodded with an air of nonchalance which told me that I would probably never hear from him again, and climbed into his Mini, zooming off to, no doubt, another depressing London flat. I turned and began to walk home, peering into the windows of estate agents that I passed to see if there was anything new which, invariably, there wasn't. I decided to stop for a coffee, sitting down at a little window table and absent-mindedly scrolling through my phone as I waited for my drink. Impulsively, I opened my property app and searched for accommodation in Peterborough, wincing when I realised that I could afford to rent a four-bedroom house for the price I was paying for a one-bedroom flat in London.

As my coffee arrived and I plonked a sugar cube into it, stirring it round and round until it dissolved, I considered my options. Perhaps moving home wasn't such a bad idea after all. Peterborough was only a short train ride from London and I worked from home two days a week anyway. I could stay in my job for the time being and commute on the other three days. It was certainly doable until I found a new job closer to home. I'd be nearer to Mum too, which I knew she'd appreciate.

What was really keeping me in London? I'd spent ten years here and they'd been wonderful, but maybe my time was up. All good things came to an end eventually and the connections I'd made were more than strong enough to last long distance. I'd lost touch with old friends back home, but there was no bad blood and I knew through social media that some of them still lived in Peterborough. It would be easy to reach out to them again, and anyway, I'd make new friends if I got a local job. It was starting to seem like an increasingly appealing prospect and, striking while the iron was hot, I finished my coffee and went outside to call my mum.

After exchanging the usual pleasantries, I cut to the chase. 'I'm thinking of moving home, Mum.'

There was a silence and I pictured her, sitting in her usual armchair with her eyebrows raised. 'But I thought you loved living in London.'

'I did. I do. It's just...' Did I tell her about being evicted and risk her getting into a panic, or skirt around it? 'Everything is so expensive here and I've been thinking about buying a place for a while now. I mean if not now, then when? I'm not getting any younger.'

'I read an article in the *Daily Mail* about how lots of people left London during the Covid pandemic for a better life and then regretted it, but they couldn't move back because they had priced themselves out of the market.'

Good old Mum, she was never one to sugar-coat anything. 'That's about people who sold property in London and then couldn't afford to buy again. I don't have property to sell, Mum. And anyway, *I* read an article about people who left London and were extremely happy with their decision. They have more money, less stress and a better quality of life.'

More silence as Mum mulled this nugget of information over. 'There's no chance of running into Jude Law in Peterborough though.'

'Mum, I've lived here for ten years and I've never run into Jude Law. Not once.'

'But you did meet that famous actor though, didn't you?'

The famous actor in question was a man who'd had a bit part in *EastEnders* five years ago and I'd had a fleeting glance of him in the local Waitrose. I'd been so excited at my first celebrity spot that I'd immediately called Mum to gloat. Which was clearly now coming back to haunt me.

'I thought you'd be pleased.' I couldn't hide my petulance.

'Oh, love, of course I'm pleased. You know how thrilled I'd be to have you living close by. I just don't want you to do it for me, that's all.'

'I'm not doing it for you. I mean, you're part of the reason but not the whole reason. I really do think it's time I got on the property ladder and there's nothing keeping me in London any more.'

'And you're sure?'

Was I sure? It seemed to have transformed from a seed of an idea to a fully blown plan in the space of five minutes, but in reality, I had been thinking about it for a while. 'I'm fairly sure.'

'Well, in that case, Anita was telling me just yesterday that her son is selling his house. It's lovely, Simone, three bedrooms and not far from the centre. I'll call her now.'

I could tell that she was brimming with enthusiasm and probably already planning what colour I should paint the walls. I tried to match her excitement. 'That's great! Thanks, Mum.'

'I'll call you back.'

After Mum hung up, I pocketed my phone and decided to go

for a mooch around the shops. I was browsing the window of a gift shop when my phone rang again.

'Anita says you should come and see the house as soon as possible and we can arrange a private sale, whatever that means.'

'Are you serious?'

'Yes, apparently it will save a fortune on fees and you can split the difference.'

'Erm, okay.' Suddenly I was very, very terrified.

'Can you come up this afternoon?'

I thought about my plans with Helen. 'Not today, and tomorrow I have Shiv's daughter's birthday party. What about next weekend?'

'He might want to put it on the market before then. Tell you what, why don't I go and see it tomorrow and I can FaceTime you as I go round? Then if you like it, you can take a day off work and come up.'

'All right. Thanks, Mum.'

'Oh it's my pleasure, Simmy.' My mother was already a woman on a mission and I wondered if she was relieved to have something to do, a project that she could sink her teeth into. My sister lived in Australia and only came back to England every couple of years so, for now at least, my possible relocation was about to become the focus of my mother's world.

As we hung up for the second time, I realised that in the space of two short phone calls, I might have changed the course of my life forever and I couldn't shake off the feeling that I'd pushed down on the accelerator of a car I wasn't sure I wanted to drive. But then I thought of my mum, bustling around with a renewed sense of purpose, finding a chink of light in the darkness that had shrouded her since my father passed. And I thought of getting the keys to my very own home, something that was all mine and couldn't be taken away from me on the whim of a landlord.

Everyone was growing up and moving on. Shiv was already there and soon Emily would be married too. Even Helen, who declared that she had no interest in settling down, was speeding up the career ladder, on the path to becoming a director at the company where she worked. Maybe it was time for me to grow up too. Perhaps it was finally time to go home.

The idea of change made me think of what the fortune teller had said to me at the fair the previous weekend. Her words, which had seemed haunting and poignant in the moment, had crossed my mind a few times since, but with each day of normal life that passed, they became more trivial. Yes, I was at a crossroads in my life but it didn't involve a man and there was certainly no offer of marriage on the cards. No, the fortune teller couldn't have been more wrong. This was about me making a life choice and I just hoped that it was the right one.

3

As I pushed open the door to the pub, I felt nervous about seeing Helen. I adored her but out of all my friends she was the most opinionated, and I was dreading her reaction to my news that I was considering moving back to Peterborough. Not only was I worried that she wouldn't get it, my relocation might feel like a betrayal to her because the two of us were so close. Helen rarely spoke to her family and referred to me as her 'person', the one she could always rely on to be there for her. We had laughed together, and we had cried together. If we were at a loose end on a Sunday afternoon, or we needed a wing-person to accompany us to a party, wedding or other event, we always called each other. But I also knew deep down that she had my best interests at heart and I hoped that she would understand my decision.

I spotted her, sitting at a corner table with a handful of other people, and I glanced around at the faces to see if I recognised any. My eyes rested on a tall, dark-haired man who I'd met briefly at Helen's house party a few weeks earlier. He'd joined the company where Helen worked about a year ago and when she'd introduced us, we'd had a chat that was bordering on flirtatious. But then he'd drifted off to talk to other people and I hadn't spoken to him again.

Helen looked up and waved me over but I gestured towards the bar, holding up my hand to mimic a drink. She nodded and pointed at her nearly empty glass, and I gave her the thumbs up. I ordered our drinks and carried them over to the table, waiting for Helen to move over and make space for me next to her on the bench, but instead she remained resolutely still, forcing me to take a seat next to the dark-haired man, whose name I couldn't remember.

'Hi.' He turned to face me and I smiled politely at him.

'Hi again, I think we met at Helen's party, didn't we?'

'That's right. I'm Jude.'

I thought of my mother's comment about Jude Law earlier that day and stifled a giggle. 'Simone.'

Helen went round the table, reminding me of the names of her other colleagues, most of whom I'd met at some point over the years, and I raised my glass in greeting. After a few minutes of group chat, people started breaking away into smaller clusters of conversations and I found myself trying to follow along to Helen's animated discussion about some work issue that had everyone up in arms.

'What do you for a living?' Jude asked me, pulling my attention away from Helen.

'I work for an insurance company.'

Helen and Emily – and Jude for that matter – worked in advertising and had interesting jobs to talk about. In contrast, there was no way to make my job sound sexy or mysterious. Believe me, I'd tried a few times over the years but the best I could come up with was some controversy over no claims discounts. I usually tried to steer the conversation on to other topics, as I did now.

'How's your job going?' I asked him.

'Yeah it's good, I work with a nice bunch of people,' Jude replied, looking around the table with a grin. 'The work's interesting. It's taken me a while to settle into a large company as I came from a start-up, but I think I'm bedded in now.'

We fell into an easy conversation, mainly discussing Jude's career and some of the crazier advertising campaigns that he'd worked on over the years. Looks-wise, he was exactly my type and I felt self-conscious, a sure sign that I fancied him. His dark brown eyes were drawing me in and I had to stop myself from staring at him too much. At one point he put his hand on my arm and I felt a jolt of electricity run through me. Was he flirting? I hoped so, but I was wary of reading the signs wrong after our previous encounter and I wished now that I'd asked Helen about his relationship status. It was so rare to meet a potential love interest these days unless I actively went looking for one online. I'd done my fair share of internet dating which had provided me with plenty of amusing stories to dine out on but no one I wanted to see again. But even after all the dates I'd been on I'd never felt this instant attraction before.

I hadn't had many serious relationships in the past, either. There had been encounters over the years but none of them had turned into anything long-term. Then I'd had my heart broken a year ago in an unrequited love affair and so had sworn off men for a while. I rarely felt lonely because I had a busy social life, but I did wonder if that would be different if I moved back home. I wouldn't be starting from scratch because I knew people in Peterborough, but in the years I'd been away, their lives had moved on without me. What if I couldn't slot back in again after all?

I finished my drink and stood up to go to the bar again. Helen saw me and sprang up too. 'I'll come with you, it's my round,' she said.

We walked over together, propping our elbows on the bar as

we waited for our turn to order.

'You and Jude seem to be getting along well,' Helen remarked.

I gave her a sideways glance. 'Yes, he seems like a nice guy.'

'You look good together.'

She was definitely plotting. 'What are you up to, Hels?'

Helen looked mock innocent. 'Nothing.'

'Helen,' I warned.

'Fine, fine.' Helen gave in easily and I could tell that she had been itching to spill the beans. 'You made quite the impression on Jude at my party the other week and he's been asking about you at work. So, I thought I'd arrange for you two to meet again.'

My eyes widened in surprise. 'So tonight is a set-up?'

Helen grinned. 'Kind of.'

My tummy gave a little flip. I glanced over at Jude, who was deep in conversation with someone else, and tried to play down my excitement. 'So he's single?'

'Oh yes, very single. Very ready to mingle.'

I giggled, feeling like a teenager. It had been a long time since I'd felt this rush of adrenaline at the prospect of something romantic. But then I remembered that only hours earlier, I'd set the wheels in motion to leave London.

'Helen, I have something to tell you,' I began.

She frowned at me. 'That sounds ominous.'

'I'm thinking of moving back home.' I omitted the part about how my mother had already arranged to view a house on my behalf.

'But this is your home.'

'Well, yes, it has been my home for a long time. But I mean my actual home. Peterborough.'

'Why on earth would you do that?'

'To be closer to my mum. To finally buy my own place. For a better quality of life.'

Helen waved away all my valid arguments, as though they were silly, insignificant things. 'No, sorry, Simone, I don't see it.'

I felt the first stirrings of frustration, but I quickly swallowed them down, anxious to avoid getting into a row with my closest friend and ruining the evening. 'I haven't made my final decision yet but I'm thinking about it. *Really* thinking about it.'

Helen looked at me thoughtfully and I steeled myself for another dismissive comment. But instead she said, 'Fair enough.'

'Really?'

'Sure. I'm not your mother, you can do what you like. Just don't rush into it, okay? Once you go, it's hard to come back. Take your time with the decision.'

'Well, that's the thing, I haven't got time. I have to be out of my flat in six weeks.'

'Oh shit, I forgot about that.'

'So as lovely as Jude seems, even if he asks me out, I'm not sure that it's a good idea.'

'If he asks you out, you're saying yes.' Helen looked forcefully at me. 'Promise me you'll say yes.'

'Hels, why are you so invested in this?'

'Because I have a good feeling about it.'

'I thought you didn't believe in fate.'

'Who the hell's talking about fate? I think you're compatible, that's all. So, promise me.'

I shrugged, knowing that to disagree would only add fuel to Helen's fire. 'Fine. I'll say yes. He probably won't ask me anyway.'

Helen smirked. 'Oh, I think he will.'

It turned out that Helen was right. As we were saying our goodbyes outside the pub a couple of hours later, Jude asked for my phone number and from the corner of my eye, I could see Helen brazenly watching us with a smug expression on her face.

While I waited for the bus home, I smiled to myself as I relived the moment when Jude had typed my number into his phone and then leaned forward to kiss me on the cheek. He'd smelled of aftershave and beer and it had given me a sensation that I hadn't experienced in a long time. I was giddy as I tried, and failed, to stop myself from looking him up on Instagram.

I still didn't know what any of it meant, though. All I could think of in that moment was that things always happened when you least expected it. I'd lived in London for more than a decade and never met anyone of note, Jude Law or otherwise, but just as I was contemplating leaving, a tall, dark and handsome man had entered my life and asked for my phone number.

It was probably too good to be true, I told myself, as the bus pulled up and I climbed on, tapped my card on the reader and looked around for a seat. These things usually were. I clambered up the steep steps to the upper deck, lurching from side to side as the bus pulled away, and found an empty seat near the back. Just as I was sitting down, my phone beeped and I pulled it out and read the message. My heart leapt in anticipation.

Lovely to see you tonight, Simone. Fancy dinner on Wednesday? Jude x

I did fancy dinner on Wednesday. And I definitely fancied Jude. I considered waiting until the morning to reply but Jude had put himself out there by messaging me right away and I didn't see the point in playing games. I hurriedly typed out a reply agreeing to the date before pocketing my phone again with a grin. Then I pulled it out again and messaged Helen.

Jude's asked me out to dinner on Wednesday!

Helen's reply was short but sweet.

Told you.

I rolled my eyes as I typed back.

All right smart arse.

Helen sent a few winky emojis in response and I smiled and put my phone back in my pocket. I was already thinking about what I could wear to the date, where we might go. And then I remembered that tomorrow I would be virtually viewing the house in Peterborough. Could I date someone from London if I lived in Peterborough? Did long distance relationships ever work? But I was getting ahead of myself already, I was high on a few glasses of wine and an evening in the company of an attractive, attentive man. What would be, would be, I decided, but at least I had something to look forward to and I had to admit that it was a good feeling.

* * *

At Shiv's daughter's birthday party the next day, I mulled it over with Helen and Emily over a *Frozen*-themed sponge cake and blackcurrant cordial. I'd filled Emily in on the potential move to Peterborough and she'd been even more shocked than Helen. But after Mum had video-called me from the house she was viewing that morning, I was more confused than ever. The house had been bigger than I imagined, with a large back garden and a home office at the end. The master bedroom even had an en suite and the thought of having all that space was so alluring that I had almost wanted to jump on the first train to Peterborough and make an offer.

But Helen urged caution. 'What's the point in having a big

house if you've got no one to share it with?'

Emily frowned. 'That's a bit harsh, Helen.'

'It's true though.'

I knew Helen's opinion already, but I was keen to hear Emily's. 'What do you think, Em?'

'I can see why it's tempting. And Peterborough's really not far from London at all. We'd still see each other all the time.'

Good old Emily, always looking at the positives. I loved her for it.

'What about Jude?' Helen demanded.

'What about him? We've not even been on a date yet, so it's hardly worth throwing all my plans out of the window, is it?'

'Just don't write him off before you've given him a chance.'

Shiv had drifted over and was listening to our conversation. 'It's a bit weird though, isn't it?'

I assumed she meant Jude asking me out just as I was thinking of leaving. 'I know, but things always happen at inopportune times.'

'I'm not talking about that. I'm talking about our old friend Mystic Maggie. Didn't she say you were going to meet someone soon? A tall, dark, handsome stranger?'

'Actually it's me who's going to meet the tall dark handsome stranger,' Emily piped up.

'Oh for God's sake, don't bring that up again.' Helen was scowling.

But Shiv had replanted the seed in my mind again. 'It is a bit weird, actually,' I admitted.

'Stop that right now.' Helen was almost apoplectic now. 'If I hear one more mention of Mystic bloody Maggie I swear I'll lose my mind. Simone's already looking for an excuse to jeopardise this thing with Jude and she doesn't need you encouraging her.'

'I'm not jeopardising anything,' I said defensively. 'I hardly know the guy. And anyway, why do you care about this so much? Have you got shares in our potential relationship or something?'

'Because you always sabotage relationships before they happen.'

I looked at Helen in shock. 'That's not true.'

'Yes, it is.' She was on a roll now. 'What about that thing with Tom?'

'Tom was a prick,' Shiv said, and I looked at her gratefully.

'What about that other guy then, Mitchell, wasn't it?'

I folded my arms across my chest, now equally seething. 'And your relationship history is a bed of roses is it, Helen?'

By now a few of Shiv's relatives were looking at us curiously, clearly intrigued by this brewing argument. Thankfully the children were too busy being entertained by a magician to pay us any notice.

'We're not talking about me,' Helen argued.

'No, we're talking about me, clearly, and I don't really understand why.'

'Come on, let's not argue.' Emily turned to me. 'What this is really about is that because we love you so much, we don't want you to move away. But *because* we love you so much, we support whatever decision you make.' She looked at Helen pointedly. 'Right, Helen?'

Helen was still scowling but she nodded begrudgingly. 'Right.'

My anger began to dissipate as I understood what had really got Helen's goat. It wasn't about Jude and it wasn't about my relationship history either. It was about me leaving.

'You guys mean everything to me, you'll always be my best friends.' I was starting to well up as I enveloped them all into a group hug and Shiv's relatives turned back to looking at the children, having lost interest in us now that the row was over. 'Promise me we'll never lose touch.'

We left the overtired kids to it soon after that, and as I rode the bus home, I thought about Shiv bringing up Mystic Maggie. It had hit more of a nerve than I'd let on at the time. I thought I'd managed to shake off the fortune teller's strange prediction, but now it was on my mind again and I couldn't resist pulling out my phone and searching for her on the internet. There were plenty of results for Mystic Maggies but none of them matched the woman I had met that evening at the fair. I looked through some social media channels too but to no avail. I racked my brains trying to remember the name of the funfair company, but I had barely even noticed the signs as we had all marched in, already eyeing up the dodgems. Basically, I realised, my chances of tracking down Mystic Maggie were slim to none.

And what good would it do even if I did find her? It's not like she could undo her prediction. *You're being ridiculous and paranoid*, I told myself, and I thought of what Helen would say if she knew I'd just spent the last ten minutes googling Mystic Maggie. She'd probably stage some sort of intervention. But then she hadn't been the one in that tent, sitting across from that odd, beautiful woman, being given what felt horribly like an ultimatum. She hadn't felt what I had felt that evening and I shivered slightly at the memory of those intense few minutes. For a brief, fleeting moment I considered finding another psychic so that I could get a second reading, one which might overwrite this one and set my mind at ease. But I quickly dismissed the idea because two wrongs didn't make a right. It would just be nonsense on top of nonsense.

No. I was a sensible, pragmatic woman and I wasn't going to let anyone mess with my head. Feeling better, I put my phone away and stared out of the window, my mind quickly becoming preoccupied with other issues, such as whether there was time to get my hair cut before my date with Jude and if buying a house in my hometown on a whim was the best or worst idea I had ever had.

4

As I got ready to meet Jude for our first date, I felt nauseous. I always got nervous before a date but this time it was even more intense. Maybe it was because Jude was Helen's friend or maybe it was because I really fancied him. Either way, the butterflies were having a field day in my stomach.

I applied some lipstick and studied my reflection in the mirror. I was wearing a plain black dress which flattered my figure but seemed bland, so I started raiding my jewellery, looking for accessories. I pulled on a chunky bangle and then rummaged around for my gold hoops, triumphantly locating one among the mass of earrings and putting it into my ear. But where was the other one? I frowned as I searched, aware that time was ticking and if I didn't leave soon, I'd be in danger of being more than fashionably late.

After a few more minutes of fruitless searching, I pulled my chest of drawers away from the wall to see if it had fallen down the back. Wincing at the dust bunnies, I stuck my hand between the gap and felt around. My fingers brushed against something metal and I grasped it and pulled it out, staring at it in wonder when I realised what it was. Years ago, the girls had bought me a name necklace for my birthday and I'd loved it so much I'd worn it all the time. But I'd lost it a few months ago and was convinced it had fallen off at the gym. I'd spent ages searching the showers, lockers and gym floor and had been in tears when I had eventually been forced to accept that the necklace was gone. I couldn't believe it had been here all along, gathering dust.

Giving up my earring search, I took the single gold hoop off and put the necklace on, smiling with satisfaction as I looked in the mirror again. It was the perfect complement to the dress and I was so thrilled that I decided it was a good omen. After slipping my phone and keys into my bag, I pulled on my boots and dashed for the door.

* * *

The pub was busy when I walked in and I tried to keep my escalating nerves in check. This was always the worst part of a date, finding the person you were meeting, hoping they were there, hoping you would recognise them, hoping you were going to have a good time. I was only a couple of minutes late in the end and I knew I might have arrived first, but I scanned the room, and after a few moments I spotted Jude towards the back, drinking from a full pint. I took a deep breath and made my way over, silently praying that it wasn't going to be awkward.

He saw me and stood up to kiss me on the cheek. 'Can I get you a drink?'

'It's okay, I'll go, you can get the next one.' I smiled and immediately hoped I hadn't sounded too forward.

But Jude showed no sign of being perturbed and I went to order my drink. A thrill ran through me as I felt his eyes burning a hole in my back and I knew he was watching me. He was just as good-looking as I had remembered, and I was buzzing with nervous excitement.

I returned to the table and Jude smiled at me. 'How's your week been?'

I wasn't sure what to say. It had been a crazy week and we were only halfway in. Mum had insisted I go and view the house in Peterborough before the owner decided to formally put it on the market, so I'd taken last minute annual leave and got the train up the previous day. I had been as impressed with the house as I'd been when Mum had video-called me from it, but at the same time the whole experience had felt so surreal that I had struggled to imagine myself living there. It had felt, fundamentally, like someone else's house which I knew was absurd because every house was someone else's before you moved in. On Mum's urging, I had spoken to a mortgage broker to get some advice and she had told me that based on the information I had given her, I shouldn't have a problem getting a mortgage, but I was yet to make an offer on the house. I just needed a bit more time to get my head around it first. It almost seemed too easy, too effortless.

But I didn't want to say any of this to Jude, so instead I simply replied, 'Yeah, fine – how about you?'

'Not bad.' He took a sip of his pint. 'I'm working on a mad crazy ad campaign for a sportswear brand so there have been a few late nights, but it's taking shape.'

'Ooh, which brand?'

Jude grinned. 'Sorry. I could tell you, but I'd have to kill you. You know how it is.'

'Spoilsport.'

'What about you? Anything exciting going on at your work?'

I snorted. 'Nothing exciting goes on at my work. I'm always a bit envious of people like you and Helen who love your job.'

'What's the dream then? If it's not insurance?'

I smiled shyly. 'You'll laugh.'

'Try me.'

'No.'

'Oh, go on!'

I laughed, enjoying the banter. 'My hobby is writing.'

He raised his eyebrows. 'What kind of writing?'

'Stories. The romantic kind.'

Jude looked enthralled. 'Are we talking happily-ever-after or bodice-rippers?'

I squirmed. 'The latter.'

'Wow, I'm impressed! And where can I read these bodice-rippers?'

'On Microsoft Word on my computer. I've never had anything published.'

'Why not?'

'I've never actually finished one. I just have these ideas and bash out some words and then life, and my insecurities that I'm writing rubbish, get in the way and I lose interest.'

'So what's the latest one about?'

I waved my hand, deeply embarrassed but also strangely compelled to share my fantasy world with Jude and see what his reaction was. I'd always kept my writing to myself and I couldn't believe I was telling someone, especially on a first date, but I was feeling reckless, and I threw caution to the wind. 'Oh, I haven't written in months. But my last plot idea was about a woman who is obsessed with air stewards and makes it her mission to sleep with one from every airline.'

Jude laughed with delight. 'Well, I would *certainly* read that.'

'I bet you would.' I knew I was blushing.

'You should finish one,' he said. 'Submit it to some publishers.'

'Oh, I don't know. Maybe one day. Until then, I'm sticking to insurance.'

'Well, everyone needs it. Tell me, Simone, how long have you known Helen?'

I smiled, glad we were on to less mortifying subjects. It wasn't that I was ashamed of what I wrote, it was that I thought people would laugh at me. I wasn't exactly known for being an extrovert, let alone a fetishist. But then, as Mum liked to say, it was always the quiet ones you needed to watch. And although Jude had laughed, I hadn't been offended, I'd been excited to share my secret with him. I tried to push images of me and Jude in the mile high club out of my mind.

'Helen and I lived together in a shared house with my friend Shiv when we were in our early twenties,' I explained. 'She introduced us to Emily, do you know her?' Emily had started as a receptionist at the advertising agency and worked her way up to PA to one of the managers.

Jude nodded with recognition at her name. 'Yes, I know her.'

'So, anyway, the four of us became a bit of a gang.'

'How very *Sex and the City* of you.'

'Well, with a few less Cosmopolitans consumed, but I'll take the compliment. What about you? Who are your crew, so to speak?'

'Odds and ends really. A couple of guys from school, various work colleagues I've picked up along the way.'

We continued in this vein, chatting about friends and work and moving on to our families. Jude was an only child and his parents, who were divorced, lived in Leeds. He didn't visit them often and felt perpetually guilty about it. In turn, I told him about my mum and how she wasn't coping too well since my dad had passed away. I spoke about my sister in Australia and how I'd been out a few times to see her over the years. And when we'd finished the first drink, there was no question that there would be a second. And then a third. The more we talked the more flirtatious we became until I could almost feel the electricity between us. Revealing my secret hobby of writing bodice-rippers had certainly done its job of breaking the ice between us.

When last orders were called and we finally made our way out of the pub, I realised I was tipsy and that we'd forgotten we were supposed to be having dinner. As if reading my mind, Jude said, 'Are you hungry?'

'Famished.'

'There's a place up the road that does the best chips I've ever tasted in my life. Fancy it?'

'More than life itself.'

'Let's go.'

As we began to walk, I felt the first drops of rain and silently cursed myself for not bringing an umbrella. Frizzy hair on a first date wasn't my desired look. Suddenly the heavens opened and we made a dash for it, laughing as the loud thunder clapped above us and the lightning lit up the dark sky. By the time we reached the takeaway shop, I was drenched.

'Wow, that storm came from nowhere,' I said, hurriedly using a damp finger to wipe under my eyes in case my mascara had run.

'I know. And on our first date too. Do you think it's a sign?'

Jude winked playfully at me, but his joke hit a nerve. *Look for the signs*. The weather had changed so quickly, and the storm had been right above us. Was it really a coincidence?

'You okay?' Jude was shaking off his sleeves.

'Yes, fine.'

'You look cute when you're wet.'

I smiled, distracted. But maybe I was reading too much into this. We'd got caught in a storm, so what? The British weather was unpredictable and it was summer, when storms often struck without warning. It was the wine, making me paranoid, I decided.

I'd feel better once I'd eaten. I looked into Jude's intensely dark eyes and tried to focus on the present.

'There's a bit of a queue,' he said.

'Never mind, there's no rush.'

As we waited, he put his hand on the small of my back and my skin tingled. Storm aside, I had a good feeling about Jude, and I dared to hope that it might be something worth writing home about. *Home.* Immediately my good mood started to vanish.

'Jude, there's something I should probably tell you,' I said.

'Uh-oh, you're married with five children and you thought this was a friendly drink, right?'

I laughed. 'No, nothing like that. It's just, well, I might be moving back to Peterborough.'

'When?'

'In five and a half weeks.'

'That's very precise.'

'That's when I have to be out of my flat. My landlord is selling and I've been given my marching orders.'

'So you're looking for places in Peterborough?'

'I'm thinking I might buy somewhere, so my plan is to move in with Mum while the purchase goes through.'

'Sounds like your mind is made up.'

'Well, it's eighty per cent made up. I wasn't going to say anything. I know we've only just met and I don't want to come on heavy. I just thought you should know.'

Jude nodded. 'Thank you for telling me. But a lot can happen in five and a half weeks and right now, all I really care about is tonight. So, if it's okay with you, let's not worry about the future yet and just enjoy the present?'

I couldn't have put it better myself. 'Starting with some chips. Which, by the way, had better be as good as you're promising, otherwise I'll be fuming.'

'Trust me, Simone, they are going to change your life.'

* * *

The chips didn't change my life but when I woke up the next morning, I wondered if Jude had. The date, the flirting, the lingering kiss outside the Tube station when we said goodnight had left me giddy. It had been one of the best dates I'd ever been on and I was already thinking about when I might see him next.

As I got up and made a coffee, my mind drifted to Tom, the last person I'd dated and the unrequited love who had broken my heart. We worked together and I'd had a huge crush on him for ages. He was movie-star hot and immensely charming to boot, and I had spent many hours mooning over him and showing the girls pictures of him on social media. But I had assumed that my crush was not reciprocated until we kissed at the work Christmas party and he asked me out for a drink. I'd immediately convinced myself that he was the man for me. Although I learned the hard way that Tom wasn't on board with my daydreams of marriage and happily-ever-afters.

Looking back, I think that although part of the reason was because I fancied him, the other part was because I was starting to feel the biological clock ticking, even if I didn't want to admit it. And Tom ticked all the potential husband boxes. This blinkered view had made me ignore some obvious red flags, like when he refused to show me any affection at work or tell people we were dating. Or when some colleagues had come into a pub where we were having a post-work drink and he'd slid so far along the bench away from me that he'd almost fallen off. Eventually, after three months of staring at my phone, waiting for him to text and feeling like all my Christmases had come at once whenever he did, he'd called it off and I'd finally realised that to Tom, I was a casual fling and nothing more.

The whole experience had bruised my pride, and my confidence, considerably, and after that I'd sworn off men for a while. I'd found that I didn't miss them. But with Jude, things already felt different, and I had to warn myself not to get carried away because it had only been one date.

Helen called as I was on my way to work. 'How did it go?' she asked.

'Good. Really good.'

'Knew it.'

'Yeah, yeah.'

'So, when are you seeing him again?'

'I'm not sure yet, Hels, it's not even been twelve hours since our last date finished.'

'Oh, I bet you'll hear from him by the end of the day.'

I frowned. 'Don't you dare go harassing the poor guy at work, Helen.'

'Oh, for God's sake woman, get a grip, I wouldn't dream of it.'

I was grinning as I hung up and walked down the steps into the Tube station, and my smile stayed with me all the way to the office. It was quickly wiped off my face when I entered the kitchen to make a cup of tea and almost collided with Tom. We worked in the same office, although thankfully in different teams, so we did bump into each other and were always polite. But I tried to avoid him wherever possible to protect my bruised heart and ego, and I didn't like being caught off guard.

'Gosh, sorry, I was miles away.' I hated how I was instantly apologetic around him, even though – as Shiv had said – he was the one who was the prick.

'Simone, it's good to see you. Actually, I was hoping to bump into you.'

He was? 'You were?'

'Yeah.' Tom flashed his devastatingly handsome smile. 'I've been thinking about how things ended between us last year.'

Terribly, I wanted to say, *because you led me up the garden path.* But I maintained a dignified silence.

'I was going through some stuff,' he said, running his hand through his hair. 'Some pretty mad stuff and I realise now that perhaps I wasn't really fully there, you know?'

This conversation was going from strange to stranger. 'Oh, I didn't know that.'

'Anyway, I just wanted to say sorry. And if you ever fancy going for a drink, well, I'd like that.'

By now I was speechless. An awkward silence ensued as I struggled to muster up some words. Eventually, for want of anything better, I said, 'Oh, um, thanks.'

Tom nodded, touched my shoulder lightly, and left the kitchen. I turned and watched his retreating back in shock. What was it with men? Nobody asking me for a drink for ages and then suddenly two. Perhaps I should consider relocating to another city more often.

I could go for a drink with Tom if I wanted to, I supposed. Jude and I had only been out once and were far from exclusive. But did I really want to open that can of worms again? For a start, Shiv would kill me. And I'd probably be setting myself up to have my heart broken all over again. I'd done enough moping about to Celine Dion to last a lifetime. I wondered what 'stuff' Tom had been referring to. A nasty break-up perhaps? Would that really explain his lack of affection towards me, his reticence to acknowledge our relationship? Or what if it was something even worse? A tragic loss? A secret drug addiction? Life in insurance wasn't exactly hedonistic but it could be stressful. Part of me felt sorry for Tom and wanted to see if he was okay. Another part was still angry with him for making me feel so insecure when we were dating. And I was also suspicious about why he had asked me out again now. Had he realised he'd made a mistake in ending things or was it because he'd had no better offers? Did he just want a casual hook-up?

It annoyed me that I was even considering saying yes. As I waited for the kettle to boil, I closed my eyes and thought of the previous evening, the taste of Jude's lips on mine as we kissed goodbye. The bashful grin on his face as I'd walked away and then glanced behind my shoulder to see him still watching me. The way I'd felt when I woke up that morning.

And then I thought about Peterborough and it was all such a confusing, messy jumble that I no longer wanted to think about anything. I wanted to bury my head in the sand and come out when it was all resolved. I made my tea and took it over to my desk, looking forward, possibly for the first time in my life, to losing myself in the heady world of terms and conditions.

5

A bright shaft of light shone directly onto my face, rousing me from sleep, and I covered my eyes with my hand and groaned. 'What time is it?'

Jude was lying on his side, watching me. 'A little after six.'

'What's wrong with you? Why don't you have proper curtains like any decent person?'

'I like to wake naturally.'

'So do I. At seven thirty.'

'Look at it this way, the earlier we wake up, the more time we have for you know what. So how about you're the passenger and I'm a flight steward for Horny Airlines?'

I slapped his arm playfully. 'Sod off.'

He reached a hand out and started stroking my arm gently, almost tickling me, and I felt the effects of sleep rapidly wearing off, my senses already heightened.

Jude and I had been dating for three weeks, barely any time at all, but we'd seen each other so often that it felt like much longer. I guess it was what people might call a whirlwind romance, which was something I'd never experienced and I was intoxicated by it, the newness of it, the excitement, the gloriously hopeful feeling that this might be something special. We were at that heady stage of wanting to rip each other's clothes off all the time and my early revelations about my writing had certainly given Jude some ideas in the bedroom. But, somehow, it wasn't embarrassing, it was liberating and I had never felt so comfortable with, or excited by, a man before.

We'd just spent the weekend together and we'd been for a pub lunch and a long walk, had a takeaway and generally just enjoyed being around each other. I was having brunch with the girls later that morning and I was half excited about seeing them so I could spill the beans on my blossoming relationship and half dreading being away from Jude, even for a few hours.

There was something nagging at me though, something lurking at the back of my mind, reminding me that life wasn't quite the plain sailing that I wanted it to be. In two and a half weeks I had to be out of my flat and I still hadn't decided what I was going to do or where I was going to live. Poor Helen was having kittens on my behalf at my lack of planning, but I was taking burying my head in the sand to new levels and I was enjoying my blissful denial. I'd decided not to make an offer on the house in Peterborough, telling my mum that it felt too soon to commit to something so big when I hadn't even viewed other properties in the area yet and she had accepted my decision without argument, even though I had sensed the flatness of her tone. She had soon rallied though, realising that it actually made the project, as she called it, a longer term one, giving her more work to do, which she embraced as though it was her dream job. Since then, she'd been sending me links to properties for sale almost daily and had visited pretty much every estate agent in the area to register her details.

I was fast running out of time to find somewhere to rent in

London and although I was sure that one of my friends would offer me a spare room or sofa, I didn't want to impose on them, not for more than a few days, anyway. I'd half hashed out a plan that I could stay with Mum for a while and commute into London, which gave me a chance to see if moving to Peterborough long term was the right decision, but the idea of being so far away from Jude did not appeal. In fact, the idea of being away from London full stop was becoming less appealing. It was like I was seeing it through new eyes again because I had someone to share it with. Jude and I had eaten out at restaurants, visited an art gallery and got last-minute tickets to a comedy night and I was falling in love with the city all over again. Or maybe it was Jude I was falling in love with. Either way, I knew I had to decide soon because the clock was ticking.

But Jude was stroking my stomach now, making my skin tingle and I pushed the thoughts of my imminent homelessness to the back of my mind and allowed myself to let go and enjoy the moment. I'd worry about the future later.

It turned out that later was in five hours' time. I'd met the girls at a café and after ordering our food, Helen launched into her interrogation.

'So where have you been hiding away, young lady? We haven't heard from you in ages.'

I grinned, half apologetic, half shameless. 'Jude and I have been spending a lot of time together.'

Helen studied my flushed cheeks and my shining eyes. 'You're smitten. You're a smitten kitten.'

'Is it too much?' I really wanted to know what my friends thought. 'Am I rushing in too quickly?'

Helen shook her head. 'I'm all for it. What's the point in wasting time? If it feels right, do it.'

I turned to Shiv and Emily who had been listening to the

exchange but up until now hadn't offered their opinions. 'What about Tom?' Emily asked. 'Is he still on the scene?'

Emily knew how into Tom I'd been and how crushed I'd felt when I realised that my feelings weren't reciprocated. 'We've chatted a couple of times at work, but I didn't take him up on the offer of a drink. To be honest, I'm too into Jude now to even contemplate it.'

'It might be worth hearing him out though. What if he's the one for you after all?'

'Tom's a player,' Shiv said forcefully.

Emily shrugged, conceding. 'As long as you're happy, that's all that matters.'

We all turned to Shiv, who had brought along two of her children and had been alternating between listening to the conversation, mopping up spilled drinks and telling them to turn their iPads down. 'I think it's brilliant. This Jude sounds like decent guy and you deserve one of them. I just wonder how it'll work when you move to Peterborough in a couple of weeks.'

'*If* she moves,' Emily interjected. 'And even if she does, it's not like she's going to Timbuktu. It's only up the road. She can still see Jude all the time.'

'So, the burning question is,' Helen said, 'are you moving?'

I put my head on the table. 'I don't know!'

'Have you written a list?' Emily suggested. 'Pros and cons?'

'Nope.'

'Let's do it now.' Emily pulled a notepad and pen from her bag, always efficient after years of being a PA. 'So, what are the pros of moving?'

'I'll be closer to Mum. I can afford to buy my own place.'

Emily jotted them down. 'What else?'

'Erm...' I thought hard but nothing else sprang to mind. 'Let's do the cons and we can come back to the pros when I think of something more.'

'Okay, so what are the cons?'

'I'll be leaving London, which I love, I'll be further away from you lot, and I'm not sure if it'll affect this thing I have going with Jude.'

Emily wrote all this down and then chewed the top of her pen. 'I mean, on first glance, there are more cons than pros.'

I grimaced. 'I know. But what if it doesn't work out with Jude and I wish I'd taken the plunge when I had the chance? If I rent somewhere in London, I'll be tied in for a year. And Mum's not getting any younger. With her only other child in Australia, I feel a sense of responsibility.'

Shiv, whose parents lived with her, said, 'I get that. But your mum would want you to be happy. And you can go up and see her all the time, she's only a train ride away.'

'We could talk about it for hours and we'd just go round in circles. I have no idea what to do.'

'Trust your gut,' Shiv said soothingly. 'It'll tell you what to do.'

'Me and my gut fell out during the whole Tom debacle, and we've not been speaking since.'

After brunch, I hugged the girls goodbye. Shiv was off to the cinema with the kids, Emily to a wedding dress fitting and Helen to meet a woman she'd recently started seeing and was being extremely coy about. I was intensely curious about this, as Helen was usually an open book, but I knew her well enough not to pry. She'd tell us when she was ready.

I was considering going home and scouring the internet for flats to rent in North London when my phone rang and I smiled when I saw it was Jude.

'Hey, how was brunch?'

'Great, thanks. I've just left.'

'Want to go see a film at the Everyman?'

I did want to go see a film, especially with him. But I was conscious that I had other things to be getting on with and I was worried that if I spent too much time with Jude, he might lose interest. Quickly, I told myself to stop overthinking. We were too old for mind games and playing hard to get. We liked each other and we enjoyed spending time together and if it was meant to be it would be. If it wasn't, then better to find out sooner rather than later.

'Sounds great, what time shall we meet?'

We made the arrangements and I pocketed my phone, turning my face towards the sun and enjoying the feeling of it on my skin. I had a couple of hours before I was due to meet Jude so I decided to head to Priory Park and sunbathe for a while, convincing myself that I could look for flats on my phone at the same time and then I wouldn't feel so guilty about the day being a write-off. I walked down the road, past the townhouses and the families on their way to Crouch End Broadway for lunch or to go shopping, and slipped in through the black metal gates into the park, finding a grassy spot and sitting down with a satisfied sigh. The grass was dry enough that I didn't need a blanket and I lay back, shielding my eyes from the sun, and felt the effects of a big brunch and the warm sun starting to take effect. Within a few minutes I was dozing off.

'Simone?'

I opened my eyes with a start and saw Tom looking down at me. 'Tom, what are you doing here?'

'I was just out for a walk.'

I frowned. I had never been to Tom's place, he'd always come to mine when we were dating – another red flag – but I was sure he lived in East London. 'What brings you over this way?'

'I'm thinking of moving to the area, so I thought I'd mooch around and check it out.'

Fair enough. 'Finally had enough of those slobby housemates you were always complaining about, have you?'

Was it me or was he wincing slightly. 'Yeah, something like that.'

'Well, enjoy your mooch.' I smiled at him and was about to close my eyes again when I sensed he wanted to say more.

'Do you fancy showing me around? I don't know this area very well.'

It was a reasonable question but I felt strange about it. Was it disloyal to Jude if I spent time with Tom? Did I even want to spend time with Tom? But then I thought about what he'd told me, about going through a difficult time, and I relented. 'Sure, why not.'

He reached out a hand to help me up and I took it, getting to my feet and brushing the grass from my dress and legs.

'Where shall we start?' he asked.

'Have you been to the Broadway yet?' When he shook his head, I said, 'Let's start there. Just so you know, I only have an hour or so and then I've got to be somewhere.'

'Anywhere exciting?'

It felt premature to say that I was meeting my boyfriend, and too much information to say that I was going on a date, so instead I just replied, 'I'm going to see a film. So, what made you think that you wanted to live in Crouch End?'

'I've heard good things about it and it's time for a change.'

'Won't you miss East London? It's very trendy.'

Tom smiled. 'Maybe I'm getting too old for trendy.'

'Nah, you're never too old for trendy. To be honest, I'd love to live round here myself but I just can't afford it.'

'You don't live far from here though?'

'Yes, but I have to leave, the landlord is selling.'

'Oh, when do you have to be out by?'

I pulled a face. 'Two weeks.'

'Where are you moving to?'

'I don't know.'

Tom looked at me with incredulity. 'You've got two weeks and you still don't know where you're moving to?'

'I don't even know which city I'm moving to.' I explained my situation to Tom, remembering that, although he was a prick, he was a charming and easy to talk to prick.

'So let me get this straight. You're being evicted in two weeks. You may or may not be moving to Peterborough. And you're seriously not stressed out by all of this?'

'Well, I might be a *bit* stressed out.'

Tom regarded me. 'You don't look stressed out.'

I grinned. 'I hide my feelings well.'

'Maybe we should get somewhere together? Save a bit on rent?'

I looked at him in horror. 'You're joking, right?'

He was poker-faced for a few moments and then his face broke out into a grin. 'Obviously.'

'Phew, you nearly had me there, Tom.'

We walked around for a while and I showed him the best cafés and restaurants, and the roads closest to the train station for commuting. With the beautiful sunshine and Tom's easy company, time passed quickly and when I looked at my watch, I realised that I should have left already.

'Sorry, Tom, I've got to dash or I'll be late for the film.'

'No worries. Thanks for showing me around, Simone. It was good to see you.'

I hesitated, wondering if I should hug him or something. I wasn't sure if this hour we'd spent together meant that we were friends now. We'd got along well, although we'd stuck to light topics and hadn't delved much deeper than the state of the London rental market. In the end, I settled for what I hoped was a warm smile and then I turned and left.

What a coincidence, I thought, as I walked towards the station, that Tom should be looking to move to Crouch End. But it was a popular area and if he really was looking for a fresh start, it was as good a place as any. I wondered again what had happened in his past, what it was that had made him – by his own admission – so reluctant to commit when we were dating. But then I glanced at the time again and, worried about being late to meet Jude, picked up the pace until I was half running to the station, all thoughts of Tom forgotten.

6

It was a week later when I finally got the fear. Jude and I were having coffee in bed when it occurred to me that in ten days' time I'd be out of my flat and I hadn't even started packing, let alone decided where I was going to live.

'Do you fancy getting a Sunday roast today?' Jude asked, looking up at me from the newspaper he was reading.

'I'd better not. I need to start packing. I need to find somewhere to live! What's wrong with me? Why have I left it to the last minute?'

Jude and I had discussed the issue a few times over the past few weeks, but I'd always given a vague answer and changed the subject, reluctant to let it tarnish the moment. Now though, I realised that the time had come to grow up and sort my life out.

'Why don't you just move in here?'

I turned to him in surprise. 'Here?'

He nodded. 'Yeah. You spend most of your time here anyway.'

My goodness, it was tempting. The idea of waking up next to Jude every morning, of going to sleep with him every night. I'd never lived with a man before and I couldn't think of a better one to make my cohabitation debut with. But there was one, rather glaring, problem.

'Jude, we've only been together for four weeks.'

'I know. But I just think, life is short. And when you know, you know.'

He knew. He *knew*! What did he know? That I was the one? That he loved me? That I wouldn't complain if he left the toilet seat up? All of the above? My mind was all over the place, my heart pounding. It would be so easy to say yes, to let myself get swept up in the whirlwind but I still had one tiny little toe on the ground telling me that this was crazy.

'It's tempting,' I admitted. 'Really tempting. But, moment of truth, Jude, I really like you and I don't want us to mess it up by moving too fast.'

'Fair enough. Look, the offer's on the table, so just think about it. If you decide it's too soon then I'll totally respect that. But if you move back in with your mum in Peterborough, does that mean that I'll have to sleep in the spare room when I come and stay?'

I laughed, relieved that he'd made things easy for me. 'Mum's not that old-fashioned. I'm sure you'll be allowed to share with me. Although thinking about it, she still has my bed from when I was a teenager and it's much smaller than this one.'

'All the better to cosy up in. Do you still have boy band photos all over your walls too? Will I be sleeping under the gaze of New Kids On The Block?'

'Actually it was Westlife. I'm younger than you, remember? But no, she took them all down ages ago. It's some sort of pastel colour now.'

'How chintzy. Well, wherever you are, I'm looking forward to visiting.'

'Do you know what, let's have that Sunday roast. I can go back to the flat and start sorting out my life after that.'

'Want a hand? I can help you pack.'

'Sure, thanks Jude.'

'But first let's work up an appetite for lunch.'

Jude rolled on top of me and I laughed, temporarily pushing my panic to the side as he leaned down and kissed me. It was a few hours later, after we'd enjoyed a delicious lunch, followed by a stroll back to my flat, our hands clasped together, that I had a eureka moment. I'd found someone I adored and he felt the same way. What was the point in denying it? And if it all went kaput then at least I could say I gave it my all. It wasn't about my imminent eviction, it was about him. Jude. A person I was quickly, and deeply, falling for.

'Oh sod it, let's move in together.'

He turned to me with a wide grin. 'Really?'

'Really.'

'I haven't pressured you into it?'

'Not at all. If anything, it'll be me doing the pressuring when you see how much crap I've got at the flat.'

Jude picked me up and swung me around and I laughed, euphoric. 'This is the best news,' he said, putting me carefully back down on the ground again. 'Hello, roomie.'

'Hello right back at ya, roomie,' I replied, burying my face in his shoulder and inhaling the warm, masculine scent of him. In that moment, I was certain that this was the right thing to do.

My warm glow lasted for a few hours, as Jude and I went back to my flat and began the slow, arduous process of sorting out my things. I quickly realised that I'd have to sell or get rid of a whole bunch of stuff because not even half of it would fit in Jude's place. But I found I didn't care. I am not a sentimental person and all I really needed was the basics and I'd be grand. With Jude's help I arranged for a charity collection in a few days and started singling out things I wanted to take with me – my clothes, shoes and jewellery obviously, books and photo albums, one armchair that I'd bought at a flea market and loved with all my heart, and some wine glasses the girls had got me for my thirtieth. Other than that, I was happy to say goodbye to the rest. It was the start of a new adventure and one which I couldn't wait to go on.

But when Jude left and I was alone in the flat again, surrounded by piles of things, I realised that I had to break the news to Mum. Immediately I was overcome with guilt and wondered if I was a terrible daughter for letting her down. Mum knew I was seeing someone but she had no idea how serious it was because I'd only mentioned a few dates. I imagined calling to tell her the news that, not only was I staying in London after all, but I was moving in with someone I'd only known for a few weeks. She'd probably be hurt and worried in equal measures and the prospect filled me with unease. But there was no point hiding from the truth any longer, it was time to confront it. I'd made my decision and now I had to face the music.

I located my phone and called Mum. But as soon as I heard her voice, I started to waver, and I had to fight to keep my voice steady.

'Mum, I've got something to tell you.'

'What is it? Is everything okay?'

'Yes, everything's fine.' I hesitated before blurting it all out. 'Listen, Mum, you know this guy I've been dating? Jude? He's asked me to move in with him and I've said yes.'

A long silence followed and I braced myself for what was to come, while simultaneously hating myself for letting Mum down. When she finally spoke, though, she sounded inquisitive rather than angry. 'I didn't realise things were so serious between you.'

'I'm sorry, I never really said, it's all happened so quickly. But he's a great guy, Mum, he makes me so happy. I want to give it a go and I'm really, really sorry.'

'What are you sorry for, love?'

'I told you I was moving home and now I'm going back on that. I'm a terrible daughter.'

'Oh, Simmy, all I want is for you to be happy. And if this Jude makes you happy then I'm delighted for you.'

'Really?'

Mum laughed. 'Don't sound so surprised. Did you know your father and I got engaged after six weeks?'

'No! I never knew that! Why didn't I know that?'

'I guess we never really talked about it. Or maybe we did and you've forgotten. Anyway, I was working as a waitress at Molly's in town, and in he walked, as bold as brass. I couldn't stop staring at him as I took his order, and when I took his food to him, I nearly dropped it all over him I was so nervous. It was love at first sight, Simmy, but I had no idea he felt the same.'

'How did you find out?'

'After he'd paid the bill and left, I went over to pick up my tip and he'd written his name and phone number on the receipt. Well, I called him that very evening and we went out together the next day. The rest, as they say, is history.'

'Oh, Mum, that's very romantic.'

'So you see, Simmy, I know you were expecting me to disapprove of this sudden decision of yours but I say go for it. And maybe pop up to stay a little more often, bring your new fellow.'

'I'd love to, Mum. We'd love to.'

We. I was part of a we now and the best thing was that Mum understood. After weeks of uncertainty, everything was slotting into place and I was as high as a kite.

'What about next weekend?' Mum suggested.

'Next weekend I'll be packing up the flat and the following one I've got Emily's hen do. But how about the last weekend of the month? We could get the train up Friday and stay until Sunday?'

'That would be lovely. I'll look forward to it.'

I put the phone down and smiled, ridiculously relieved at how well the conversation had gone. Deciding to bite the bullet, I opened the group chat between me, Helen, Emily and Shiv and furiously typed out a message.

So, Jude's asked me to move in with him, and I've said yes!

I stared at the phone, waiting to see if the ticks would turn blue to show that everyone had read the message. Within less than a minute, I saw Shiv was typing.

OMG! You two move mad, I love it! Congratulations hun xx

I grinned and waited to see if Helen or Emily would reply but there was no response from them. After a minute or two, I put my phone down and turned to face the piles of things again. All of a sudden, sorting out and packing up the flat didn't seem like such a horrible chore. Not when I had something so exciting to look forward to on the other side.

* * *

A few days later, I bumped into Tom in the kitchen at work again. He was making a cuppa and he gestured at the kettle and held up a mug, silently asking if I wanted one too.

'That would be lovely, thanks. Milk, no sugar.'

'I remember.'

'How are you?' I asked him. 'Found anywhere to live yet?'

'I've got a few viewings lined up this week. How about you?'

'Oh, um, yes.' Surely, now that me and Jude were moving in together, I could call him my boyfriend? And maybe it would be good to let Tom know, just in case he still harboured any ideas of something happening between us. It would cement whatever this thing between us was firmly as a friendship. 'I'm moving in with my boyfriend, actually.'

Tom raised his eyebrows. 'I didn't realise you even *had* a boyfriend.'

'We've not been together long, it's all a bit of a whirlwind,' I said, wondering why I was trying to justify it to Tom. What was this hold he had on me that made me so apologetic all the time? There was something about ridiculously good-looking men, I decided, a quality they possessed that seemed to turn women into mush. Not that I fancied him any more, I reminded myself, which meant that I just needed to relax and be myself around him.

'Well, congratulations, I guess.'

He looked a little deflated and I wasn't sure if it was because he genuinely fancied me or he was nostalgic for a relationship of his own. I concluded that it was probably the latter because the way he'd acted when we were dating, issues or no issues, had been tepid at best.

'What about you? Any women in your life at the moment?' I don't know what possessed me to ask, other than a desperate need to make conversation.

'No. There was someone. It didn't end well.'

Ah, I thought. So that was it after all, the difficult time he'd been referring to. Tom and I had dated last year and I immediately wondered if there had been any overlap with this person. That would certainly explain a few things. And what if it was someone from work? I mentally ran through a list of potential people it could be. Maybe Sophie from accounts. I'd seen her talking to Tom at the water cooler several times. But it could easily have been someone he met online, or through friends, and anyway, what did it matter now that I was with Jude?

'I'm sorry to hear that. If you ever want to talk about it, I'm here.'

Tom looked at me, his expression sad. 'Thanks, Simone. Hey, congratulations, I'm happy for you.'

'Cheers.'

I took the tea he was proffering, waved goodbye and headed to my desk, stopping when I saw a bouquet of flowers resting on my keyboard. I looked around the room self-consciously, but everyone had their heads down. After placing my tea down on the desk, I found the little envelope attached to the cellophane wrapper and opened it, pulling out the card.

I can't wait to be your roomie. Lots of love, Jude xxx

I tried to hide my smile, embarrassed to be in full view of the open-plan office, but Sarah, who sat opposite me, looked up with a knowing smile.

'Got an admirer have we, Simone?'

'Something like that.'

'Well good for you. I hope he deserves you.'

'Oh, he definitely does.'

As I lifted the flowers to tuck them under my desk, not wanting them to be the centre of attention for the rest of the day, I felt something loose moving in the pink bag they'd come in. Carefully, I pulled the flowers out and gasped when I saw the glint of metal at the bottom of the bag. It was a sharp knife with a long, yellow handle. I picked it up slowly, staring at it. What was a knife doing in my beautiful bouquet of flowers? How had it got there? And, more importantly, why was it there? Suddenly the flowers didn't seem like a thoughtful gift, they felt like a threat.

'What have you got there?' Sarah was looking at the knife, frowning.

'I found it in the bottom of the bag.' My heart raced as I turned the knife over in my hand.

'The florist probably left it in there by mistake when they were cutting the flowers.'

My hand shook as I carefully placed the knife back into the bottom of the bag, not sure what to do with it or how to react. 'Do florists use knives?'

'Yes. That's how they cut the flowers so cleanly. You okay, Simone? You've gone pale.'

'Yes, I'm fine.'

It was just a shock to find a knife, that was all and it didn't take away from the thoughtfulness of Jude's gesture. It wasn't like it had been placed there deliberately. Had it? Of course not, why would anyone give me a knife? The flowers had been delivered directly by the florist so I couldn't see how anyone would have meddled with them. But I needed proof, just to put my mind at ease, so I turned on my computer and googled florists' knives. Sure enough, plenty of results came up. Satisfied with the explanation, and cross with myself for even suspecting anything sinister, I tucked the flowers under my desk out of sight and swivelled around in my chair to see if anyone was looking. But the only person's eye I caught, on the other side of the office, was Tom's.

7

'Right, Helen, it's time to spill the beans.' I looked at my friend sternly from over the top of my coffee cup. Helen had arrived late for our lunch, looking flustered and uncharacteristically unkempt, and I strongly suspected that she'd been with the new woman in her life.

Helen looked at me with mock-innocence. 'I don't know what you mean.'

'Yes you do. Who are you seeing and why are you being so secretive about it?'

'I'm not being secretive.'

'Then tell me.'

'Hey, aren't you moving out of your flat tomorrow? Shouldn't you be packing?'

'Don't change the subject. Who's the lucky lady? Oh wow, are you blushing? Well, as I live and breathe, Helen Eades is *blushing*.'

'Stop it.'

'I will not stop it. Start talking. Now.'

Helen looked down at her coffee. 'I'm a bit embarrassed.'

'Why?'

'She's quite a bit younger than me.'

'Oh, you're a cougar now, are you?'

'I hate that term.' Helen scowled before adding, 'But yes, I am.'

'How much younger are we talking?'

'About eight years.'

'Oh, Helen, that's nothing. Jude's seven years older than me.'

'I know but she's very different to anyone I've been with before.'

'In what way?'

I could have sworn that Helen was squirming. 'I usually go for go-getting, successful types who are older than me. But she's what I can only describe as... a bit of a hippy.'

'Maybe that's what you need though, Helen. I mean, you're a go-getting, successful type and perhaps someone who's different to you is the secret to a happy, balanced relationship? They do say opposites attract. What's her name?'

'I don't want to say.'

'Why not? She's not famous, is she?' I was thoroughly enjoying my interrogation of Helen.

Helen, on the other hand, was not. 'No. Can we just leave it please, Simone?'

'Fine, we can leave it, for now. But I'm not done with you yet. Do Emily and Shiv know?'

'No, and I'd like to keep it that way. Just until I've got my head around it all, okay?'

'Your secret's safe with me. Now what's the plan for Emily's hen do next weekend?'

Although we were Emily's closest mates in London, she'd asked her sister and her oldest friend from school to be her bridesmaids, which had relieved us of the task of planning her hen do. They'd hired a cottage on the south coast and we were all travelling down after work on Friday and staying until Sunday. I was looking forward to it, especially now I'd sorted out my housing issues. The charity collectors had been and gone and the house was full of remaining boxes, which meant that the place increasingly felt less like home. I thought I'd be devastated to be leaving but, apart from the occasional pang of nostalgia, I hadn't given it much thought because I was too excited about moving in with Jude. I had already fallen in love with his split-level flat, with its little roof terrace out the back where we'd sit at the end of the day, watching the sun go down. I could sit there forever, not wanting anything more, never wishing to be anywhere else. Jude had cleared out some drawers and space in the wardrobe for me and had made room in the living room for my armchair. When I'd gone round the other day, he'd marked out the spot with a square of masking tape and stuck a Post-it note in the middle on which he'd written '*Simmy's armchair*', and I loved him a little bit more for it.

'I've booked tickets for the six o'clock train from Victoria,' Helen was saying. 'Have you booked yours yet?'

'Not yet, I'll get on it this afternoon. What are your plans for the rest of the day?'

'Probably work, I've got a new campaign coming up. How about you?'

'I've got a bit more packing to do then I'm done. Jude's driving over tonight and we're going to take stuff over to his in carloads. I've barely got enough to warrant a removal van.'

'Wow, it's really the end of an era, isn't it? We had so many good times in that flat of yours.'

'I know.' I was wistful suddenly, thinking of the many raucous dinner parties we'd had round at mine, or the impromptu Saturday afternoon barbecues we'd arranged in the garden.

'But it's the start of an exciting new era too,' Helen added quickly.

'I am doing the right thing, aren't I, Hels?'

'Of course you are.'

'You'd tell me if I wasn't?'

Helen put her coffee down and took my hands. 'Simmy, you are my person. If I thought for one second that you were doing the wrong thing, I'd shout it from the rooftops.'

I squeezed her hands, relieved. 'I know you would. Thanks, Hels.'

We finished our drinks and went our separate ways, but instead of going home I decided to pop to the shops and buy a little house-warming gift, something new to mark the start of mine and Jude's new living arrangement. I was browsing kitchenware when I spotted someone from the corner of my eye. She had shiny jet-black hair and I couldn't stop staring at her. Something about her was familiar and I couldn't put my finger on what it was.

Then it came to me: she was the fortune teller. I froze, torn between staying where I was and confronting her. But what would I say? I watched the back of her head as she picked out a greeting card and went to pay and then, on impulse, I started to follow her out of the shop, anticipation growing inside me as I considered meeting her again. But as she began to walk down the street, she turned and looked in through the shop window and my heart sank. It wasn't her after all. Feeling silly, I quickly turned around and returned to the kitchenware. In all probability, the fortune teller was long gone, travelling with the fair to other parts of the country and I'd never see her again.

It was the first time I'd thought about her in a while and I realised that, just as she'd predicted, I'd met a man. Not only that but I'd faced a dilemma over whether to move to Peterborough or stay in London and give this thing with Jude a chance. And I'd chosen Jude. And what else was it she'd said? Something I'd lost would be found again? It made me think of my name necklace, lost down the back of the chest of drawers for months.

A shiver ran up my spine as I compared what she'd said to me to the choices I had recently made. Was Jude the man she had been talking about? Should I have moved to Peterborough instead? But how could I change my life based on the loose predictions of a funfair fortune teller with no real credentials? It would have been madness to throw away my chance of happiness on the ramblings of so-called Mystic Maggie. Anyway, the predictions she'd made for Emily and Shiv hadn't come true and were unlikely to do so.

Look for the signs, she'd said. I thought about the thunderstorm on my first date with Jude, the knife I'd found in the bag of flowers. But there were rational explanations for both. The problem was that when someone told you to look for signs, you began to see them everywhere, even when they were nothing but everyday occurrences. And I didn't want to live like that.

I considered calling Helen so she could talk some sense into me, but I changed my mind. I didn't need Helen to tell me that it was all nonsense, I'd worked that one out for myself. I just had to forget about Mystic Maggie and get on with my life. With a renewed sense of purpose, I picked out a pair of mugs and some candles and went over to the till to pay for them.

But as I walked to the bus stop, the fortune teller's words continued to echo around my head.

* * *

I'd never seen so much penis paraphernalia in my life. Emily's sister and friend had gone all out with the decorations and we sipped our cocktails from penis-themed straws, while phallic helium balloons floated all around us. At the head of the table,

Emily was wearing a tiara and a banner which said 'Bride To Be'. She had a huge smile on her face and a slightly glassy expression which told me that she'd started on the cocktails long before Shiv, Helen and I had arrived in a taxi from the train station. It looked like we had some catching up to do.

There were twelve of us in total, and after all the introductions had been made, we'd fallen into easy conversation. Emily's sister Becky had told us the plan for the weekend, which involved a night in with pizzas this evening and a trip to the beach tomorrow followed by dinner and a pub crawl. It had been a long time since I'd had a crazy night out and I hoped my body was up for it.

'Time for some games,' Becky announced, and we all simultaneously groaned and grinned. 'Starting with Mr and Mrs. Every answer Emily gets wrong, she has to drink a shot.'

Poor Emily, I thought, although she looked delighted by the prospect.

Becky pulled out a piece of paper and read out the first question. 'We'll start with some easy ones. What's Mark's favourite film?'

'*Jurassic Park*,' Emily said immediately.

'Correct! What's his favourite pizza topping.'

'Pepperoni!'

'Correct. Okay, Em, let's see how well you know your man. What is his favourite thing about you?'

Emily looked thoughtful. 'My boobs?'

We all erupted with laughter. 'Afraid not,' Becky said. 'It's your generosity.'

'Ah man.' Emily picked up a pre-filled shot glass and downed it in one.

The game continued in this thread for a while and I sat back and enjoyed the spectacle, wondering what I would want to do for my own hen do. As fun as this was, I wasn't really the penis straw type and I'd rather go out for a lovely meal at a nice restaurant with some close friends. It was crazy that I was even thinking about my hen do. I'd always hoped to get married eventually but as time went on and I'd stayed single, I'd accepted that it might not be in my future. Now, though, I was daring to daydream again, imagining walking up the aisle, Jude waiting for me at the end. Going on a honeymoon together. Maybe even having children. We'd discussed it after only a few dates and when he'd said that he wanted kids, I'd been completely honest with him about my condition, warning him that it may not happen naturally. Perhaps it should have felt strange, being that intimate with someone so early on in our relationship – I couldn't imagine ever having had this conversation with Tom – but it had felt easy and comfortable, and Jude had said that he understood and that there were more ways than one to become a parent. I had loved his reaction and I hoped that we could cope with anything that life threw in our way, as long as we had each other. I smiled, happy to be celebrating with Emily and giddy with the joy of a new relationship when the possibilities seemed endless.

The game ended and we all dispersed to have a break before the next one. Emily sidled up to me, looking guilty, and waved a packet of cigarettes at me. 'Fancy joining me outside?'

'Emily, I thought you'd given up years ago!'

'I did, but if you can't be a bit naughty on your hen do, when can you?'

'Fair enough. I won't join you but I'll come and keep you company.'

We slipped out through the patio doors and sat down on rattan chairs in the garden, which overlooked the sea. It was too dark to see the view now, but I knew it would be spectacular in the morning.

'Are you having a good time?' I asked her, as she lit up and inhaled deeply.

'The best. Thank you for coming.'

'Oh, I wouldn't miss it for the world. How are you feeling about the wedding?'

'I can't believe it's so soon. We've been planning it for so long it felt like it might never actually happen, but now it's just around the corner.'

'You'll be a beautiful bride, Em.'

'Thanks. What about you? Would you like to get married some day?'

I smiled shyly. 'Yes. And for the first time in a long time, I'm actually feeling positive that it might happen.'

An expression passed over Emily's face, so quickly that I almost missed it but she was too drunk to hide it completely.

'What is it?'

'Nothing, it's nothing.'

'Emily, tell me, please.'

Emily looked like she was agonising over something and if she'd been sober perhaps she would have glossed over it, but the alcohol had made her looser-lipped. 'This thing with you and Jude, I just worry sometimes.'

She had my full attention now. 'Why?'

'I don't know, it's just happened so quickly. You've only known each other for a few weeks and you're already moving in together, and...'

Emily stopped. 'Go on,' I said impatiently.

'I just feel like it's all on his terms. He was the one who decided that you should move into his flat. And then he made you get rid of *all* of your stuff, like you're throwing away your past, all the things that belong to you, and anything that isn't his, until you're left with nothing.'

I was appalled by her words. 'Emily, it isn't like that at all. Jude didn't put any pressure on me to move in with him; he suggested it and I agreed. And it was my decision to get rid of most of my stuff. I'm just not a sentimental person. Anyway, I'm taking my armchair.'

'One armchair, Simone. Are you aware of how absurd that sounds?'

I was becoming defensive now, eager to defend Jude. 'It doesn't sound absurd at all. Jude's got a lush flat, full of lush furniture, and I'm just not that interested in holding on to mine.'

'But what if it doesn't work out? Could you not have put all your things in storage just in case?'

I'd been so swept away by Jude and the thought of us living together that I'd gone in full throttle without even pausing to seriously consider putting my belongings in storage, but I was feeling too prickly to admit that to Emily. 'Look, it's just *things*, Emily. It can all be replaced.'

'I guess so. Just, promise me something, Simmy.'

'What is it?'

'Be careful, okay? Don't lose who *you* are. Because you're pretty amazing.'

'Oh Emily.' My anger was already ebbing away at the sight of the bride-to-be, drunk as a skunk and looking like she might cry. 'So are you.'

'I'm sorry I said anything. Me and tequila have never been a good combination.'

'Come inside, I'll get you some water to dilute all that booze.'

I pulled her up from her chair and we headed inside hand in hand. Emily was immediately dragged away by her old schoolfriends and never did have that glass of water, something I suspected she regretted at two in the morning when she had her head down the toilet bowl.

The following morning, she somehow managed to rally and when I spoke to her, she acted as though nothing had happened between us the previous evening. Perhaps she didn't even remember.

But I remembered. As Shiv and I were getting ready together in the bedroom we were sharing, I told her what had happened and asked her what she thought.

'I can see her point about the stuff,' Shiv said. 'I'm sure things are going to work out with Jude, but if for any reason they don't, you've lost all of your belongings.'

'I know,' I admitted. 'In hindsight I should have put it all in storage for a few months but I was so excited about moving in with Jude that I ignored the practicalities. But honestly, I'm not lying when I say that I'm not attached to all that stuff, it's just like old clothes to me.'

'I'm thinking more financially,' Shiv said. 'It'll cost you a fortune if you have to furnish a whole new place from scratch.'

'Why does everyone think it's not going to work out between me and Jude?'

'We don't think that,' Shiv said diplomatically, and I didn't like the way she'd used the word *we*. It could have been the hangover making me paranoid, but I got the distinct feeling that my friends had been talking about my relationship.

'Maybe you should meet him,' I suggested. Helen and Emily already knew him from work, but he'd yet to be officially introduced to the gang as a whole, over dinner.

Shiv smiled. 'I'd like that. And seriously, Simone, don't worry about what Emily said. She loves you and she's just looking out for you, but it's clear to see that Jude makes you happy.'

'Thanks, Shiv.'

We heard Becky shouting from the bottom of the stairs, telling everyone that we were leaving in five minutes, and I started to gather up my stuff. 'Are you going to brave the British sea?'

'Absolutely not. I've got my beach towel, my book, my sunhat, and no children. Once we hit that sand, I don't plan to move a muscle all day except to eat and drink and even then, I'd really rather someone brought it to me.'

I laughed. 'I'll see what I can do.'

We headed downstairs where the rest of the group had already gathered and started to make our way outside to walk down to the beach. Helen hung back and linked her arm through mine.

'Everything okay?' she asked.

I nodded. 'Everything's fine.'

As we reached the beach and I saw the waves lapping the shore, I smiled contentedly, pushing my conversation with Emily to the back of my mind. Life was good, the sun was shining and all I wanted to do was bask in it and look forward to the day ahead, and my future with Jude.

8

When I got back to Jude's flat on Sunday evening, I was exhausted. I'd had a great time on the hen do but a weekend of partying, followed by a long train ride home, had taken its toll and all I wanted to do was take my make-up off, put my pyjamas on, throw a pizza in the oven, and collapse on the sofa. But although Jude couldn't have been more welcoming, I still didn't feel a hundred per cent at home in his place yet. *Our* place, I corrected myself. I'd only been living there a week, though, and it would take time to settle in and get used to cohabiting.

Jude was in the kitchen making a pasta sauce. He turned when he saw me and came over to kiss me. 'How was it?'

'Brutal,' I said, dumping my bag on the floor. 'But fun.'

'Was it all cocktails and strippers?'

'Not a single, real-life penis in sight. But plenty of plastic ones.'

Jude grinned. 'I'm making dinner, you hungry?'

'I was craving pizza, actually.'

'Well, this is better for you than pizza and the sauce is already on.'

'Okay. Well, do you mind if I take a shower first?'

'Go for it, it'll be another twenty minutes or so.'

I headed to the bathroom, taking my clothes off and sighing with pleasure as the hot water from Jude's power shower drenched my weary body. Fifteen minutes later I was dressed in jeans and a T-shirt, still too self-conscious to go into full-on pyjama mode in front of Jude. I sat down in my armchair and watched him cooking.

'Jude?'

'Mmm?'

'Do you think I should have kept my stuff from the flat?'

Jude turned to look at me, a wooden spoon in his hand. 'You don't like my stuff?'

'I love your stuff. And I know there wasn't much room for mine. I'm just wondering if I should have put it in storage, you know, just in case.'

Jude frowned. 'Just in case what?'

'Well, in case it doesn't work out between us.'

'Blimey, Simmy, you've only been here seven days and you're already thinking of breaking up. Am I that terrible to live with?' He said it with a smile, but I knew he was only half-joking.

'You're wonderful to live with and I'm not going anywhere. It's just something the girls said.'

Was it me or did he look a bit peeved? 'What did they say?'

'Just that maybe we've rushed into this.'

He abandoned the pasta and walked over, crouching down next to the armchair and taking my hand. 'We have rushed into it. But it still feels right to me.'

I squeezed his hand. 'It feels right to me too.'

'Are you regretting getting rid of your things? 'Cause if you like, we can call the charity and get it all back, I'm sure it's not too late.'

'Oh God no, can you imagine? I'd be mortified. Anyway, it doesn't matter, forget I said anything.'

'If you like, we can go shopping next weekend and pick out some new bits for the flat, things that we've chosen together, so it feels like you've put your stamp on the place too?'

'That sounds lovely but we're going to visit Mum next weekend.'

'Oh yes, I forgot. Well, the weekend after maybe. There's no rush.'

I nodded. 'Sounds good. Now, where's this pasta, I'm starving.'

He stood up and saluted. 'Coming right up, madam. And maybe once you've enjoyed your in-flight meal, you'll join me in the mile high club?'

'Maybe not tonight.' It was the first time I'd said no to sex with Jude but I was far too tired and hungover to take my clothes off again.

Jude looked surprised but he shrugged. 'Fair enough. Sounds like you've seen enough male genitals for one weekend.'

'More than enough.'

I watched him as he walked over to the kitchen and drained the pasta, admiring his tall, lithe body, still slightly stunned that he was mine. He was right, I decided, there was no rush. We had the rest of our lives to get to know each other better, to make a home together. Over time, the flat, or wherever we ended up living, would morph into a combination of us, not belonging to one but to both. And despite my friends' concerns, I knew in my gut – which had finally decided it was talking to me again – that I was doing the right thing.

* * *

The next day at work, I was having lunch on the wall outside the office when Tom appeared, carrying a sandwich.

'Mind if I join you?'

'Not at all.'

He sat down and started unwrapping his sandwich. 'I've found somewhere to live.'

'Oh, that's great news. Is it in Crouch End?'

'Yes, on one of the roads you recommended. I'm moving in a couple of weeks.'

'Congratulations.'

'You'll have to come round and see it when I'm settled. After all, if it wasn't for you, I wouldn't have found it.'

I wasn't sure what Jude would think of me going round to my ex's new flat but I didn't want to admit that to Tom. 'Sure, that would be lovely.'

'Are you going to the afterwork drinks on Friday?'

'No, I'm getting the train up to my mum's house for the weekend.'

'She lives in Peterborough, right?'

I glanced over at him, surprised that he remembered. 'Yes, that's right.'

'Oh well, maybe next time.'

We chewed our sandwiches in silence for a while. I'd like to have said it was companionable but there was still something about Tom that set me on edge, and I could only think it was the remnants of my old, unrequited love.

Tom started talking about some new work policy and I was glad to be on safe ground. After a few minutes his phone rang, and when he looked at the screen, I saw panic flash across his face. He quickly put it back in his pocket, but I could tell the missed call had shifted his mood.

'Everything okay?'

'It's my ex,' he said. 'She won't stop calling.'

'A recent ex?'

He winced. 'Yes and no. We were on and off for a long time. Now we're definitely off and have been for a while but she won't let it go.'

'She still loves you?'

'She's a fucking psychopath.'

I was stunned by Tom's words, and the venomous way in which he said them. 'In what way?'

'She's obsessed with me. At first I thought it was kind of sweet, until I realised her true colours.' I saw genuine fear on Tom's face as he continued talking. 'She kept turning up at places she knew I might be, she called my friends, my family. Once, I went out for a drink with a friend and she followed the girl home and confronted her, accusing her of sleeping with me.'

'Oh, Tom, I'm sorry. That sounds awful.'

'I broke up with her after that but, I don't know, for some stupid reason I went back to her again. And again.'

'So how did it finally end?'

'I came home from work one evening and she was burning my clothes in the garden because she thought I was cheating on her with our neighbour. It was because she'd seen us talking together that morning. I was only giving the woman some post that had gone through our letterbox by mistake! When she realised she'd made a mistake, she was all tears and apologies, but I was done. I packed what was left of my stuff and moved in with a friend.'

That explained why Tom had needed to find somewhere new to live. But it also meant that he'd got back together with this girl after we'd stopped dating last year. He may even have been reconciling with her while we were together, which would explain his detached behaviour towards me. And what if there was even some overlap? I wasn't angry, exactly, because we were never serious, but it smarted a bit that he'd potentially chosen a psychopath over me.

I also wondered if I'd dodged a bullet. If this girl had been aware of my existence, she might have followed me home and confronted me too and I couldn't resist bringing the subject up with Tom. 'Did she know about us when we were dating?'

'No.' He shook his head firmly but didn't expand on the matter.

I thought about how he'd behaved when we were together and wondered if he'd deliberately avoided showing any affection towards me in public so that this ex, whoever she was, didn't find out that we were a couple. Had I read our fleeting relationship completely wrong? When I thought he'd been rejecting me, had he actually been protecting me? But then he'd ended things and presumably got back together with this girl, so he'd clearly still been thinking about her. I tried to ignore the indignation that was starting to creep in.

'I'm really sorry, Tom.'

He gave a forced smile. 'So am I. Sorry I ever laid eyes on her. Anyway, when I move into my new place, hopefully it'll be a fresh start. She doesn't know where it is and I intend to keep it that way. But I can't stop her calling. I block her number, but she just gets a new pay-as-you-go phone and calls me from that.'

'Do you think you should go to the police?'

'And tell them what? That my ex is still into me? They'd laugh me out of the station.'

'It sounds more serious than that.'

'I can handle it.' Tom stood up, indicating that the conversation was over. 'Anyway, I'm sorry to throw all this on you.'

'Not at all. I'm always here if you want someone to talk to.'

'Thanks, Simone.' He touched my shoulder and then headed back into the office.

I stayed outside for a few minutes longer, mulling over everything Tom had told me. It just went to show that you could never judge a book by its cover. All this time I'd thought he was arrogant but he'd actually been dealing with emotional trauma. Perhaps if he'd told me about it at the time, things might have been different between us. But then he'd gone back to her so his heart must have been with her anyway. Or she'd still had a hold over him.

I wondered how he had got himself into that position in the first place, why he didn't see the red flags sooner. Tom was a very attractive man and he could probably have any woman he wanted, and yet he'd chosen her. Surely there must have been alarm bells ringing from the start of their relationship? And, once he'd realised how controlling she was, why had he kept going back to her? Because he loved her, I guessed, and love could be blind.

Still deep in thought, I looked at my watch and realised with horror that I had a meeting in four minutes. I threw my sandwich wrapper into the nearest bin and dashed inside.

9

We shuffled along the pew to make way for Helen, who was wearing the most incredible fascinator I'd ever seen. Jude gave me a look, which I read as *What the heck is that thing on her head?*

Shiv was not so subtle. 'Helen, are you doing your bit for conservation by allowing birds to nest on top of your hair?'

'Oh, sod off.' Helen sat down at the end of the row and gave Shiv the finger. 'Hello, Jude.'

'Hello, Helen.'

I was sandwiched between Jude and Shiv, who had left the kids with her in-laws and had loudly declared that she and Avyaan were looking forward to a day off parental duties. Shiv looked stunning in a blue silk dress, and Jude and Avyaan had chatted while we waited for Emily's wedding ceremony to start. I'd been elated that they seemed to be getting along so well.

Jude and I had been together for a few months and things were going so brilliantly that I sometimes had to pinch myself. We were still in the early throes of our relationship, where it was fresh and exciting, but we'd also settled into living together as though we'd always done it. After a hilarious shopping trip where we'd egged each other on to buy garish things, the flat was starting to feel more like ours rather than just his. He'd been out with me and the girls a few times and I had sensed their approval before they'd voiced it to me at the debrief the next day. I hoped that it had put an end to Emily and Shiv's reservations about him.

We all fell silent as the back door opened and the choir started singing. I stood and craned my neck to get the first glimpse of Emily, who looked beautiful as always in a designer dress. But then my head turned towards Mark at the front of the church. I always thought it was more interesting to see the look on the groom's face as his bride walked down the aisle and I was rewarded with the purest expression of awe and joy on his face. I felt myself starting to well up and tried to fight back my tears, but I wasn't quick enough.

'Are you crying, you old wuss?' Shiv whispered, giving me a nudge.

'No.'

'It'll be you next.'

I glanced nervously at Jude, worried in case he'd overheard, but he was staring stoically ahead. 'Shh,' I hissed, and Shiv gave me a knowing look.

After the ceremony we all piled into a taxi and travelled to the hotel where the reception was being held. A few of us had decided to stay overnight and after we'd checked in and deposited our bags in our rooms, we headed towards the function room where staff were waiting to greet us with trays of champagne. As we picked up a glass each and clinked them together, I looked around at my friends and Jude and I had never felt so happy.

When we were called to our tables, I was pleased to see that I would be sitting with Helen and Shiv, as well as a couple of Emily's friends we'd met at the hen do. We had a raucous time, enjoying the free-flowing wine and settling into the evening, and when the band started playing, I couldn't wait to take to the dance floor. We all cheered as Emily and Mark got up for the first dance, and as soon as they gestured for us to join them, I sprang up from my seat and turned to Jude.

'Come on then, mister.'

Jude grimaced. 'I hate dancing.'

'Who hates dancing?!'

'Me.'

I grinned, still thinking that this was a joke and that any moment he would stand up, take my hand and lead me on to the dance floor. But he remained in his seat, a stubborn look on his face.

'Come on, Jude, just one dance. It's a wedding, for goodness' sake.'

'Sorry, Simmy, you go, have fun. I'll be here, watching your sexy moves.'

I looked at all the couples who were making their way to the dance floor and my heart sank. I'd had no idea that Jude was so anti-dancing, but then it wasn't the sort of thing you discussed with a new beau. *Tell me, do you hope to get married some day? Do you want children? What are your thoughts on dancing?* Still, his refusal to join in was threatening to put a serious dampener on the evening. I felt someone appear by my side and Helen took my hand. 'Come on, gorgeous, dance with me.'

I let her pull me on to the dance floor and we smiled as we embraced each other and swayed along to the music, but, surrounded by couples, I felt silly.

'Who doesn't like dancing?' I repeated to Helen incredulously, trying to conceal my disappointment.

'Lots of people. Me for one.'

'But you're still up here, dancing.'

'That's true. Don't overthink it though, Simmy, it's not a big deal.'

How could I explain it to Helen? That I was hurt my boyfriend didn't want to dance with me? That it changed the way I felt about him just a tiny bit? That it somehow tainted the evening in my eyes? I knew I was overreacting, but I was struggling to laugh it off.

The song ended and was replaced with an upbeat number and soon a group of us were dancing in a circle to 'YMCA'. *Sod him,* I thought uncharitably, as I threw my hands up into the air. *He's the one missing out, not me.* I remained resolutely on the dance floor, making a point I wasn't entirely sure I understood myself, ignoring Jude who was sitting alone at the table watching me. Finally, after about half an hour, I was exhausted and thirsty and I admitted dancing defeat. But when I turned towards our table, Jude's chair was empty. I picked up my glass of wine and wandered out to check the lobby and hotel bar but there was no sign of him. After ten minutes had passed, I concluded that he couldn't be in the toilet and I started to panic. Had I gone too far and pissed him off? What if he was up in our room, sulking, or worse, what if he'd gone home?

I slipped out through the French doors onto the patio outside and looked for him in the dusk light until I saw a figure about thirty metres away, standing by the lake. It was him. I put my wine glass down on a table and made my way over, stopping when I was standing beside him.

'You're cross with me.' He didn't look at me when he said it.

'Yes,' I admitted. 'I know it's silly, but I felt rejected when you wouldn't dance with me.'

'My last memory of my parents together was when they were dancing at a cousin's wedding. The next day they told me they were getting divorced.'

'Oh, Jude, I'm sorry. I had no idea.'

'I've refused to dance since. Does that sound ridiculous?'

I put my hand on his arm. 'No, of course not. I really am sorry.'

He turned to me then. 'Hey, is this our first fight?'

I smiled. 'I believe it might be.'

'Does that mean we get to have make-up sex?'

'Well, yes, I think we qualify for that now.'

He grinned and then his face turned serious. 'Okay, cheesy moment time. I've never met a woman I've cared about so much that I wanted to dance with them. Until I met you.'

'Jude, you don't have to, it's okay.'

'I know I don't have to, but I want to.'

He took me in his arms and started swaying along to the faint music we could just about hear in the distance. I fell into the rhythm, resting my head on his shoulder and closing my eyes. The cloud that had formed over me had already disappeared and all I saw was blue sky again. I slipped my hands under his jacket and felt his warm body through his shirt. As I pulled him towards me, I thought that I would never get bored of touching him, of being near him.

'I love you,' he said, and it was the first time we had spoken those words to each other.

'I love you too.'

'I want to spend the rest of my life with you, Simmy.'

'I want to spend the rest of my life with you too, Jude.'

He broke away suddenly, making me start, and I looked at him in shock as he got down on one knee. 'Jude, what are you doing?'

'Will you marry me, Simone?'

I stared down at him wide-eyed. We'd only been together a few months, to get engaged so soon was madness, wasn't it? A million thoughts raced through my head. *If I say no, will he ever forgive me? Do I want to say no? What will my friends say? Does he actually want to marry me or is this a mad, spur-of-the-moment thing?*

But then I remembered what my mum had said to me. *When you know, you know*. And I knew.

I looked down at him and when I spoke, my voice was unwavering. 'Yes. I will.'

* * *

We decided not to tell anyone our news that evening because we didn't want to steal Emily and Mark's thunder. In some ways it made it even more special, this secret between us, and we kept stealing glances at each other and sharing knowing looks. Jude even braved the dance floor a couple of times, looking awkward as hell, but doing his best, and it made me love him even more. By the time we stumbled to bed at one in the morning, there was no chance of make-up sex. We both passed out the moment our heads hit the pillows, our hands clutched tightly together.

I woke up early, with a dry mouth and a banging headache, and when I turned to Jude, he was still fast asleep. I closed my eyes and tried to go back to sleep but my mind was whirring too much. I was engaged! I couldn't believe it. I wanted to wake Jude up and ask him if he still meant it, to check he hadn't changed his mind. But instead, I gave up on sleep and reached for my phone. There were no messages because everyone else was still asleep, the lucky sods, so I browsed Instagram and thought about how I might announce my engagement, enjoying visions of a happy selfie or a picture of me holding up my ring finger and revealing a sparkler. Of course there was no ring yet, but hopefully it would only be a matter of time. I didn't need anything fancy or custom-made; a simple high street ring would do the trick for me.

Jude stirred and I watched him, hoping he might wake up. But instead he turned on his side and started snoring softly so I decided to message Helen and see if she was awake.

You up yet?

She replied immediately.

Yes. Hungover and hangry. Fancy breakfast in half an hour?

I looked guiltily across at Jude. I should probably wait for him, but I was eager to break the happy news to Helen and I was famished too. I sent back a thumbs-up emoji and got up to use the shower. By the time I was dressed and ready to go, Jude was still in the land of nod, so I left him a note telling him where I'd gone and crept out of the hotel room.

The dining room was empty when I arrived, except for an elderly couple on one side of the room and Helen on the other. I walked over to her and kissed her on the cheek, then nodded my thanks at the waitress who was hovering with a pot of coffee.

'At least we're beating the breakfast rush,' I said, as I took a sip of my coffee. 'You going for a cooked breakfast?'

'Abso-bloody-lutely. This body needs protein. Pronto.'

'Tell me about it.'

We ordered our breakfasts and then looked at each other from across the table.

'It was a good night, wasn't it?'

'It was,' Helen agreed. 'I haven't danced that much in ages. Speaking of dancing, was everything okay with you and Jude? I saw he gave in eventually and got his boogie on.'

'Oh yes, that's all sorted.' I was grinning like a Cheshire cat, unable to hide my excitement.

Helen narrowed her eyes at me. 'What's going on?'

'I... um... we... got engaged last night.'

Helen stood up, nearly sending the crockery flying, and dashed around the table to hug me. 'Oh, wow, congratulations!'

'Thank you.'

'You kept that quiet, you dark horse. When did it happen?'

I explained about finding him by the lake and the conversation we'd had. 'Then he got down on one knee and popped the question.'

'Go Jude.'

'You don't think it's too soon do you, Hels?'

'Yes,' Helen said, and my heart plummeted. But then she added, 'But who bloody cares. I'm thrilled for you, Simmy, I really am.'

'Why are you thrilled for Simmy?'

We looked up to find Shiv and Avyaan standing over our table.

'I'm engaged!'

'What? When?'

'Last night, but we kept schtum because we didn't want to take the shine away from Emily and Mark.'

'Congratulations!' Avyaan high-fived me but Shiv remained quiet and an awkward silence followed as we all looked at her, waiting for her to congratulate me too.

Finally, she said. 'I'm thrilled for you, Simmy, I really am. But it's a bit sudden, isn't it?'

'Yes.' I tried not to sound defensive. 'But we love each other and it feels right. I've never felt so certain about anything in my life.'

Shiv seemed to mentally check herself and her face broke out into a smile as she leaned down and kissed me. 'Congratulations hun, I'm so pleased for you.'

Shiv and Avyaan sat down next to us and were ordering their breakfasts when Jude arrived, in a crumpled shirt, rubbing his eyes sleepily. 'Tell me there's coffee.'

I signalled to the hovering waitress and she came over and filled Jude's cup.

'I hear you're making an honest woman of our Simmy,' Helen said, and I panicked, suddenly afraid that Jude hadn't meant to propose, that it was all a big mistake.

But he beamed, gave me a wink and said, 'I think you'll find it's Simmy making an honest man of me.'

'Well, I'm dead pleased for you both,' Helen said, and Avyaan reached over to shake his hand. 'So when's the big day?'

'Oh we haven't even started talking about it...' I began, at the same time as Jude said, 'Christmas.'

I looked at him in surprise, wondering if we'd discussed it last night and I didn't remember, but I was positive that we hadn't gone into that much detail. From the corner of my eye, I could see Shiv raising her eyebrow quizzically and I knew she'd picked up on my confusion. Determined to show that everything was fine, that my husband-to-be wouldn't dream of deciding on our wedding date without discussing it with me, I said, 'We've got a few things to iron out first.'

'Christmas is two months away,' Shiv exclaimed. 'You'll never be able to get everything sorted in time, and all the best venues will be booked up.'

'Who needs a fancy venue?' Helen seemed to be conveniently ignoring the fact that we were, at that moment, sitting in a fancy venue. 'Registry office and a few pints down the local pub sounds ideal to me.'

Still smarting that Jude had mentioned a Christmas wedding before we'd had a chance to talk about it, but hell-bent on not revealing how I felt to my friends, I said, 'I think somewhere between the two will be a happy medium for us.'

The food arrived and we all tucked in, merrily dissecting the events of the previous evening, and then Emily and Mark arrived and we crowded around them, giving them the fuss they deserved. By the time we were done, we had to check out and then we shared a taxi with Helen to the station and sat with her on the train back to Central London. It wasn't until we were walking back to the flat that Jude and I had a chance to talk alone.

He took my hand and squeezed it. 'Hello Mrs-Pearce-to-be.'

'Hey.' It was only at that moment that I was able to reveal my annoyance.

Jude picked up on my tone immediately. 'What's up?'

'I'm just a bit confused about this Christmas wedding thing. I mean, if you'd like a Christmas wedding then I'm happy to talk about it, but it sounded like your mind was already made up, without us even discussing it.'

Jude's face fell. 'Uh-oh, have I royally messed up?'

I was tempted to tell him no, that it was all fine, but I stuck to my guns. 'I don't want a big fancy wedding like Emily but it's still an important day for me. I'd like to at least have some input.'

'Of course, oh Jeez, I'm sorry, Simmy, I've gone about this all wrong.' Jude hung his head, ashamed. 'It's just that when we were watching *Love Actually* the other week you told me that Christmas was the most romantic time of the year, so I thought you'd be happy.'

I thought back to our movie night and realised, grudgingly, that he was right. 'I did say that,' I admitted.

'And I got a bit carried away and had these grand visions of a Christmas wedding, with red and gold and maybe some snow, and I'm a total idiot who should have discussed it with you first.'

My bad mood was quickly evaporating. 'That does sound lush.'

'Listen, Simmy, I love you and I would get married to you any day of the year. You pick a date and I'll be there. Big wedding, small wedding, I don't care as long as you're the bride. And I promise I'll never be so gung-ho about something so important again.'

'A Christmas wedding would be nice,' I conceded. 'But can we arrange everything in time? Shiv was right, venues and bands and so on get booked up months or even years in advance. Maybe we should look to next winter instead.'

'Can you wait that long?'

I stopped and looked at Jude. 'No. Can you?'

'No.'

'I tell you what, let's get home, order a takeaway and discuss what kind of a wedding we'd like. Then we'll make some calls, and if it's doable, we'll do it.'

Jude's face lit up. 'I reckon it's totally doable.'

I felt myself getting caught up in his enthusiasm. 'Me too. But we are forgetting one thing.'

'What's that?'

'We haven't told our parents.'

I was confident that Mum would be okay about it, given how well she'd reacted to the news about me moving in with Jude, but I hadn't even met his parents yet. Was it strange that we were engaged before any introductions had been made? What if they hated me?

As if reading my mind, Jude said, 'My parents will love you.'

'Won't they be cross that you're getting married to someone they've never even met?'

'Nah, they'll be cool.'

'Still, we should go and see them. Your mum at least.' I knew he had a better relationship with his mother, who he'd lived with after the divorce.

'Sure,' he said non-committally.

'When?'

'Soon.'

'I'm going to call Mum this evening. Maybe you should do the same?'

'Sounds like a plan.'

I had to accept that Jude wasn't as close to his mum as I was to mine. Every family was different. But right then, I couldn't wait to break the news to Mum. 'What about a ring?'

'Oh yeah, we kind of need one of them.'

I punched his arm playfully. 'Oh Jude, you old romantic.'

'Tell you what, let's go shopping after work tomorrow and buy you something bling.'

'Tiffany's?' I suggested with a wink.

'Whatever my beautiful lady desires.'

'You know they're, like, thousands and thousands of pounds, right?'

'Then not whatever my beautiful lady desires.'

I snuggled into him. 'It's fine, Jude, I don't need an expensive ring. I just need you.'

He put his arm around me. 'And you have me, Simmy. Every single inch of me.'

10

It didn't take long for my work colleagues to notice the new sparkler on my wedding finger, which Jude and I had picked out together the day after we got back from Emily's wedding. I'd had to wait over a week for it to be resized, but I'd picked it up the previous day and now wore it proudly on my finger. Word spread like wildfire, and by midday I'd been congratulated by about twenty people and I was both elated and exhausted.

I slipped out at lunchtime and perched on my usual spot on the wall outside, zipping my coat up to the top. Autumn was well and truly here but it was dry and I enjoyed the fresh air. A few minutes later Tom appeared and sat down next to me. We'd started having lunch together a few times a week, an unofficial agreement rather than anything prearranged, but I enjoyed his company and had started looking forward to seeing him. Over the past few weeks, I'd become more relaxed around him and now I found that I could talk easily without getting nervous and flustered. My crush, it seemed, was well and truly over.

'I hear congratulations are in order,' he said.

'Oh yes, thank you.'

'Let's have a look then.'

I held out my hand and he took it and studied the ring. 'Very nice. When's the wedding?'

'December twenty-first.'

Against all odds, Jude and I had managed to pull off organising a wedding venue at short notice. We'd both agreed that we wanted a civil ceremony followed by a small reception of no more than forty people, and we'd chanced upon a venue in the city that had a licence for civil weddings as well as a full catering service in a lovely function room. Even better, they had managed to squeeze us in. We still had to organise the wedding dress, photographer, band, cake and flowers but we were well on our way.

Mum had been delighted when I told her the news. She had met Jude a few times and was already a big fan. There wasn't much to dislike about him, he was practically perfect. Thoughtful, kind, funny and easy on the eye to boot. I still couldn't believe my luck that I had found him.

Mum had insisted that she contribute financially to the wedding, and although I'd argued at first, I'd been secretly pleased when she didn't take no for an answer. I had savings, and so did Jude, but we didn't want to blow it all on a wedding because we were hoping to buy a house together. It turned out that London wasn't so inaccessible when there were two people contributing to the deposit and mortgage, or at least small pockets of London weren't. We'd have to move to a cheaper area and we were happy to do that, but we'd agreed to get the wedding out of the way first, because there was so much to do in a very short space of time.

'Wow, that's only a few weeks away,' Tom was saying now.

'I know but we didn't see the point in hanging around. We're not having a huge wedding.'

'Well, I'm really pleased for you.'

'How are things with you? Is your ex still calling you all the time?'

'She seems to have stopped. For now.'

'That's great news.'

'We'll see. I'm not counting my chickens yet.'

'Maybe she's met someone else.'

'Poor bastard.'

'But it gets you off the hook at least.'

'That's true.'

'How's the new place?'

'It's great. You should come and see it.'

'Definitely.' I said this but actually had no intention of going to see it because while Tom and I had become work pals, of a fashion, we definitely weren't the 'hanging out at each other's flat' kind of pals.

'Are you going out for Gemma's leaving do later?' Tom asked.

'Yes, I'll be there. How about you?'

'Yep. I'll buy you a drink to say congrats.'

'Thanks, Tom.'

We finished our lunch and returned to our desks together, although a couple of hours later we stopped again to give Gemma her leaving present and have some cake. By four o'clock everyone was restless and eager to head to the pub, and at four thirty we decided to down tools and call it a day. We all piled into the lifts and made our way to the pub down the road, where the boss had put a company card behind the bar, much to everyone's delight.

'I hear we have some celebrating to do,' our manager declared, holding up his glass and looking at me. I smiled, embarrassed that I was taking the attention away from Gemma, but she held up her glass too, looking genuinely pleased for me.

'Cheers, guys,' I said, and we all took a sip of our drinks before dispersing into smaller groups. Within a couple of hours, there were a fair few people who were three sheets to the wind, including, I suspected, Tom, who was visibly swaying as he stood by the bar. I knew that things would probably start getting raucous soon and I was glad for an excuse to leave.

I headed over to Tom. 'I'm off now as I'm meeting a friend for dinner.'

'Wait, I'll walk you out.'

He followed me outside, and as soon as the door had closed behind us, he grabbed my arm and said urgently, 'Simone, there's something I need to tell you.'

'What is it? Is everything okay?'

I thought he was going to say his ex-girlfriend had found out about us dating and was out for my blood or something, but instead, he lurched towards me and said, 'I like you. I really like you.'

And before I realised what was going on, he'd leaned in and kissed me. It took my brain a second to catch up with what was happening, but as soon as it did, I abruptly pulled away.

'Tom, no!'

Tom looked mortified. 'I'm sorry, I shouldn't have done that.'

'No, it's fine, don't worry. I really like you, Tom, you're a great bloke, but you know I'm with someone else.'

'I know. I'm an arse. I'm so sorry.'

'Stop apologising. Honestly, let's just pretend it never happened, okay?'

He was clearly relieved. 'Thanks. I appreciate that.'

'Now, go and have a good night and I'll see you tomorrow.'

He turned and went back inside, but I stood outside the pub for a minute to get my head straight. What a strange, unexpected turn of events. I'd fancied Tom for so long, wishing he felt the same way I did, and now that I was happily with someone else, he wanted me. Talk about a twist of fate. But as much as I'd liked

Tom once, it was Jude I loved and it was Jude who I wanted to spend the rest of my life with.

Then, as I started to leave, I suddenly got a creepy feeling that I was being watched and I looked behind me, wondering if Tom had come back out to talk to me again. But the door to the pub was firmly closed and, peering through the window, I saw no sign of him. I glanced around but I couldn't see anything untoward so I set off down the road, still slightly on edge. I kept looking back over my shoulder but although there were people around there was no sign of anyone tracking me. By the time I reached the Tube station ten minutes later, the sensation had worn off.

* * *

Helen was enthralled when I told her what had happened with Tom over dinner.

'So when he had the chance with you, he didn't take it, and now he wants you? Now that's what I call karma.'

'Now I know more about him and his past, I can understand why he behaved the way he did back then. I'm not angry with him any more. If anything, I feel sorry for him.'

'Well, it doesn't matter now anyway, you're a taken woman.'

'Speaking of taken women, how's it going with you and your young flame?'

'I'm not sure it's going to work out.'

'Oh? Why not?'

'We're just so different, I can't see a future in it.'

'Still not ready to tell me her name?'

'Nope.'

'I've never known you to be such a dark horse, Helen, you really have me intrigued.'

'Anyway.' Helen clearly wanted to change the subject. 'How are the wedding plans going?'

'Great,' I enthused. 'We love the venue we've chosen and it's a relief that they'll sort out all the catering. I've got an appointment with a florist on Saturday and I've emailed a few cake makers. So, I'm storming through the to-do list.'

'What about Jude?'

'He's in charge of the band and photographer. We're not bothering with wedding cars.'

'What, you're going to get the Tube in your wedding dress?'

I laughed. 'Why not? It'll be quite the talking point. Anyway, I'm not planning on wearing a traditional gown. I'm thinking of something red, actually.'

'Have you met his parents yet?'

'No, he keeps putting it off.' I was starting to get a little paranoid about it. He'd told them that we were engaged and a few days later we'd received a lovely card from his mum. I was beginning to wonder if it was me he was keeping from his parents, or vice versa. But when I confessed this to Helen, she was more pragmatic.

'Some people just aren't that close to their parents. And you know the old saying. "A son is a son till he gets a wife, but a daughter is a daughter all her life".'

'I guess so.'

'Anyway, what about your hen do? Any ideas about what you want or would you prefer it to be a surprise?'

I'd asked Helen, Emily and Shiv to be my bridesmaids. 'I'd like to go for a lovely dinner somewhere with my nearest and dearest, that's easy for everyone to get to.'

'Well, thanks for making life so easy for us. I still need a guest list and email addresses though, so can you send them over?'

'Sure, I'll do it at the weekend. Speaking of which, Emily will be back from her honeymoon in a couple of days. We should do something nice to welcome her back.'

'Gosh, I can't believe you're getting married so soon after Emily. I feel like we spent years talking about her wedding and we've only talked about yours for five seconds.'

'It's crazy, I know. Sometimes I can't believe it myself.'

'I'm the last single girl standing.'

'Oh there's plenty of other single girls still standing. Lucky for you.'

'We'll still meet up, won't we, Simmy? For our coffees and dinners and so on?'

'Of course we will. You're not getting rid of me that easily.'

We finished dinner and said our goodbyes, and by the time I got back to the flat, I was shattered and ready to hit the sack. But I knew immediately from the look on Jude's face that something was wrong.

'Hey,' I said, looking at him quizzically.

'Have a good evening?' His tone was frosty.

'It was great.' I sat down next to him but he moved a couple of inches away from me. 'Jude, what's wrong?'

'Anything you want to tell me?'

'I don't think so, no.'

He looked at me and his face was a picture of anger and hurt. 'I saw you. With that guy.'

I knew he must mean Tom, but my immediate reaction wasn't guilt, it was confusion. How on earth had he seen us? What had he been doing at the pub?

'How did you see us?'

'You were quite hard to miss, Simone, you were both standing on the street for all to see.'

'But what were you doing there?'

'Is that all you care about right now? Not that you were kissing another man, but that I caught you?'

'Listen, Tom is a work colleague and he was drunk. He tried to kiss me, I told him it wasn't happening and that was the end of it. If you really were there, then you'll know I'm telling the truth.'

Jude appeared to mull this over. 'You don't just kiss someone out of the blue like that. There must be some background.'

I had nothing to hide and I told him everything. 'Tom and I dated briefly last year. It didn't work out and that was the end of it. There's nothing between us and there hasn't been for a long time. I don't know what got into him tonight, but I can assure you that I have no feelings for him.'

'I've a right mind to go and punch him in the face.'

'Jude!' I'd never seen this side of him before.

'Does he know you're with someone else?'

'Yes, he does. Like I said, I don't know what got into him, other than a skinful of booze. He was very apologetic afterwards and I know that it will never happen again.'

The hostility was already leaving Jude's face. 'I'm sorry I jumped to conclusions.'

'It must have been a shock to see something like that. I'd have been livid too, if I were you. But Jude, what were you doing there in the first place?'

'I forgot you were going out after work and I decided to surprise you at the office and take you out to dinner. I was walking past the pub when I saw you with him.'

'You should have just come over and spoken to me. We could have cleared this up in no time.'

He hung his head. 'I know. I'm sorry.'

'Never mind, it's all cleared up now. I love you, Jude, I'd never cheat on you. Never.'

He put his arm around me. 'I know. I'm an eejit.'

'Yes you are, but you're my eejit.'

We sat on the sofa for a while, wrapped up in each other's arms, and I exhaled, relieved that we'd been able to clear the misunderstanding up so easily. Jude may have jumped to the wrong conclusions but at least he wasn't too proud to admit when he was wrong. He'd listened to my explanation and he'd believed me, and that was the most important thing.

I was still keen to lighten the mood between us, though, to make sure that things really were okay. 'Hey, we never did have that make-up sex after Emily's wedding.'

'You're right.'

'Well, there's no time like the present.'

I looked at him, waiting for his reaction, hoping desperately that he wasn't still brewing on what he'd seen. But then he said, 'Okay, madam, get ready for your in-flight entertainment.' And he pulled my legs out from under me, making me squeal, and pushed his lips down on to mine.

As I wrapped my legs around him and kissed him back, a thought crept into my head, but I pushed it away. I was overthinking things, being melodramatic. We'd just had an extremely honest conversation, full disclosure, and it had made us stronger for it. There was no way that I was sabotaging something so special because of my misplaced paranoia.

But the thought, while fleeting, had been there. *Jude wasn't just passing by. He was watching me.*

11

The ladies had really pulled it out of the bag. The restaurant was picture-book perfect, one of those hidden gems that you didn't even know existed, that you could walk past on the street a thousand times without ever realising it was there.

There were ten of us, my true nearest and dearest. The only person missing was my sister but she was flying over for the wedding. Mum had come down from Peterborough and was chatting with Emily, asking about her wedding and honeymoon. I couldn't believe that I was getting married in a week's time. It had been the craziest, and best, period of my life. Jude and I were as high as kites and falling more in love with each other every day. Neither of us had mentioned the incident between me and Tom again and now it felt as though it had never happened. We'd been too busy with other things, consumed with wedding and honeymoon plans. We were going to spend Christmas with Mum and then go to South Africa a few days later and we'd be bringing in the new year on a safari. It had meant that we'd blown some of our house deposit savings, but we'd decided it was worth it. In many ways, it felt like our last adventure before married life and who-knew-what after that.

There were so many exciting things happening over the next few weeks that I was almost ready to burst. The only thing that still troubled me was that I hadn't met Jude's parents and we'd run out of time to arrange it before the wedding. Jude had said that they were both coming and were looking forward to meeting me but something about it didn't feel quite right. Whenever I discussed it with Helen, though, she always reassured me, telling me to count myself lucky that I wouldn't have an overbearing mother-in-law.

At least it meant that we could plan the wedding we wanted without any interference, because Mum had left us to it too, and I was so pleased that Jude had suggested Christmas. It had been the perfect idea and everything had fitted easily into place. As I looked around at my friends, all chatting amongst themselves, I felt such contentment and I wondered if life got any better than this.

One of my work colleagues, Ruth, was talking about her own wedding to a captive, female audience. 'It was all going perfectly until I started walking down the aisle and then I got that crampy feeling in my stomach, you *know*, the warning sign that the time of the month had arrived. I was three days early, for goodness' sake, how unlucky is that?'

We all clucked sympathetically, imagining her horror as she had to endure a long ceremony, standing in a pristine white dress. 'What did you do?' Emily asked.

'I was too embarrassed to say anything so I just stood there, hoping that the odds would be in my favour, but the whole time I was saying my vows, I was absolutely terrified. As soon as the ceremony was over, I dashed to the loo at the back of the church. It was not what you'd call a dignified exit from my own wedding. Fortunately, I got there in time.'

'Oh, you poor thing,' Emily said.

Ruth turned to me. 'Word of advice, Simone. If there's any risk at all that you might be about to surf the crimson tide, take precautionary measures!'

I laughed along with the rest of the ladies but then I got a sinking feeling in the pit of my stomach, and not the one that Ruth was talking about. Subtly, I reached for my phone and opened my health app, looking to see when my last period was. Seven weeks ago. That wasn't unusual for me as I was often irregular. But my heart started beating rapidly as I considered the possibility. Surely not? The chances must be slim to none.

'You okay?' Helen was looking at me with concern.

'I need the loo,' I gasped, standing up and hurtling towards the toilets, hoping that my own undignified exit didn't raise any eyebrows among my friends and family.

Wordlessly, Helen followed me, and as soon as we reached the loos, she said, 'What's going on?'

'I'm three weeks late.'

'Christ, Simone! And you've only just realised?'

'I'm often late, it's not really anything unusual.'

Helen's face relaxed. 'Okay, so why are you stressing?'

'I don't know, I just have this weird feeling. I can't explain it.'

'Do you not use contraception?'

I grimaced. 'No, I came off the pill after me and Tom finished and I swore off men. And I was so convinced that I wouldn't conceive naturally I've been a bit careless with Jude.'

Helen pulled out her phone and did some fast googling. 'Okay, there's a chemist up the road that's open until nine. You stay here and I'll go get a test.'

'I can't just hide in here, Helen, everyone will wonder what's wrong with me!'

'Fine, go back out and then when I come back, make your excuses.'

'Okay.'

Helen dashed off and I returned to the table, trying to act normally. Everyone was telling stories about their own weddings and I listened and laughed in all the right places, but I knew I wouldn't be able to relax until I'd done a test. *It'll all be a fuss about nothing, and then I can go back to enjoying my evening*, I told myself, but at the same time I wondered if that was the outcome I was even hoping for. My mind was scrambled, my thoughts and feelings all over the place. I could see Mum watching me and I smiled reassuringly at her, trying not to show my anxiety. The last thing I wanted to do was raise any kind of alarm when it was most likely a storm in a teacup.

Helen reappeared fifteen minutes later and beckoned me over. I stood up, smiled apologetically at the crowed and headed back towards the loos.

'Here.' Helen pulled a test out of her bag. I grabbed it and locked myself in a cubicle to do the deed. My only experience of pregnancy tests was what I'd seen in films and on television shows, when couples waited ten agonising minutes to get the results, so when the second blue line started appearing immediately after the first, I stared at it in disbelief. Surely not? *Surely not?*

I stood up and unlocked the door, opening it and coming face to face with Helen. She knew immediately from the look on my face what had happened, and her hand shot to her mouth.

'Oh my good Lord.'

I looked at her wide-eyed. 'I can't believe it.'

'How did this happen?'

'I don't know. I honestly thought that I had no chance of ever having kids naturally.'

Helen, to her credit, didn't chastise me for my naivety. 'How do you feel?'

'Stunned. Shocked. Terrified. I've been drinking, Helen! What if I've done some terrible damage to the baby?'

'Don't worry about that, Simmy, lots of women drink before they realise they're pregnant. And anyway, it's not like you've been on the shots every night. But how do you *feel*? Have you and Jude talked about kids?'

I nodded, still dumbfounded. 'Yes, we both want children. But this was not how I imagined it at all. We're not even married! I'm supposed to be going on honeymoon in two weeks!'

'You can still do those things, mate.'

'But don't I need to see a doctor? Can I travel? What if something happens while we're abroad? Oh God, Helen.'

Helen took my arm and guided me towards the sinks, leaning me up against them. 'Okay, calm down, deep breaths. First thing Monday, make a doctor's appointment. They'll tell you what you can and can't do. Whatever happens, it doesn't have to have any impact on the wedding, okay? Did you get travel insurance?'

'Yes.'

'Okay, so if you need to cancel or postpone the honeymoon, you can. All these things are material, Simone, they can be sorted out with a few phone calls or emails. The most important thing is, are you pleased or not pleased about this?'

I looked at her, my face as white as a sheet. And then I said, 'I'm pleased.' And as I said it, I knew that I meant it. It had happened much quicker, and far more easily, than I had expected but I wanted to be a mother and I knew that Jude would make an amazing father.

Shiv appeared, sticking her head around the door. 'What's

going on in here? You guys have been ages, people are starting to worry.' She took one look at me, and the pregnancy test that I was still clutching on to and gasped. 'Are you serious?'

I nodded. 'I can't believe it.'

Shiv rushed over and hugged me. 'This is amazing news, Simone!'

'But the timing!'

'Oh, never mind the timing. I was pregnant when I got married, although don't ever tell my parents that, they still haven't worked out the maths. How do you feel?'

I wondered if I'd be answering questions about how I felt for the next nine months. Nine months? Oh my goodness. It was still sinking in.

Emily appeared then. 'What's going on in here, guys?' She looked at each of us, her gaze finally resting on me and then moving down towards my hand. 'Is that what I think it is?'

'Yes.'

'Are you?'

'Yes.'

Emily gave a high-pitched squeal. 'Oh, wow, Simone!'

She ran over and hugged me and soon the four of us were in some sort of group embrace, half laughing, half crying. I could have stayed there forever, in the warm, safe cocoon of my friends' arms but after a couple of minutes Shiv said, 'As lovely as this is, we'd better head outside before people really start to worry.'

I nodded. 'You're right, let's go.'

'Will you be okay?' Helen asked.

'I'll be fine, just cover for me, okay? I'm not going to drink any more but I'm not ready to tell people. So, make out like you've been pouring me drinks all night.'

'Don't worry, we've got your back.'

We headed back to the table and I sat down, fielding off questions from everyone else about where I'd been, telling them that I'd felt a bit unwell but that I was fine now. I was so relieved that I'd decided to have a sedate hen do rather than a raucous night out. All I wanted to do was get through this dinner and go home to Jude. I wondered how he was going to react to the news. I hoped he'd be thrilled but a small part of me fretted that he'd worry it was too soon. Not only would all our plans for the next few weeks now be up in the air, but we hadn't even got married yet, let alone found a house to buy. I knew people often said that pregnancy happened when you least expected it but I never, for one moment, imagined that it would happen to me.

I somehow made it through the meal, doing my best to act as normally as I could, while Helen, Shiv and Emily gallantly deflected any attention away from my untouched glass of wine. When the bill came and a few people started talking about going on to a bar, I politely declined, saying that I was still a bit peaky and everyone was sympathetic, offering theories about pre-wedding nerves or saying that if I was coming down with something it was better to get it out of the way before next weekend. Never did I think that I'd be so pleased to leave my own hen do.

On the street outside, Mum sidled over. 'Everything okay, love? You've been awfully quiet.'

I wanted to tell her, but I needed to tell Jude first. 'I'm fine, Mum, honestly. Will you be okay getting back?'

'Yes, I'm booked on the ten-thirty train back to Peterborough so I'd best be heading off.'

'I'll see you next Saturday. Thank you so much for coming.'

Mum hugged me tightly. 'I'm so proud of you, Simmy.'

I waved her off and then said goodbye to my workmates, who were all heading out for another drink somewhere, with Shiv and Emily tagging along too. Soon it was just me and Helen left.

'Want to share a taxi?'

'Yes please.'

We booked an Uber and climbed in, and as the car pulled away, I rested my head on Helen's shoulder. 'Thank you for tonight. I don't know what I'd do without you.'

She took my hand. 'Any time. And for what it's worth, you're going to make an amazing mum.'

'Thank you.'

'And Jude's going to make an amazing dad too.'

'You do like him, don't you?'

Helen squeezed my hand. 'Of course I do. What's brought this on?'

'I don't know, just something Shiv and Emily said a while back, about everything being on his terms.'

'Look, I genuinely think he's one of the most decent blokes I've ever met, and you know I wouldn't say that if I didn't mean it.'

I smiled, relieved to hear her words. 'Me too.'

'Everything okay between you two?'

I closed my eyes. 'Everything's perfect.'

When the taxi pulled up outside the flat, Helen had to nudge me awake. 'You were drooling on my shoulder,' she said.

'Oh gosh, sorry, I must have nodded off.'

'Has that been happening a lot recently?'

'Yeah, I've been pretty tired but I thought it was because I was so busy with wedding planning.'

'Well, now you know the real reason why.'

'I guess so.'

I climbed out of the taxi, waved goodbye to Helen and let myself into the flat. Jude was still up, watching TV and drinking a beer. He looked at me in surprise.

'You're back earlier than I thought you'd be.'

'Yep.'

I took my coat off and went to sit down next to Jude on the

sofa. He looked at me in concern. 'Are you okay? You're looking a little pale.'

'I'm fine. Listen, Jude, we need to talk.'

'Uh-oh.' His face fell. 'That doesn't sound good. Don't tell me you're having second thoughts about the wedding?'

'No, nothing like that.' I turned to face him. 'Jude, I'm pregnant.'

Jude looked at me in shock, opened his mouth and then closed it again, and I waited for his reaction. When none was forthcoming, I said, 'I know, I can't believe it either. I had no idea. It wasn't until someone mentioned something about their wedding and how they were caught out and, oh forget it. It doesn't matter how I worked it out. The fact is, I'm pregnant.'

Jude still looked like he'd been stunned and I wondered if he was going to freak out. But then suddenly his entire face lit up and he leapt up and punched the air. 'Yes!'

I exhaled, releasing the breath I didn't even know I'd been holding. 'I take it you're pleased?'

Jude threw himself at me, pulling me to him. 'Simmy, I couldn't be happier. When you said that it might not happen easily for us, if at all, I prepared myself for a long, difficult journey. But this is just incredible. How did it happen?'

'I honestly don't know. I wasn't on the pill because my chances of conceiving were so low.' I realised I'd never actually told Jude that and hoped he wouldn't be angry, but he didn't seem to care. 'Maybe because I wasn't even thinking about it, or stressing about it? I don't know.'

'Ah, who cares. It's a miracle.' Jude put his hand on my stomach. 'This baby is our miracle.'

'But Jude, it throws a lot of things up in the air. We may not be able to go on honeymoon.'

'Who cares about that, I've been on plenty of holidays. This is more important.'

Jude's joy was infectious and any last shred of doubt I'd had about the timing of my surprise pregnancy vanished. 'We're going to be parents, Jude!'

His eyes were misty now. 'I know. I can't believe it.'

We sat on the sofa, in each other's arms, and I daydreamed about the future, picturing Jude, me and this miracle baby we'd been blessed with. I couldn't believe how much my life had changed in just a few months. If you'd told me at the beginning of the year that I'd end it married and pregnant, I'd have laughed it off but now here I was.

Someone did tell you. It hit me, out of the blue. I hadn't thought about Mystic Maggie in weeks but suddenly I was back in that tent, looking into her intense, dark eyes as she foretold my future. Hadn't she said that I would meet someone soon? She'd even mentioned the patter of tiny feet and I'd been offended by her comments at the time, finding them insensitive and flippant. But she'd been right. She'd been right about everything.

Look for the signs. The missing necklace that I'd found months later. The sudden thunderstorm on my first date with Jude, the knife in the flowers. The fact that I hadn't even met Jude's parents yet. I had made myself dismiss them all, yet now suddenly I wasn't so sure I should have done. My mind was a jumble of confused thoughts that I couldn't piece together. Had I really stood at the crossroads that Mystic Maggie had predicted? Had I made the choice she warned me against? And did that mean the clock was about to start ticking? Five years of being happily married, she'd said, and then a tragedy. I felt nauseous then and I put my hand to my mouth.

'Are you okay?' Jude pulled away and looked at me.

How could I tell him? He'd think I was ridiculous. But my

anxiety was starting to spiral and I had to say something because if I didn't, it would fester.

'Just before we met, the girls and I went to a funfair and saw a fortune teller. She told me I would soon meet the man of my dreams, but if I married him, a terrible tragedy would befall me five years later. She even mentioned that I'd have a baby. Jude, I'm freaking out.'

Jude, to his credit, didn't laugh at me. But it was obvious that he didn't take it seriously either. 'Simone, you're a woman in her thirties. Being told that you're going to marry and have children is a pretty safe bet for someone who's being paid to predict your future.'

'I know, but why did she say all that stuff about a tragedy?'

'Who knows, maybe she was just not a very nice person and wanted to mess with your head? It's all a load of rubbish.'

'That's what Helen said too.'

'What did she predict for the others?'

'Helen refused to see her. From what I remember, she told Emily she'd meet someone tall, dark and handsome and that she'd get a promotion at work. And she told Shiv she'd travel abroad.'

'And have any of these things happened?'

'No.'

'Then I rest my case. No one can predict your future, Simmy.'

His words soothed me, and I snuggled into him again. 'I know, but I still think it's weird.'

'My mum's friend used to write the horoscopes for her local paper. She once admitted to me that she made them all up. Literally, she wrote whatever came into her head.'

'Really?'

'Really. So, forget about this so-called fortune teller and focus on what's important. This time next week, you're going to be Mrs

Pearce. And soon there's going to be a baby Pearce. Heck, we'd better start looking at places to live, I'm not sure this flat is very baby-friendly.'

I looked around. 'You're right. Gosh, we've got a lot to do, haven't we?'

'Yes. But we're doing it together, and you know what? I can't wait.'

I reached up and kissed him, trying to push any thoughts of Mystic Maggie to the back of my mind. Jude was right, we had far more important things to think about. 'Me neither.'

12

I'd never been fussed over so much in my life. Emily was on her knees straightening the hem of my scarlet dress, Shiv was rubbing lipstick off my teeth and Helen was smoothing out my festive bouquet of sumptuous red roses, berries and pine cones. She stood back and admired me.

'Oh, Simmy, you look beautiful.'

'Thank you.'

'Are you cold?'

'No,' I lied, ignoring the goosebumps on my arms from the December chill. I did have a cardigan to wear after the ceremony, but I was determined to walk down the aisle without it.

'Are you ready?'

Was I? I couldn't believe I was finally here, on the cusp of saying my vows. The week had gone by in a flurry of activity. I'd managed to get a doctor's appointment but she had just referred me to the maternity services of a local hospital and advised me that I could travel if I wanted but to make sure I had adequate insurance. After much discussion, Jude and I had decided to go ahead with the honeymoon. We'd also started registering our details with estate agents so that we could start looking in earnest for a family home as soon as we got back. And on top of that, there had been a million and one last minute wedding preparations to arrange.

I wasn't sure whether my pregnancy symptoms had ramped up a notch or I was simply more aware of them now, but my tiredness seemed to have increased tenfold and I felt nauseous in the mornings, unable to stomach anything but dry toast, crackers and sweets. I'd finished work on Wednesday and it had been a relief not to have to go into the office and force myself through a day's work. My colleagues had given me a bottle of champagne, which I hadn't been able to tell them I couldn't drink, and they'd all contributed to a lovely card wishing us congratulations. On my last day, Tom had come over to wish me good luck for the big day. Although we were both trying to act normally around each other, things had become strained between us since he'd tried to kiss me and I wasn't sure we'd go back to the easy banter we'd only just started to develop before it happened. Tom had no idea of the trouble that kiss had almost caused me and there was no point in telling him because it would only make him feel guiltier.

But why was I even thinking about Tom? I was about to marry the man of my dreams and he was the only person I wanted on my mind. I loved Jude more than any man I had ever known and I couldn't wait to become his wife, and the mother of his child. Any doubt I'd had about him after the Tom debacle, or my chat with Emily at her hen do, were completely gone and I had never been more certain of anything. I looked at Helen. 'I'm ready.'

I'd asked Mum to walk me down the aisle and she had bought a fancy new outfit for the occasion. I was so used to seeing her in jeans and a jumper that the sight of her standing by the door, dressed up to the nines and waiting for me, made me so emotional that I had to fight back tears. As she took my arm she leaned in and said, 'I'm so proud of you, Simmy and your dad would have been too.'

'Thanks, Mum.'

The girls, resplendent in dark green, fell into step behind us as we walked into the room where the civil ceremony was being held. I wasn't nervous, I was one hundred per cent excited, anticipation racing through me. I saw Jude at the other end of the room, looking handsome in his grey suit, and when he caught my eye a huge smile spread across both our faces and I knew we were both thinking the same thing. We were the luckiest people in the world.

As the registrar greeted us and began the ceremony, I was barely listening to her words, barely concentrating on anything but the man standing in front of me who was about to become my husband. The wedding guests were nothing but a blurry sea of faces, fading into the background so it seemed like me and Jude were the only people in the world. Just fifteen minutes later, I was officially Mrs Pearce. The guests cheered as Jude and I shared our first kiss as husband and wife and then we clasped hands and walked up the aisle, smiling at all our friends and family who had come back into focus again and were beaming at us and waving. I saw Helen delicately wiping away a tear and Emily clutching Mark's hand. Shiv gave me a thumbs up. It was the quickest, and most glorious, walk of my life.

When we finally exited the room and the doors closed behind us, we looked at each other.

'Hello, Mrs Pearce,' he said.

'Hello, Mr Pearce.'

'How are you feeling?'

Jude asked me this about twenty times a day now that I was carrying his child. 'Wonderful.'

'I'm sorry you can't celebrate with a glass of champagne.'

'I don't need champagne to enjoy this day. It's already perfect.'

Jude leaned in and kissed me. 'You're perfect.'

Our moment of calm was brief. Soon the door opened, and the guests started to pile out, stopping to congratulate us, shake our hands or give us a hug, and I grinned at everyone, thanking them, while also wondering when I might be able to sit down. Having to hide my pregnancy from forty people wasn't going to be easy but I was nowhere near ready to announce it yet. I leaned into Jude, and he put his arm around me, propping me up. I knew he could sense my tiredness and I loved him so much for having my back that I thought I might burst.

When Jude's mum appeared, he finally introduced us, and I gave her a hug.

'I'm so sorry we haven't had the chance to meet yet,' I told her.

'Me too.'

She gave me a smile that didn't quite meet her eyes, and as she walked off, I leaned into Jude. 'I think your mum's annoyed.'

'Why would she be annoyed?'

'Because she's never met your bride before?'

'What? No, that's just her manner. Don't worry about it.'

In any case, I didn't have much time to worry before the next guest was hugging and congratulating me, and when Jude's dad appeared a few minutes later, he was full of smiles as he welcomed me to the family. I beamed at him, brimming with happiness. If Jude's mum was angry, then Jude would have to sort it out with her. After all, it was his fault that we hadn't met. Still, I made a mental note to spend some time with her at some point during the evening.

I'd always imagined that my wedding would be a raucous affair with everyone, including me, dancing until the early hours, but I knew that I'd be ready to retire by eleven. However, I wasn't disappointed that things hadn't turned out the way I'd imagined because they'd turned out better. I'd met the man of my dreams and we were going to spend the rest of our lives together. I'd spent my entire adult life thinking that I might not be able to have children and yet it had happened so quickly and unexpectedly, it felt like a miracle, like the gods were saying that Jude and I were a good match and we belonged together. Or maybe it was just my wedding day, sprinkled with a hefty dose of pregnancy hormones, which were making me sentimental.

We'd decided against a top table and instead Jude and I were sitting with Mum, my sister, Helen, Shiv, Avyaan, Emily and Mark. I'd asked Helen if she wanted to bring her mystery girlfriend to the wedding, but she'd said that they weren't together and offered no further information. I hadn't probed her on it because if she wanted to talk to me, she would.

I was sitting between Jude and Mum, and as we sat down to eat, Mum leaned in towards me and whispered, 'How are you holding up?'

I assumed she was talking about the overwhelming nature of a wedding. 'Great, thanks, Mum.'

'It can be hard going in the first trimester.'

I turned to her in alarm. 'How did you know?'

She smiled. 'I didn't for sure, but I do now. I suspected it after you started acting all strange at your hen do when that girl was going on about her wedding day near miss. And I've been watching you like a hawk all day. You haven't had a drop of alcohol.'

'I couldn't believe it, Mum, I'm still in shock.'

'It's what you and Jude want, though, isn't it?'

'Yes, absolutely. We just weren't expecting it to happen so soon, if at all.'

Mum squeezed my knee under the table. 'It's wonderful news.'

'You don't think we've rushed into this, do you, Mum?' As I

said it, I held my breath, praying for her to say the words I was hoping to hear.

'Like I told you before, Simmy – when you know, you know.'

I exhaled shakily. 'Thanks, Mum.'

Sensing a few pairs of eyes on us, Mum changed the subject and continued in a louder tone. 'I'd like to propose a toast. To the bride and groom.'

Everyone on our table lifted their glasses into the air and then guests at the other tables cottoned on to what was happening and did the same. 'To the bride and groom,' they all called back.

I closed my eyes, savouring the moment, drinking in every second of it, trying to memorise this feeling so that I wouldn't forget it. When I opened them again, Jude was looking at the middle of the dance floor with a frown. I followed his gaze.

'What's up?' I asked.

'Something's wrong with the cake.'

My eyes landed on the beautiful white cake we'd ordered which had just been wheeled out on to the dance floor ready to be cut after dinner, and then my hand shot to my mouth. The top tier had streaks of red running down it. It looked hideous, almost like it was dripping in blood.

'Oh my God,' I said as I stood up and rushed over, with Jude behind me. We reached the cake and stared down at the red drips which looked like something from a horror movie.

'Did you order it like this?' Jude asked.

'Of course not,' I snapped.

'Then what happened?'

'Is it... is it blood?'

Jude and I looked at each other. I didn't know what he was thinking but I knew exactly what I was. *It's a sign*. The fear which I had been forcing myself to push away with increasing frequency was back. The cake was the clearest warning I'd had yet that danger lay ahead and for a moment my whole world stood still. I could sense people's eyes on us, alert to the fact that something wasn't right. *Is she here?* I thought, even though I knew it wasn't rational. *Is Mystic Maggie here?* It was like I could feel her in the room, watching me.

Then Jude started chuckling and I stared at him, wide-eyed. 'What's so funny?'

'It's your dress,' he said.

I glanced down at my dress. 'What are you talking about?'

'Look.' He pointed to the little bride and groom cake toppers. I'd asked the cake designer to paint my dress red, to match the real-life one, and now I could see that the dye had run.

Jude reached a finger out and licked one of the drops. 'Mmm, tasty.'

I was nearly in tears, though. 'It's not funny, Jude. It's horrific.'

'It does look a little morbid, I'll give you that. Did you check the cake this morning?'

'No, it was delivered straight to the venue.'

'Well then, lesson learned. Anyway, it still tastes good and that's the main thing.'

Jude gave me a kiss and moved away to talk to some friends who were beckoning him over. For him, the drama was finished. But I stood, staring at the cake, wondering how a tiny bit of red dye could make so much mess. Was that really what had happened? I wanted to believe it, and yet something was preventing me. Mum came over and stood beside me, taking my hand.

'What happened here then?'

I explained about the dye. 'It's ruined,' I cried, trying not to let my tears fall.

'Oh, love, it's only a cake. I think it looks quite atmospheric.'

'What if it's a sign?'

Mum frowned. 'A sign of what?'

'That me and Jude shouldn't have got married.'

Mum squeezed my hand. 'Stop that. It's just wedding day nerves, love. We all get them. And you're full of hormones too from the pregnancy. Trust me, this isn't a sign.'

Mum's words soothed me and I tried to calm down. 'Okay,' I said quietly.

Mum was studying the cake, her head cocked to the side. 'I reckon I can fix this up in no time.' She beckoned to a passing waiter. 'Help me get this to the kitchen, will you?'

Mum and the waiter wheeled the cake off, and when they emerged a few minutes later, the top tier had been removed and the cake was pure white again, as though nothing had happened. But my memory wasn't as easy to erase. As we tucked into dinner, all I could see was red.

'Your mum's done a good job fixing the cake,' Jude remarked, and I looked over at Mum, who was looking at me with a reassuring smile on her face.

'Yes.' It was all I could muster.

Jude looked at me in concern. 'Are you okay, Simmy?'

I forced a smile. 'Yes, I'm great.'

As I said it, I realised how much I wanted it to be true, how determined I was to shake off this feeling of dread and enjoy myself again. It was my wedding day and I wasn't going to let the questionable handiwork of a cake maker ruin my moment. All the people I loved most in the world were in this room, wanting to celebrate with me and I was going to have a good time. With a final glance at the cake, I took Jude's hand and held it in my own.

It was nearly midnight when we finally decided to call it a night. I was exhausted from talking to so many people as Jude and I worked our way around the room. I'd sat down next to his mum but after only a few minutes I'd been whisked off to meet someone else and we hadn't had the chat I was hoping for. But I told myself that there was plenty of time for that, now that Jude and I were husband and wife. I couldn't believe I'd made it to the end completely sober, but I was high on life and love, and it was stronger than any amount of champagne I could have consumed. Anyway, it seemed that my guests had consumed more than enough on my behalf. By the time the DJ had finished packing up, a small huddle of guests had formed, including Helen, Shiv and Emily, and were talking about going to a late bar.

I looked at Jude. 'I'm done in but you're welcome to go with them if you fancy it.'

He laughed. 'Are you kidding me? It's our wedding night, Simmy, and the only person I want to spend it with is you.'

'But just to manage your expectations, I'm going to fall asleep the second my head hits the pillow and there's a very good chance I won't even take my make-up off.'

Jude put his arm around me. 'I'm happy to watch you sleep all night.'

'That actually sounds a little creepy.'

He laughed. 'Okay then, I'll watch you sleep for, like, a minute and then I'll probably pass out too. I'm knackered. Shall I get us a taxi?'

'Yes please.'

Jude moved away to book a cab and Helen replaced him by my side.

'Did you have a good night, Simmy?'

I smiled, pushing away my memory of the ruined cake. 'The best. You?'

'It was awesome. Didn't I tell you it was a good idea to get you two together?'

'Oh yeah, you've told me about a dozen times, mate. Bet you

didn't think you'd be attending our wedding so soon, though, did you?'

Helen shrugged. 'I had a good feeling about it from the start. And I know you guys are going to be really happy together.'

I opened my mouth to tell her that the fortune teller's chilling prediction had got to me again, but then Jude drifted back over. 'The taxi will be outside in five minutes.'

I gave Helen a hug. 'Enjoy the after party, Hels. Have a drink for me.'

Blowing kisses at the remaining guests, I followed Jude out of the room and onto the pavement outside. The Christmas lights hanging above us lit up the midnight sky and the air was frosty but dry. I snuggled into Jude and felt butterflies in my stomach, despite my exhaustion, at what was yet to come.

My life was about to change forever, not just because I was married now but because I was soon to become a mother. I was scared, excited and overwhelmed. But most of all, I was happy. The whole evening, bar the cake, had been magical. It was time to forget about silly signs and move on with the next chapter of my life. And although I was old and wise enough to know that it wouldn't always be easy, I was certain that with Jude by my side, I could tackle anything.

PART II

13

They took it in turns to torment me. One would start and then, as soon as they were beginning to tire, the other would take over, wearing me down until I was an empty shell with nothing left to give. How long had it been like this? Months? Years? Decades? Centuries? I had lost track of time, every day merging into the next, so that I could hardly remember what life was like before and I could barely contemplate what it might be in the future. It was just, this.

Ivy and Samuel had been born at thirty-five weeks. Apparently for twins, that was pretty good going but to me it felt like they'd stolen time away from us, precious time that we needed and craved. We'd scarcely even got our heads around the fact that we were going to be parents before they were thrust into my arms, one on each side and, as I looked down at them, all I could think was, *how am I going to manage?*

They were a blessing, of course they were. We knew we were incredibly fortunate. We'd just wanted a few more weeks, a little more time to prepare, to steady ourselves in the calm before the storm. To complete on the sale of our new house and be able to move and unpack. To not be living among looming towers of cardboard boxes, knowing that the worst was yet to come. For Jude not to be in Paris when I went into labour, an unavoidable work trip which he'd justified by saying he could be home quicker than if he'd gone to York for the day.

Sometimes I think that if I'd just had a bit more time to prepare then everything would have been okay. I usually have this thought in the middle of the day when I'm sitting on the sofa, trying to ignore the chaos around me – toys scattered across the floor, the constant screaming, the reeking smell of a soiled nappy – yet so acutely tuned into it that I'm trapped inside it, unable to escape. I think of the six hours I have left before Jude comes home and I wonder if we'll all survive until then. And then I wonder if I even want Jude to come home, if it isn't easier without him.

And then one of my tormentors will toddle up to me, wiggling their stinky bottom from side to side, and say, 'Mama!' And then the other one, desperate not to be left out, will hurry over too, clambering onto the sofa and burying themselves into me, almost as though they are trying to get back inside me. And I will kiss the top of their heads, breathe in the scent of them and feel at once an acute sense of being numbingly overwhelmed, a visceral protectiveness and a strange contentment that I can't explain because it's involuntary, something I feel without thinking.

And slowly, in this moment, I start to come back to myself. I think of getting the children down for their naps, of snatching an hour to myself while they sleep, of taking them out in the buggy later and going to M&S so I can buy a nice bottle of wine for when Jude gets home from work because I've just realised that it might possibly be Friday today. I reach for my phone so I can text Jude and ask him if he fancies a Thai takeaway that evening. And then, like a light switch, I am no longer trapped in the long, hopeless tunnel of despair, I am facing towards the light, and I am slowly, steadily, moving towards it. I can feel it and I know that it is going to be okay.

Everyone said the early years were difficult. After that, people went one of two ways; either their faces contorted in sympathy when they realised that twins took difficult to a whole new level or they tried to cheer me up by saying that our babies would always have a playmate and that would, in the long term at least, make things easier. Of course, I didn't really get it until it happened. I smiled coyly, stroked my bump and thought of all the ways that I was going to be a better mother, a different mother to those people. And then I had them and I realised that I was just like everyone else, shocked to my core, exhausted beyond my wildest imagination, surviving, not thriving and living each day like its own, separate eternity.

When Jude and I first got married, I could not imagine what was to come. We went on honeymoon, saw elephants and lions and rhinos and snuggled up under a blanket in our South African lodge, sipping hot tea and feeling elated to be alive, to be experiencing this incredible earth that we lived on. Dare I say it, we were smug.

When we got home, we ploughed straight into hospital appointments and house viewings and returning to work, trying to get into the swing of an everyday life that was the same as we had always known yet also vastly different. At the twelve-week scan, we had clasped hands and prayed for our baby to be okay. And then we had learned that it was not one baby that we needed to pray for but two and we had laughed and cried and panicked in equal measures. But we had held steady, an unbreakable partnership, as solid as a rock. And I had believed, just as I had on the day we married, that we could cope with anything as long as we had each other.

I still believe that, even after all we have been through. There have been times when I have doubted it of course, times when I have questioned our marriage, my sanity, but these episodes have been temporary, never permanent, a consequence of the highly stressful situation we found ourselves in. Overall, I would say that we have been extremely happy.

But it wasn't without its tests. The twins made a dramatic entrance into the world and were whisked off to the neonatal ward to be monitored. Whereas other mothers got to hold their baby to their chest and go home twelve hours later, we spent five days in hospital, watching our babies, waiting for our turn to be discharged. And then when we were, we weren't sure if we were thrilled or disappointed because life was easier, safer, in hospital than it was at home, where we were on our own, in charge of these two beautiful beings with no idea what they wanted.

The first few months were the hardest of my life. I didn't sleep, I forgot to eat and self-care went out of the window. Jude was incredible, as I'd known he would be, but he had to go back to work after a couple of weeks and I was on my own, confused, exhausted, afraid. My mum was my hero and I still don't know what I would have done without her. She travelled down to London regularly, helping us move into our new house, a three-bed terraced about a mile away from Crouch End, where prices were cheaper. She minded the babies while I slept, took them out when she knew, without asking, that I needed a break, and told me I was doing great. Inevitably, though, the time would always come when she had to go back to her own life and I wondered how I would survive without her. The days passed slowly, the nights even more so. For a long time, I thought this was my life now, that it would never change, I would always feel this way. People said *this too shall pass* but I didn't believe them.

And then it did pass. Not completely, of course, but slowly, almost without me realising. The twins got into a routine, largely thanks to my mother. I started sleeping more, the babies started eating solids, smiling, giggling. Their first birthday party came and went and we ordered a cake and served sandwich platters and fruit kebabs. My eagerly awaited return to work didn't materialise because I realised I didn't want it, and Jude was earning enough for me to stay at home for a little longer. I became a housewife, something I had never contemplated before. But I needed to do something, so I started writing, not like I had done previously, typing out a few hundred words and forgetting about it, but really writing. And then the twins turned two and started going to nursery and I wrote even more until I had finally finished a short story. It wasn't the one about the woman who wanted to smash the mile high club, because after giving birth, my appetite for bodice-rippers had waned, but it was a proper story and I had written it.

Now the twins are two and a half and life is returning to normality. The new normal, you might say, not the old. It's still hard, it's still exhausting but I have some time again, time to think, to breathe, to plan. There will be no more children in our future, of that we are both agreed, and I'm starting to get this wonderful sensation that we are entering yet another new chapter, one where we are parents, and always on duty, but we are slowly reclaiming some of our lives back.

Throughout all of this, Jude has been my rock. Every night he comes home and he scoops up our children, makes them giggle and takes them off for their bath and I listen to them and feel grateful that I have him, that I married him, that I still love him and that he still loves me. We don't see his parents, but I've given up pushing Jude on it because, to be honest, I've got enough on my plate. We send cards, and photos of the twins, and I've made it clear that they are always welcome to visit. Not all families are close but I'm determined that my one will be. Because I have a family now and sometimes I have to pinch myself.

It's been the hardest two and a half years of my life, but am I happy? Yes. Do I regret anything? No. In a few months the children will start preschool and I can barely believe it. Tomorrow, Mum is coming down and she's going to babysit so that Jude and I can go out for Emily's birthday dinner, and I can barely believe that either. What felt like the longest, slowest period of my life is already starting to speed up. Jude and I are having date nights again, I'll soon have five days a week to myself and before I know it, Ivy and Samuel will be starting school and our life will change again. I'll be a school mum, making new friends, worrying about reading and phonics, fretting over whether they should have school dinners or packed lunches.

The twins began to fuss now, rubbing their eyes and whingeing and I knew it was time for their nap. Scooping one up in each arm, something that was becoming increasingly difficult as they grew taller and stronger, I took them up to their bedroom and changed their nappies. Then I gently placed them in their toddler beds, kissed them gently on their foreheads and crept out, closing the door softly behind me.

Downstairs, I turned on my laptop and tried to do some writing but I couldn't concentrate so instead I reached for my phone and opened the Find My app. I liked to check in on Jude, not because I didn't trust him but because knowing where he was, seeing the little dot of his phone on a map which told me that he was at the office, made me feel reassured and safe. Then I sent a message to Helen.

Can't wait to see you tomorrow. It's been so long since we all went out!

In truth it had probably been six months. I loved the girls just as much now as I always had but being a new mother took over your life and I didn't see them as much as I would have liked.

Helen was still single and showing no sign of settling down. Shiv had been a beacon of knowledge and advice, but her children were older and she was in a different stage of life, one of football practice and violin exams and secondary school applications. And Emily, still happily married to Mark, hadn't yet announced the patter of tiny feet and we didn't bring it up because we all felt that if she wanted to tell us about it, she would do in her own time. I was acutely aware, though, that it might be hard for her to see me with my children and I was always careful not to moan around her, to harp on about how exhausting or brutal it was, because I knew it was what she dreamed of for herself.

I smiled as my phone pinged with a reply from Helen.

Can't wait either. So much to catch up on. See you at 8 xx

I tidied up some of the toys and emptied the dishwasher, and before I knew it, an hour had passed, and I could hear Ivy and Samuel stirring on the baby monitor. I gave them a few minutes and then headed upstairs. A snack and another round of nappy changes later and we were ready to face the world. Ignoring their protests, I strapped them into their seats and manoeuvred the buggy out of the front door, enjoying the feeling of daylight on my face as I strolled down the road towards the high street. I smiled at a mum that I passed, someone I recognised from a Wednesday toddler group, and in the afternoon sunshine I felt excited and hopeful for the weekend ahead.

Something caught my eye, a poster taped to the railings of the park, and I paused for a moment to read it. It was an advert for a funfair which was coming to town in two weeks and my first thought was that I might take the twins. Although they would be too young to go on most of the rides, they might enjoy the bright lights and the noise, and it would be a nice thing to do as a family.

But then a second thought came to me and it took me by surprise as it was something that hadn't entered my mind for a long time. *I've been to that fair.* It was years ago now, another lifetime, but it all started coming back to me as though no time has passed. Me, Helen, Shiv and Emily meeting by the gates on a summer's evening, heading into the fairground, riding the waltzers and sitting astride the ponies on the carousel. Then deciding to go and see the fortune teller and her giving me that strange prediction that had stayed with me for some time. What was it she'd said? My brain was so addled from the baby years that it took me a while to recall. I'd marry the man of my dreams but my happiness would only last five years.

Then it all came flooding back, and before I knew it, I was mentally calculating how far in I was. Jude and I had been married for just over three years which meant that I had two left. The thought disturbed me, even though the iota of sanity I still had left as a new mother told me there was nothing to fear. I looked down at the tops of Ivy and Samuel's heads, reliving the moment when the fortune teller said that I would soon have children, and tried to ignore the feeling of dread that washed over me. I instinctively lifted a hand and gripped on to my name necklace that I still wore every day, remembering my joy at finding it behind the drawers, something the fortune teller had foretold too. I thought about the odd things that had happened, the knife in the flowers, the red-stained wedding cake, things I had convinced myself weren't signs.

And for a second, my world started to close in on me and my breath caught in my throat. Had there been any more signs? I didn't think so but what if I'd missed them? Then Samuel started crying and I had to stop and placate him, and by the time we were ready to set off again, rationality had returned and I was just a mother again, on her way to M&S, and the idea of being able to predict my future seemed ludicrous. And then Ivy threw her favourite cuddly toy into the path of an oncoming car and started wailing even harder than her brother and when I eventually reached M&S, what felt like three hours later, I barely even remembered what my own name was any more, let alone that of a long-forgotten fortune teller.

It came back to me though, later that evening, when the children were in bed and Jude and I were drinking the wine I'd bought, alongside the Thai takeaway I'd been dreaming of all afternoon. A piece of vegetarian spring roll lodged in my throat and I took a sip of water and contemplated confiding in Jude. But it seemed so silly, so trivial compared to the complexity of our lives, Jude's busy career, the twins' development and so I swallowed it down, along with my spring roll, and didn't breathe a word.

We were happy. We had each other, we had our children. Our family was complete. We were both looking forward to this new post-baby stage in our lives and I wasn't about to let anything stand in our way. *Go away, Mystic Maggie*, I thought. *You're not getting into my head again.*

But our thoughts don't always do as they're told, do they? And sometimes it's the ones you hope to forget the most that linger, reminding you of their presence when you least want them. Persistently infiltrating your mundane, everyday musings, sometimes disappearing for a while before reappearing suddenly, feeding on your insecurities or anxiety, until before you know it they've doubled in size and there's nowhere for them to hide any more.

And by the time that's happened, it's too late to stop them.

14

The restaurant that Emily had chosen for her birthday meal was trendy and buzzing, and as Jude and I walked in, hand in hand, I felt horribly underdressed.

'Do I look okay?' I hissed to Jude.

'You look gorgeous.'

He leaned in and kissed my cheek and I clutched his hand a little tighter, grateful he was there.

'This restaurant is far too trendy for us.'

'Speak for yourself.'

I giggled and looked around the room, immediately spotting Emily, Mark, Shiv, Avyaan, Helen and a few other people sitting at a long table, popping olives into their mouths.

'Over there,' I said, and we walked over towards the table, holding our arms out as people stood up to hug us.

'You made it!' Emily looked chuffed to see us both as I kissed her on the cheek.

'Happy birthday, Em.'

'Thank you for coming.'

'We wouldn't miss it for the world.'

I sat down next to Helen and gave her arm a squeeze. 'On your own tonight?'

'We can't all be part of a smug married couple, you know.'

'Well, I don't know about smug. But it's nice to be out. And I'm only asking because I got the impression that maybe... you're seeing someone new?'

'Never mind me, tell me how those ghastly godchildren of mine are doing.'

'Terrorising the neighbourhood as usual.'

'Tell them I said "excellent work". And how's the writing going?'

I blushed a little. 'I've finished my short story, I'm going to start sending it out to magazines.'

'Wow, Simmy, that's awesome.'

'I doubt anyone will be interested but hey, at least I can say I tried.'

I didn't miss my job, not one bit. I missed the people, and the camaraderie of being in an office, but not the job itself. Jude, on the other hand, was thriving. A few months after the twins were born, he'd been given an offer he couldn't refuse at a different advertising agency which meant more responsibility and more hours, and as he sat down opposite me, Helen immediately started interrogating him about what he was working on. I ordered a drink and half listened to their conversation, while also eavesdropping on Shiv's chat with a couple of the dinner party guests about the upcoming elections. By the time the waitress came to take our food order, I'd had a glass of wine and was feeling tipsy, a stark reminder that I rarely went out these days.

I heard the sound of cutlery tapping on glass and I turned my head to see Emily, poised to speak and looking shy. The table fell silent as all eyes fell expectantly on her.

'Firstly, I'd just like to thank you all for coming tonight, it means a lot to me to be able to celebrate my birthday with you.'

We all cheered and 'hear-heared' before quietening again and waiting for her to continue.

'It turns out that tonight is a double celebration because I have some exciting news.'

We all waited, glasses hovering in the air, to find out what Emily's news was.

'You're now looking at the PA to the CEO of Sable and Sable!'

'Wow, Emily, that's amazing!' Shiv was the first one to speak. I looked at Helen and guessed that she already knew but was waiting for Emily to enjoy her moment in the spotlight.

'Thanks,' Emily said, beaming. 'It's a lot more responsibility and the CEO is already keeping me ridiculously busy, but it's a huge pay rise and I never thought I'd be considered.'

'Congrats, Emily, that's brilliant,' Jude said, holding up his glass, and I echoed his sentiment. Emily worked hard and deserved her success and as I saw Mark put his arm proudly around her, I was filled with happiness for her, and for myself for being out among grown-ups and talking about things that didn't involve toilet training and teething.

The food started to arrive and Jude leaned into me. 'You having a good time?'

'Great, how about you?'

'Yeah.'

We grinned at each other, mutually enjoying the rare treat of being out together, and I made a mental note to arrange more date nights. It was good for us to take some time out and be reminded that we still had a life away from the children, that we were still us.

'I never thought it would happen to me,' Emily was saying. 'I thought I'd climbed as high as I was ever going to get. And then out of the blue I got this email from the CEO's outgoing PA telling me that she was retiring and that they were looking to fill her shoes.'

I sipped my wine and listened, enjoying Emily's telling of the story.

'They didn't even advertise the role externally, they arranged for me to have an interview and offered it to me pretty much immediately. It was like it was written in the stars.'

Written in the stars. My smile froze. Perhaps if seeing that funfair sign hadn't jogged my memory of our trip to the fortune teller, Emily's comment would have passed over my head, remaining innocuous and irrelevant to my own life. But the two events had come too closely together and I couldn't stop myself from thinking about the predictions that Mystic Maggie had made.

'You okay?' Helen asked me.

I had to say something. But I tried to make light of it, not to make it any more of a big deal than it needed to be. 'Do you remember when we went to see that fortune teller at the funfair?'

Was it me or did Helen pale slightly at the mention of Mystic Maggie? But before I had time to analyse her reaction, her expression quickly shifted to disinterested. 'Vaguely.'

'Well, I saw that there's a funfair coming to town again in a couple of weeks and it's got me thinking about that night.'

'What about that night?'

I put my knife and fork down on my plate. 'Everything she told me would happen has happened, and now Emily too. Remember she said that Em would get a promotion at work?'

'To be honest the thing I'm most shocked about is that you even remember. It's been years since that happened!'

'I had forgotten about it,' I admitted. 'But it's on my mind again. Don't you think it's odd?'

'What, that Emily has finally got a promotion after years of slogging away at her job?'

Helen had a point but I wasn't ready to concede yet. 'What about me, though? She told me I'd get married and have children, two things I never thought would happen.'

Helen looked mock-alarmed. 'Holy moly. She told a thirty-something-year-old woman that she'd get married and have kids? This woman must have a gift!'

'All right, smart-arse.' Helen's scathing response riled me a little and prevented me from telling her about the signs. But her pragmatism also helped to alleviate my anxiety. Helen was right, nothing that Mystic Maggie had said was particularly outlandish, they were things that probably would have happened to me and Emily anyway. But there was one thing that was still lingering. 'Still, why do you think she put a five-year limit on my happiness? What was it she saw that made her so certain that I was heading for a tragedy?'

'Christ, I can't believe we're still talking about this after all these years.'

'Three and a bit years, to be precise.'

Helen raised her eyebrows. 'Not that you're counting though, right?'

'Which means I have just under two years before it all goes to hell.'

I looked up to see Jude listening intently to our conversation. 'What are you two talking about?'

'Your wife has lost the plot,' Helen said. 'I blame those godchildren of mine, they've exhausted her to the point of insanity.'

Jude laughed but I could see concern on his face. 'Are you okay, Simmy? You're not seriously worrying about what that fortune teller told you, are you?'

I glanced from Jude to Helen and then back to Jude again. Jude looked worried and Helen looked scathing. And then I checked to see if either Shiv or Emily were listening in, but they were both preoccupied with talking to other people. I was on my own, against two cynics, and I realised that I wanted Helen and Jude to be right anyway.

I smiled. 'No, of course not. Now, are we having dessert or what?'

* * *

I couldn't resist taking the kids to the funfair, though. I told myself that it was for Ivy and Sam, but I knew deep down that I was hoping that Mystic Maggie would be there. I needed to look her in the eye and see her for the fraud she was before I could truly forget about her prediction and move on with my life again. Or perhaps I was hoping that she would remember me and confess that she'd got it all wrong, maybe even apologise and tell me that, in fact, I was destined for a long and happy life despite marrying the man she had warned me against.

It didn't matter, as long as I came away knowing that I had nothing to worry about.

I was tired and ratty by the time I strapped the twins into the buggy and made my way towards the park. Ivy and Sam had both been up in the night with stuffy noses, taking it in turns to cry out, and Jude was away on a work trip so I'd been on my own, trying to soothe them while also mentally calculating the maximum amount of sleep I could possibly get that night and realising with horror that it was no more than three and a half hours. In the morning, they had been grouchy from lack of sleep, with constant rivers of snot streaming out of their noses and had both decided that they didn't want to nap, stealing my precious one hour of peace and quiet. By the time it reached 3 p.m., when the fair opened to the public, I was half considering abandoning my plan and trying again the next day. But, I reasoned, we could all do with a bit of fresh air and the buzz from the fair might cheer us all up and exhaust the twins enough to give us all a better night's sleep later.

They fussed in the buggy and I had to continuously pass them rice cakes in order to prevent a full-on meltdown, but as soon as we reached the fair they both fell silent, looking around at the rides and the lights in stunned awe. I bought some ride tokens and pushed the buggy through the short grass, casting my eye around at the attractions to see if I could locate the little tent I remembered so well. But this was a small fair, consisting mainly of child-friendly attractions, and I realised with disappointment that it was not the same one that we had been to before. There was no carousel with hand-painted horses, no waltzers and no Mystic Maggie.

'Mama! Mama! Want to go!'

Samuel was pointing at a little train and I walked over and handed over some tokens to the bored-looking ride attendant before lifting the twins out of the buggy and squeezing into a tiny little carriage with them. Ivy and Samuel bounced around with excitement, their bunged-up noses temporarily forgotten, and I was pleased that I'd dragged us all out of the house. As the train set off, going round and round in a little circle, the twins giggled and shrieked and I took a couple of photos of them to send to Jude. Already my bad mood was beginning to lift, the fog of exhaustion no longer seeming so overwhelming. That was the thing when you had children, you could go from rock bottom to sky high in seconds. With the sun on my face and the prospect of Jude coming home from his trip later, I was smiling again as I cuddled Ivy and Samuel to me and gazed out of the glassless window of our carriage.

As I scanned the crowds outside, I noticed a man staring directly at me. A second later we had passed him but a jolt of recognition ran through me and I craned my neck as the train continued travelling round in a circle until we reached him again. He was still looking intently in our direction and I tried to place him. Was he a dad from the twins' nursery? Someone who worked in one of the cafés we regularly frequented? By the time we passed him a third time, the man still hadn't turned away and as the train slowed, I turned my head, trying to locate him.

'Again, again!' Samuel cried.

'Sam, darling, let's try another ride.'

'Want to go again!'

'Ivy want to go again too!'

I didn't have the energy to resist, and I fished some more tokens out of my pocket, leaned out of the carriage and handed them over to the ride attendant. As I did, I looked to where the man had been standing but he was gone, leaving me with an odd sensation that I couldn't quite place. Before I had time to digest it, we were away and the twins were shrieking and screaming, 'Choo choo!' and I eagerly scanned the crowds again but couldn't see the man.

Two more goes later, I'd run out of tokens and I manhandled a weeping Samuel and Ivy out of the carriage and back into the buggy.

'Mummy is going to buy some more tokens,' I told them, trying not to think about the amount of money I'd already managed to spend in less than fifteen minutes. I pushed the buggy towards the token booth and stopped at the back of the queue, praying that it wouldn't take too long because I knew that Ivy and Sam were ticking time bombs who could explode at any moment.

'Simone?'

I recognised his voice before his face. 'Tom!'

'I thought it was you on the train. How are you?'

He moved towards me as if to kiss me on the cheek and then stopped, perhaps changing his mind, and he looked so conflicted that I decided to make things easier for him and gave him a hug. I noticed, though, that he didn't hug me back and stepped away as quickly as he could, looking left and right as though we were being watched. He had aged in the years since I had seen him last and flecks of grey peppered his slightly receding hair, but he was still disgustingly handsome. In contrast, I knew that I was looking far from my best.

'Are these your children?' he asked, looking down at the twins.

'Yes, this is Ivy and Samuel. They're two and a half.'

'We missed you at work after you left. I think everyone was hoping you'd come back after maternity leave.'

'I thought I would too, to be honest. Do you still work there?'

'Oh no, I left a while ago now.' Tom's eyes were darting about again.

'Are you here on your own?' I asked him.

'No, my partner's here somewhere with our daughter, Camille. I just came to get some more tokens. I really ought to go find them, she'll be wondering where I've got to.'

'Oh, shall I come with you? I'd love to meet Camille. How old is she?'

'Nine months. Listen, I'd better go but it was great to see you, Simone.'

Before I could protest, Tom had dashed off and I followed him with my eyes for as long as I could, but he was quickly swallowed up by the crowds. I thought I saw him later, talking to a woman. The woman had her back to me and her long dark hair was tied up in a tight ponytail. I craned my neck to get a better look but then my phone rang and I saw it was Mum wanting to FaceTime. I held the phone in front of the twins so that she could say hello and by the time I looked up again there was no sign of Tom or the woman.

We stayed for another half an hour or so until the twins began to grow tired. We didn't see Tom again and the fair was so small that I assumed he'd left. It wasn't particularly surprising that I'd run into him because I knew he lived nearby, assuming that he was still in the same flat. But what was surprising was how he'd reacted to seeing me again. It was as though he'd been afraid to hug me or even talk to me. But why? Surely he wasn't still embarrassed about what had happened between us all those years ago? It had been such a minor, trivial incident and we'd both moved on, we had families now.

'Mama, want home.'

I looked at Ivy, who was wriggling in the buggy, and picked up the pace, keen to get back to the safe sanctuary of our house before one of us had a meltdown. Jude would be home in a couple of hours and the twins would be so delighted to see him. Then this weekend I was meeting the girls for lunch, a blissful two hours of child-free time. Whatever was up with Tom had nothing to do with me. But, as I walked away from the fair, I still hoped that he was okay.

15

I was drying my hair when my phone pinged, signalling that I had a new email. I reached for it, expecting it to be junk, but stopped short when I saw who the sender was. It was from a magazine I'd pitched my short story to and I already knew what it was going to say because I was well rehearsed by now. *Thanks for your submission, but it's not quite right for us...*

I opened it, expecting the worst, and had to read it a few times before I could truly digest the words. Then I read it one more time just to be safe. And then I screamed, 'Jude!'

He came running in, with Ivy clinging on to his back. 'What is it? Is everything okay?'

Wordlessly, I handed him the phone and he took it and read the email, his eyes widening. 'Oh my God! Simmy, this is amazing!'

The magazine wanted to publish my story. *My* story! I'd spent years writing on and off, I'd dreamed of this moment for so long and now it had finally come. But how could it be real? Surely it was a mistake? I half expected to get another email any moment from the editor telling me that they'd cocked up, that the email was meant for another person. But I took the phone back off Jude and re-read the message, just to check they'd used my name and the title of my story. It was all there, in black and white. I, Simone Pearce, was soon to be a published writer.

Jude put Ivy down on the bed and came over to hug me. 'Congratulations, I'm so proud of you.'

I closed my eyes and breathed in the scent of him, fresh from the shower. Could life get any better than this? I had a wonderful husband, two amazing children and now I'd been given this incredible opportunity which, if I was lucky, could become a career.

'I'm so happy,' I murmured into his ear.

'We must celebrate!'

'Well, actually, I'm going out with the girls tonight,' I said, a little sheepishly.

Jude took it on the chin. 'Well, at least you get to celebrate, that's the main thing.' He picked Ivy up again. 'Me and the two tots of terror will have a blast watching *Paw Patrol* and *Peppa Pig*.'

'I can cancel? We could get a takeaway instead?'

'Not at all. You go out and have some fun, you deserve it. Tell you what, why don't I drop the kids at preschool this morning and you can take it easy, maybe even go and get your nails done or whatever it is you fancy doing?'

'Really?' I always did the preschool runs because Jude had to be in the office by nine o'clock.

'Of course. My first meeting isn't until ten. I'll go get them ready now while you finish up here.'

'Thanks, Jude, that's amazing.'

I watched him leave with Ivy and sighed with pleasure. Jude was an incredible dad, and husband. He worked long hours but even when he came home, exhausted from a day's hard graft, he always put a smile on his face and had the twins giggling within minutes. For a while now, I'd felt a little inadequate by comparison. Ivy and Sam were at preschool every day and I still wasn't earning any money or contributing financially to the household. But maybe that was about to change. I picked up my phone and started drafting a response to the email. The editor wanted to arrange a call and I wondered if it would be too forward to say I was free all day today. I decided to throw caution to the wind and sent off a reply.

I heard the twins chatting in the background and remembered that soon I would have to start thinking about primary schools. I couldn't believe we'd reached that stage already. I was feeling more like myself again these days. I'd finally found my groove with my new role as a mother but I'd also found some of me again, through my writing, and it felt like the perfect combination.

I finished drying my hair, dabbed on a bit of make-up for good measure, and by the time I emerged from the bedroom, Jude had the twins dressed and ready to go.

'Bye, Ivy, bye, Sam.' I kissed them both and handed their lunchboxes over to Jude.

'I'll be back by six thirty so you're not rushing to meet the girls.'

'Thanks.'

I waved as they all left the house and smiled as the front door closed. I had some time to myself and something to celebrate and I wasn't going to waste a moment of it. Throwing some things into my handbag, I left the house too and started making my way towards the high street. I'd get a coffee, I decided, and browse the shops for a bit, perhaps get my nails done like Jude had suggested. The world was my oyster, and I was more than up for it.

It was warm out and it gave me a glorious sense of calm and freedom. I passed a steady stream of commuters dashing to the train station and their lives felt a million miles away from my own.

How long had it been since I'd been one of them, rushing to catch the train, my mind full of meetings and work deadlines? How much had changed in a few years. I daydreamed about becoming a writer, earning a living and finally being able to contribute financially, and it filled me with excitement. When I hit the high street, I decided to sit down for my coffee and I ordered a croissant to boot as I was feeling frivolous. I was just about to find a table when I felt someone behind me and I turned around and found myself looking straight at Tom. I hadn't seen him since the funfair and, until now, I'd forgotten all about our encounter.

'Hey,' I said. 'Fancy meeting you here.'

He smiled and I thought that he looked more relaxed than the last time I'd seen him. 'Hey, Simone, how's it going?'

'Great, actually. I've just been told that one of my short stories is going to be published!' The words were out of my mouth before I'd even thought them through and although it probably sounded boastful, I was feeling too impulsive and excited to care.

'Wow, that's great. I remember that you used to write when we were dating.'

I was surprised that he remembered. 'I've just ordered a coffee. Do you have time to join me?'

'Sure, why not.'

I waited for Tom to order and then we found a vacant table and sat down opposite each other.

'Were you on your way to work?'

'No, actually, I'm having some time out from work at the moment.'

'Ah, I see.' I couldn't tell from his tone whether this was a good thing or a bad thing.

Reading my mind, Tom added, 'I took some parental leave and Camille has just started her settling-in sessions at nursery, so I'll be back in the office in a few weeks.'

'Oh, that's lovely. So how have you found fatherhood?'

Tom ran his fingers through his hair and I sensed that the question held more meaning than I had intended. 'Wonderful, Camille is amazing.'

'But?'

He looked at me. 'How do you know there's a but?'

'I can just tell.'

We paused our conversation while our coffees arrived, and then I waited for Tom to continue. 'It's not been an easy year,' he said. 'There's been a lot going on.'

'Well, parenting is tough.'

'Yes, but it's not just that.' He looked at me, as if trying to decide whether to tell me more and then eventually he said, 'My partner hasn't been well.'

'I'm so sorry to hear that. I must admit, when I saw you at the fair a few months ago, I did wonder if something was wrong. You seemed a little on edge.'

'Yeah.' He looked down at his coffee and I got the feeling that something was very wrong.

'Tom, what's going on?'

When he looked at me again, I could see the strain on his face. 'Do you remember I told you about my ex? The one who was extremely possessive?'

'Yes.' I already knew what was coming.

'We got back together. She's Camille's mother.'

'Oh, Tom.'

'I thought it would be different,' he said, and it was as though once he started talking he couldn't stop, like he'd had no one to talk to for so long that he'd been storing it all up, waiting for the right moment. 'She told me she'd got some help, that she was much better now, that she loved me and that things would be different. And I wasn't sure at first, but she *did* seem different and I decided to give it one more go. At first things were good, better than good, they were great.'

'Okay.' I nodded encouragingly.

'Then she fell pregnant and I was shocked because we'd never discussed children and I'd thought she was using contraception. I could have sworn she'd told me that she was but when I raised it she was so angry with me, saying how dare I accuse her of lying, and I wondered if I'd got it all wrong, if I'd jumped to the wrong conclusions.'

I didn't tell him what I was thinking, which was that this girl had clearly duped him into this, because what was the point? It wouldn't make him feel any better.

'So I did what I thought was right and I proposed. She moved into the flat and we tried to make it work.'

'But it's not working?'

'She hasn't changed, Simone. If anything, she's worse. And she's convinced I'm seeing someone else. If she'd seen us together at the fair she would have lost it. That's why I was afraid to talk to you. I can't talk to anyone, even the mums at the baby group I take Camille to. The only reason why I'm with you now is because I know she's at work. But at the back of my mind I'm already thinking, what if she's tracking me? How can I explain why I'm here?'

'Tom, you can't live like that. It's not healthy for you or Camille.'

'I know, but what choice do I have? I can't take Camille away from her mother. And to be honest, I'm not sure I'll ever be able to escape now.'

'You shouldn't feel like you have to escape a relationship. It should be a two-way partnership.'

Tom smiled sadly. 'That's because you're in a healthy one, Simone.'

He was right and I realised this now more than ever. Jude and I were a team, we tackled life together and I had never felt more grateful for the man I married. When I looked at Tom, all I felt was pity, for his situation and for his daughter, and I reached over and put my hands over his. 'Tom, I'm sorry. I don't know what to say other than that I'm here if you ever want to talk.'

He squeezed my hands and smiled at me, and we sat there for a short while, in companionable silence because the moment didn't require any words. I wanted to tell him he should leave her, to warn him that he was in an abusive relationship, but he already knew that. What he really needed wasn't advice but simply a friend. Someone to listen and not to judge.

Eventually, Tom moved his hands away, signalling that he wanted to change the subject. 'Anyway, enough about that, tell me about this exciting magazine deal.'

And although I felt bad gloating after everything he'd just told me, I sensed that we both needed to talk about something happy and I relished sharing the story. I was going to be paid the handsome sum of two hundred and fifty pounds for my efforts, but it wasn't the financial gain I desired, it was the recognition that something I'd written was good enough to be published.

'I always knew you'd be a success, Simone,' Tom said, when I had finished.

'Really?'

'Of course. I'm so thrilled for you.'

'Well, it's only one article in a magazine, it's hardly a *Sunday Times* bestseller.'

'Everyone has to start somewhere.'

I looked down at our finished coffees and my empty plate littered with croissant crumbs. 'Listen, Tom, I meant what I said earlier. I'm here for you if you need me, any time.'

'Thank you. I appreciate that.'

We both started putting on our coats and making our way

towards the door. I felt bad for leaving Tom, but I didn't know what else to do. I couldn't call or text him to see how he was doing as I'd only make things worse with his girlfriend, and I certainly couldn't pop round to check in on him without causing trouble. I would just have to keep my distance and hope that he was okay. And if I was being honest, although I was worried about him and wanted to help if I could, part of me was reluctant to get too involved. Tom was an ex and not someone I was close to. And my life was so chaotic with the twins that I often felt like I was at full capacity and that just one more thing in my life would cause everything to spill over and become a great big mess. Sometimes I felt like I was on the edge of something – disaster, insanity, chaos, I wasn't sure what – but something was stopping me from toppling right over. And I had no desire to add one more element to my life that might be the tipping point.

As we were saying goodbye, Tom said, 'This may seem like a strange question but have you ever been approached by anyone? A woman you didn't know?'

I shook my head. 'No, not that I can think of.'

He exhaled. 'Okay, good.'

The penny dropped and I felt a jolt of alarm. 'You think your ex found out about us?'

'I'm almost positive that she didn't and it was so long ago now that it doesn't really matter. But I just wanted to ask because of something she said a while back that made me wonder.'

'What did she say?'

He shook his head. 'It doesn't matter.'

But I wasn't letting it go, not if I had become unwittingly involved in Tom's messy life. 'Tom, what did she say?'

He looked ashamed and embarrassed as he spoke. 'That she knew I'd been seeing other women and that they'd get what they deserved.'

An involuntary shiver ran up my spine. 'Do you think she meant me?'

'No, Simone, honestly I don't. If she did, she'd have done something by now. I genuinely think she was bluffing and I'd actually forgotten about it until I saw you at the fair.'

'Did she see us together there?'

'No, definitely not.'

I tried to stem the rising panic. 'Do I need to watch my back?'

Tom shook his head vehemently. 'No. God, no. Forget I said anything.'

'Okay.'

I hoped Tom was right. We had dated years ago and I was now married with two children. I clearly wasn't a threat to his ex and I was in no way involved in his life or his relationship. I had nothing to worry about. I smiled at him, relaxing again. 'It was good to see you, Tom.'

'You too, Simone, let's do it again some time. I'll be in touch.'

As I watched him leave, I suspected that I wouldn't hear from him and I couldn't help but feel a little relieved. I was happy to return to my own life, which seemed so blissfully uncomplicated in comparison. Yes, the past few years had been challenging and yes, it wasn't all sunshine and roses in my marriage, but I was happy, which was more than I could say for poor Tom. I didn't take what I had for granted, I was grateful for it, but it been a choice. I had chosen to marry Jude and it had been the right decision. So, now was the time to appreciate it.

I wandered up the Broadway, glancing in shop windows as I headed towards the nail salon to see if they could fit me in. I paused when I reached a bakery and considered picking up some cupcakes for the twins to have as a treat later. There was a beautiful wedding cake in the window and I smiled before remembering what had happened to the cake at our own wedding. It seemed like a million years ago now, a minor blot on an otherwise perfect day, but I instinctively looked up at the little cake toppers. The bride was wearing a traditional white gown and holding a bouquet of pink flowers, with not a hint of red in sight. But then I looked at the groom and I recoiled in horror. At first glance the little topper looked perfect in a grey suit and pink tie, just as Jude had worn, but his head was missing.

I stared at it, blood draining from my face and my mind racing as I battled between logical reasoning and irrational fear. The head had simply fallen off, it was probably lying on the shelf behind the cake. But it felt like more than that to me. It felt like a sign.

Something bad is going to happen to Jude. It hit me, hard and fast, like a blow to the stomach. The fortune teller's words were echoing around my head again, reminding me of the clear warning that she'd given me all those years ago. How much longer could I bury my head in the sand and tell myself that I had nothing to fear? A knot of anxiety tightened inside me, making my heart race and my hands shake, but I still couldn't tear my eyes away from the cake.

A child screaming behind me made me jump. Slowly, the sounds of the busy Broadway came back to me. A car horn, people chatting, the beeping of a pedestrian crossing nearby. I turned away from the cake, abandoning any thoughts of buying cupcakes in my desperation to get away from the bakery as quickly as possible. I thought about calling Jude, or Helen, but they were both at work and I didn't want to disturb them. Anyway, what would I say? If I told them I'd been freaked out by a beheaded cake topper in a shop window, they'd laugh at me.

They'd laugh. Gradually my heart rate began to slow down and my hands steadied. Of course they'd laugh because it was ridiculous to find a link between a cake in a window and my own life. It was the funfair poster that had brought it all back to me and now I was looking for signs that weren't even there. What about the good signs? Jude and I were still blissfully happy, despite some people saying we had rushed into getting married. We had two happy, healthy and amazing children. I was about to have a story published in a magazine. Life was good and I should appreciate it, as I had told myself just minutes earlier. Feeling better, I continued towards the salon, trying to distract myself with thoughts of what colour to paint my nails. But no matter how hard I tried, the image of the decapitated groom remained etched in my mind.

16

I knew from the second that Jude walked through the door that he was in a foul mood. It happened from time to time, when he'd had a testing day at work, when it was just that little bit too hard to turn on the smiles and pretend that everything was okay. But this time my immediate reaction was to panic. *Something bad has happened.*

'What is it?' I asked, bracing myself.

He didn't respond and fear crept over me. 'Jude, what's wrong?'

He ignored me again and walked into the kitchen. I heard him open the fridge, pull out a beer and rummage around in the drawer for a bottle opener. When he didn't return, I went to find him, my mind racing with worst-case scenarios. Had he been made redundant? It would be awful, but we'd get through it. As long as he was okay, we'd get through it. But what if he wasn't okay? What if he was sick? *It's the tragedy the fortune teller foretold. It's come early.*

'Jude, you're scaring me. What's happened?'

'Are you fucking him?'

His question was so absurd and unexpected that I couldn't work out what, or who, he was talking about at first. 'Excuse me?'

I had never seen such venom on his face. 'Are you fucking him?'

'Jude, I have no idea what you're talking about.' I was scared by Jude's anger and I was confused too, but I was also relieved because although Jude was furious, he wasn't sick.

'Don't lie to me.'

Even then I had been caught so off guard by his accusation that I didn't piece it together. 'You're going to have to be more specific because I'm really confused right now.'

He sighed heavily, as though he was talking to someone stupid. 'I saw you with him again, Simone. The guy you used to work with. The guy you kissed outside that pub.'

It hit me then and it was so ridiculous that I almost laughed but I stopped myself just in time. 'Are you talking about Tom?'

'I don't know what his fucking name is.'

'Shh.' I craned my neck, silently indicating that the twins were just next door. 'Jude, what's got into you? I bumped into Tom in the café and we had a drink. That is literally it.'

'You know, I believed you the first time. When I saw you two kissing with my own eyes and you denied it all, you made me feel so stupid for jumping to conclusions. But you knew exactly what you were doing, didn't you?'

What on earth was going on here? 'Jude, come on, let me explain.'

'Have you been fucking the whole time behind my back?' He was no longer bothering to keep his voice down and I no longer bothered to try and hush him.

'Jude, this is out of control. I hadn't seen Tom in ages, and then we bumped into each other this morning and had a drink together. If you must know, he was telling me that he's in an unhappy relationship.'

I realised as soon as the words were out that it was probably the worst thing I could have said.

'Oh, I see, so he's decided to find a new one with you, has he?'

'No. No! You've got this all wrong.'

'I saw you holding hands, Simone. Don't try to deny it.'

I put my head in my hands. 'I was comforting him, Jude. He's been through a really crappy time and I was providing a listening ear.' At the back of my mind I was thinking, *How does he know this? Why was he even anywhere near the café?* And what worried me most was that I'd had these thoughts before. But they had been years ago, before we'd got married and had the twins. They paled in comparison to everything we had done together since. Yet here we were again, and I had no idea how we'd got here.

'Am I not enough for you, is that it?'

I tried to take his hand but he snatched it away. In the background I could hear the twins bickering and I knew it wouldn't be long before one of them was screaming. 'Jude, you are everything to me. You are my life. I would never, ever cheat on you. I love you.'

He looked at me then, really looked at me, and I saw a slight softening in his face. But then it hardened again. 'How can I believe you?'

I tried to take his hand again and this time he let me. 'Jude. I'm your wife. I have never lied to you and I never will. I love you and I would never hurt you like that, ever.'

His face crumpled and I knew in that minute that whatever had possessed him, whatever had taken over his rational thoughts, was gone. 'I'm sorry,' he said, and I was shocked to see that he was crying. I prayed that the twins would hold out for just a little longer so that Jude and I could see this conversation through to some sort of conclusion.

'What's going on?' I said softly. 'This isn't like you.' But even as I said it, I knew that it wasn't quite accurate. It had happened before. Years ago, yes, but it had happened.

He buried his head in his hands. 'I don't know.'

'Talk to me, Jude.'

When he looked up, his eyes were red. 'My mum had an affair when I was a boy. That's why my parents split up.'

I stared at him, wide-eyed. I knew his parents had divorced when he was young, but he'd never revealed the reason why and I hadn't thought to ask. Now I couldn't believe I'd been with him for so long and not known this.

'I had no idea.'

'I never talk about it because my mum raised me and she did a good job, and I don't want to tarnish that. But it's why my relationship with her is difficult, and with my dad too. It's like I feel I should be on his side, and I feel guilty that I'm not and sometimes it's easier just to avoid them both.'

'Oh, Jude, I'm so sorry.'

'I guess it's just left me a little bit exposed. I know I work long hours and I travel, and you're here with the twins, and I feel guilty about that and then sometimes a little paranoid.'

'I understand.' And in that moment, I really did. 'But you have nothing to be paranoid about.'

He gripped my hands tightly then, almost in desperation. 'I know. And I'm sorry.'

There have been a few, rare occasions in our marriage when I've wondered if we got together too soon, if by rushing it we omitted some important moments or details of our lives and that, as a result, we were constantly playing catch up. Now was one of those moments.

'What were you doing at the café, Jude?' I knew if I didn't ask, I'd always wonder.

He shrugged. 'I'd dropped the twins at preschool and fancied getting a coffee to take on the train with me.'

It was such an obvious explanation that I felt bad for even doubting him. 'I'm sorry that you saw what you saw. But it really was nothing. Like I said, I've not seen Tom in ages and we literally bumped into each other by chance.'

'I know that. I get it.'

As if on cue, Ivy started crying and we both looked at each other and got up. 'I'll go,' Jude said. 'You'll be late for your dinner with the girls.'

With all the drama I'd almost forgotten about it and I had half a mind to cancel. 'Maybe I won't go,' I said tentatively.

'You have to go. You've had some amazing news today and you need to go out and celebrate. Honestly, Simmy, we're good.'

I put my hand on his arm. 'You sure?'

He covered my hand with his own. 'More than sure. Go on, go and get glammed up.'

After the conversation we'd just had, the last thing I wanted to do was to leave him on his own. I couldn't think of anything worse than getting into the shower and putting my make-up on. I hesitated, torn between two loyalties. But part of me needed to talk to the girls about what had just happened, to help me make sense of it all. Jude had jumped to a crazy and ridiculous conclusion and it still troubled me that he didn't trust me. But then he'd also given me a completely valid and understandable reason why. My mind was scrambled and I craved the company of Helen, Shiv and Emily more, in some ways, than my own husband. I listened as Jude picked up Ivy and started soothing her in the high-pitched sing-song tone he reserved just for our children. And then I darted for the shower.

* * *

When, much later, well-meaning people asked me what the trigger was for what happened next, I can pinpoint it to the exact moment. Usually, they don't believe me. They say things don't happen that suddenly and that it must have been more gradual, but I don't agree. Yes, there were warning signs, fleeting thoughts or longer periods of worry, but they passed before they did any significant damage. They were just small blots on what I perceived to be an otherwise picture-perfect canvas.

Perhaps it wouldn't have happened if I hadn't bumped into Tom earlier that day. If Jude hadn't accused me of cheating on him. If I hadn't seen that damn cake with the beheaded groom in the bakery window. If Shiv and Emily hadn't said what they'd said about my marriage, making me question my own version of events. Mostly I think that if Emily hadn't mentioned *her* and set the wheels in motion, they wouldn't have fallen off completely. But the reality is that it could have been any one of these things, or all of them combined, that set me on my path to self-destruction. Or maybe it would have happened anyway. Maybe it was written in the stars.

Our friends speculated too, of course. They said I was burned out from caring for two beautiful but demanding children. They said I should have gone back to work, had a break, got some help. They dissected my relationship with Jude, looking for cracks. Everyone needed something, or someone, to blame for what happened to me. They wanted to find a cause, anything to justify my behaviour, mainly because they loved me and they didn't want to admit that it was my fault.

Before I even walked into the restaurant that night, I knew that I was going to get drunk. My mind had decided before my body had sat down, before I'd ordered my first drink. I wanted to obliterate everything that had happened that day and lose myself in the glorious numbness of alcohol. It was no longer about celebrating the incredible thing that had happened that morning, which seemed so long ago now, but about forgetting what had happened since.

But first I had to let it all out and so my first words to my friends weren't, 'I'm going to be published,' or 'A magazine wants to run my story!' They were, 'Jude lost it this evening and accused me of having an affair.'

The table was silent, as the girls all stared at me, dumbfounded. If I'd wanted their full attention, I'd certainly succeeded. And then at once, they were all talking.

'How on earth does he think you have time for an affair? You have young twins, for goodness' sake,' was Shiv's contribution.

'Oh, Simone.' Emily looked at me with sympathy.

And then it was Helen's turn. 'We need shots. Now.'

Shiv and Emily laughed because we hadn't done shots together for years, but I couldn't even muster a smile. The drinks were duly ordered, and the girls all turned to me, waiting for me to continue. Was I breaking Jude's confidence by telling them about his parents and the reason for their split? My loyalty was, first and foremost, to my husband above anything else. But these women, they were like my sisters, and I wanted to confide in them. I had to.

When I was done, they all looked at each other, waiting for someone else to speak first. It was Shiv, who tentatively said, 'I love Jude, you know I do, but this is crazy, Simone.'

I glanced at Emily, who was nodding her agreement, and then at Helen who, as a Jude loyalist, was clearly trying to stay neutral.

I needed them to understand. I needed them to be on my side but not to turn against Jude either. 'I guess though, when you think about what happened with his parents, it makes sense.'

'I guess,' Shiv said diplomatically, 'but his reaction still seems irrational. So he saw you having coffee with another guy, so what?'

'He saw us holding hands, Shiv. It was innocent of course, but I can see how he got the wrong impression, especially when he recognised Tom as the same guy who tried to kiss me.'

Shiv still didn't look convinced. 'Then he should have asked you about it. He should have given you the chance to explain before he flew off the handle.'

'In fairness,' Helen said diplomatically, 'Simone didn't tell Jude about what had happened. If she had, maybe he wouldn't have reacted in the way he did.'

'He didn't give her a chance,' Shiv protested. 'He just went straight down the rabbit hole. And let's face it, it's about more than this one, isolated incident.'

'How do you mean?'

A ball of dread began to form inside me as I saw Shiv and Emily exchange glances. I knew that glance. I knew it well. It told me that they'd talked about me and Jude before, that they had already discussed our relationship and made judgements about it, without me even knowing.

'Jude loves you so much,' Emily began tentatively. 'Everyone can see that. But sometimes we worry that he's a little... controlling?'

I was incredulous. 'Controlling? Are you serious?'

'We don't want to upset you,' Emily said quickly. 'We know he's a great dad. It's just, there have been a few incidents that have worried us a bit.'

How had this happened? I'd expected sympathy from my friends and now I had the horrible feeling that I was under attack, or at least my marriage was.

'What incidents?' Helen jumped to my defence, as oblivious to this as I was. If Emily and Shiv had been talking about me and Jude, it seemed that they hadn't included Helen.

'Well, do you remember when you first got together and you gave up all your stuff to move in with him? And then he decided that you were having a Christmas wedding without even discussing it with you?'

I almost laughed. Those things were so long ago and they seemed trivial to me now. 'Is that it?'

'No, that's not it.' Shiv seemed to be getting into her groove now, almost as though she was relieved to finally be saying what she had clearly been thinking for ages. 'After you had the twins, it was like he locked down your family. We hardly ever saw you and when we called you, trying to arrange to come and see you, he often answered and said it was a bad time.'

'It probably was a bad time,' I argued. 'If Jude was answering my phone, then it would have been because I was napping and he wanted to let me rest. And everything was so chaotic that we just needed to get our heads around things for a while, establish a routine for Ivy and Samuel. But I still saw you guys, it's not fair to say that I didn't, and Jude certainly never stopped me.'

'What about when you decided not to go back to work? You were on the fence about it, and it was Jude who told you not to do it. It was Jude who said you should stay at home.'

It was like my friends were rewriting my history from an entirely different perspective and I was becoming increasingly angry with them. 'Jude told me I didn't have to go back because he knew that I didn't enjoy my job. But it's not like he made me a Stepford Wife for Christ's sake. He encouraged me to write, he even signed me up for that short writing course.'

'Yes. He signed you up without even checking with you.'

'It was meant to be a nice surprise!'

'It just feels like every major thing that has happened to you since you met Jude has been decided by him, not you.'

I was almost in tears now and I turned to Helen, desperate for an ally. 'Tell them that's not true, Hels.'

'I think you've said enough.' Helen shot a warning glance at Shiv. 'No one ever really knows what goes on inside another couple's relationship.'

I was grateful but I also knew that Helen had omitted something important. She had stuck up for me, she had intervened to stop Shiv and Emily's attack, but she hadn't disagreed with them. Paranoia was seeping in now, eating me up from the inside, making me doubt my own version of events even though I knew them to be true. What was happening to me?

'We didn't mean to upset you,' Emily said quickly. 'It's just because we care about you and we want you to be happy.'

'I *am* happy.' I wasn't in that particular moment, far from it, but overall I was still convinced that I led a charmed life, with a wonderful and thoughtful husband.

'Let's leave it there then,' Helen said, with a note of finality in her voice. 'Anyone else have any news to share?'

This was my moment to tell the girls about my magazine offer, to bask in their awe and congratulations, but I was still feeling too prickly from our unexpected and deeply unpleasant conversation, and I shook my head and took a large gulp of my drink instead.

'Well, actually, I've got some news,' Shiv said, and we all turned to her, grateful for the change of subject. 'Avyaan has been offered a job in his company's California office and we've decided to go for it.'

'What the...? Are you serious?' Helen looked even more stunned by this conversation than the one we'd just been having.

'I know it seems sudden, but we've actually been talking about it for a few weeks now and we just feel that it's too good an opportunity to pass up. They'll pay relocation fees and we've found a great school for the kids, and, well, the idea of year-round sunshine is just too enticing. Mum and Dad are going to stay on in the London house and my sister's moving in with them.'

Of all my friends who could have dropped this bombshell, Shiv would have been last on my list. She was a homegirl through and through, she was born and bred in London and had never strayed far from her family. And now she was telling us that she was packing up and moving thousands of miles away? I couldn't believe it.

'This is amazing!' Helen was saying. 'How exciting! When do you go?'

'In six weeks. Once we agreed, it all started happening quickly. Tell me I'm doing the right thing, girls? Because I'm all over the place about it.'

'You are definitely doing the right thing,' Helen said. 'Life's too short not to take opportunities like this when you get them and I, for one, can't wait to come and visit.'

'Me neither,' Emily added. 'You lucky things.'

I still hadn't spoken and I knew that if I didn't say something soon, I might offend Shiv. Although a small part of me was feeling uncharitable after everything she'd just thrown on me, I also knew that she was a good person and what she needed right now was some reassurance.

'I'm shocked, I'll admit,' I said. 'But I'm thrilled for you. The kids will love the California life. I bet you'll all be cool surf dudes within a few weeks.'

'Oh, I don't know about that.' Shiv was grinning as she said it, probably already imagining long, heady days on the beach. 'I'm going to miss you guys so much.'

'You'll come back, though, right? This is only temporary?'

'We've said we'll give it a year and after that we'll reassess.'

'Once you leave, you never come back,' Helen said with certainty. 'I've seen it happen time and time again. The expat lifestyle's just too good to return to Blighty.'

'I feel bad about leaving my parents though, they're getting on and soon they'll need more help. I don't want to leave it all to my sister. I suspect I'll be travelling back and forth quite a lot.'

'Hey,' Emily said suddenly. 'Does anyone remember that fortune teller we saw a few years ago? She said I'd get a promotion and Shiv would go abroad. Well, it turns out that she was right after all, how funny is that? What did she say to you again, Simone?'

And there it was. The trigger. A small thing, granted, and yet I knew, in that moment, that no matter what my friends or Jude told me after that, no matter how hard they tried to reassure me or reason with me, there was no going back. I had just gone past the point of no return.

The clock was ticking and I could no longer drown out the noise or pretend that I couldn't hear it. I couldn't ignore the signs. I'd tried over the years but it had defeated me in the end. Perhaps I'd known deep down that it would because it had always been there, in the background, it had never really left me, it had been waiting for its moment to pounce, to catch me at my most vulnerable.

I'd had four out of my five years of happiness. We were approaching the end, but the end of what? My husband's life? My children's? Our marriage? I didn't know and the worst thing was that I was completely powerless to change a thing. The only thing I could do was wait and see if the prophecy came true, while praying that it didn't.

As I continued drinking, trying to listen in to my friends' conversations, laughing in all the right places, I had already left the room. My mind was drifting, the alcohol fuelling my paranoia.

I had done everything that the fortune teller had warned me about. I had gone into it with my eyes wide open but I had done it anyway, thrown caution to the wind and chosen love over all else. A love that I still felt, in every bone of my body, was real, despite what my friends had told me tonight. They didn't know Jude, but I did and I knew he was the real deal. He had his problems, we all did, but he was a good man, of that I was certain.

So, if I could turn back time, how could I have chosen differently? How could I have let my chance of happiness with Jude slip through my fingers because of an unsettling encounter with a mysterious stranger in a tent? It would have been ludicrous to have taken the other path. I had to conclude that if I *could* rewind the clock, I would have done exactly the same thing.

Did I regret my choice to marry Jude? No. Was I afraid? Yes. I was terrified.

Tick tock. That was all I could hear now, above the laughter of my friends and the noise in the restaurant, the clinking of glasses and the scraping of chairs. *Tick tock.*

17

Jude answered on the seventh ring. I preferred it if he answered on ring two or three. When it got to four, I started to worry. By the time it reached eight, I escalated to a full-on panic and if it went to answerphone, that was my cue to implode. He had answered just in the nick of time.

'Simone, I'm in a meeting.'

'Sorry, just checking in, I won't keep you.'

I heard him sigh. 'Everything okay?'

'Oh yes, everything's fine.'

'Simmy,' he spoke quietly, barely above a whisper. 'This has to stop.'

'I know, I'm sorry. I love you.'

'I love you too.'

He still said 'I love you', which was something. I wondered if the time might come, at some point in the future, when he no longer said it. I feared it more than anything. And yet I couldn't stop.

I called him three times a day, no more and no less. I wanted to call more but I'd found a strange sort of equilibrium, whereby three was just about enough, any less didn't cut it. It was a compulsion, something I had to do otherwise I couldn't relax. Once I'd done it, it was like someone had released a pressure valve and I felt the tension fizzing out of me. Sometimes I promised myself that I wouldn't call again, but a couple of hours later, the pressure would start mounting again and the only way to release it was to pick up the phone and make the call.

My day now centred around these calls. Up until Jude left for work, everything would be okay. We'd get up, have a coffee, make some toast, get the twins ready. We were like any normal couple. But as soon as he closed the front door, the first pangs of fear would start to kick in. What if he was hit by a car on the way to the station? Or involved in a train crash? Or caught up in a terrorist attack in London? As soon as I dropped the twins at preschool, I immediately opened the Find My app so I could track Jude. Sometimes he was still underground and had no signal, so I would check again and again until the dot marking his location appeared.

For a few minutes, that little dot was enough to ease my anxiety but soon the fear would take over again. I made my first phone call between nine thirty and ten in the morning. By that time he was at his desk, and after a quick exchange, we'd hang up and I'd tell myself to stop worrying and attempt to get on with my day. Sometimes I met a friend for coffee or stopped by the shops to pick up milk or bread. By the time I got home, though, the panic would be growing again. I would open up my laptop and try to do some writing, but I always became distracted.

Instead, I would look up terrifying childhood health conditions. What if one of the twins got meningitis? Would I be able to recognise the symptoms? They always had snotty noses, one of them was always grumbling about a tummy ache. But what if it was more serious than I thought and I didn't get them to the hospital in time? Sometimes, when I couldn't sleep, I would go into their rooms, sit on the floor between their toddler beds, and watch the rise and fall of their chests. I could sit there for hours, just watching them sleep, knowing they were safe. But when they weren't at home with me, I had no such peace of mind. Every child they played with was a virus carrier waiting to infect my babies. Every tree they clambered up was an accident waiting to happen. And their busy, chaotic preschool was full of potential death traps.

Thinking of all the hazards they might be facing while I sat at home, helpless, I would log into the app where the preschool staff uploaded photos and updates about the children's day. If there were new photos of the twins, I'd devour them, studying Ivy and Samuel's little faces and telling myself that there was nothing to worry about. If there were no photos, which there often weren't, I'd wonder if something was wrong, if one of them were sick or if there had been an accident. I'd called the preschool a few times to check and the staff had been lovely but even I knew that I was going too far, that my calls were bordering on neurotic. I fretted that they had me down as *that* crazy mother, that they were all talking about me, laughing about me.

After I'd convinced myself that no one was in danger, for the moment at least, I usually opened Google and spent some time searching for Mystic Maggie, hoping for the day when a new page or profile I hadn't seen before came up, but it never did. Then I searched for funfairs coming to North London, adding any new ones to a spreadsheet I had created, but it was April and the season for fairs hadn't properly kicked in yet. The first one on my list was on the May bank holiday and I had already added the date to my calendar, telling myself it was for the twins, not me. But the truth was that my obsession with finding Mystic Maggie was growing stronger each day, as though only she could make all this go away now, only by seeing her again could I shake off the cloud of dread hanging over me. She would tell me that she had made a mistake, or she would laugh at my gullibility, and then I could breathe a sigh of relief and get on with my life.

Until then, though, I couldn't relax and by lunchtime I would have made my second call to Jude. He was so accustomed to it now that he often answered immediately, like he'd been waiting for me. Most of the time, he tried to make out as though this was a perfectly normal conversation, as though we were like any other married couple. How had my morning been? What was I having for lunch? He was about to head out to get a sandwich, he would tell me. Probably cheese and ham. Sometimes he'd be in a rush and our exchange would be quick, curt even. Whenever that happened, he always sent me a text message a few minutes later with a few heart emojis.

The third call usually took place between four and five. By then I had picked the twins up and brought them home and I would consider myself on the final stretch. In a couple of hours, Jude would be back from work and I could relax for the evening, knowing that my family were safe at home and that nothing bad could happen to them. But those two hours seemed like an endless stretch of time, and as the twins played or watched television, I would pace around the house. *Just one more call*, I would tell myself. *And then I'm done.*

The irony didn't escape me. It had been Jude who my friends had accused of being controlling. Jude who had been suspicious of me, who was worried that I was having an affair. But I was the one who was calling him constantly, checking his whereabouts on my phone, trying to account for his every move. The difference between us was that I didn't for a second suspect adultery or betrayal. I just needed to know that he was okay.

It had only been a few short months since that dinner with the girls. A tiny sliver of time in the grand scheme of life and yet so much had changed. Shiv had moved to California and her Instagram grid was full of photos of the kids at the beach, or at their new condo which had a shared pool. It wasn't just that she had moved, it felt like she had travelled to another planet, a place so far removed from my life in London. Helen had gone to ground, which she sometimes did when she was in the throes of a new relationship, but I had no idea who she was seeing. And Emily had gone quiet too, presumably busy with her job, marriage and life. She and Mark didn't have children and so their lives were different to mine and Jude's, peppered with long weekends away and last-minute holidays to exotic places. It felt like the beginning of the end, the inevitable dissolution of our group after fifteen years of friendship. We had gone off on different tangents, the four of us, and while I knew that the love between us was still there, and that we would always be there for each other, I had to accept that we would no longer see each other as much as we had. The problem was that it had happened when I needed them the most.

Jude thought I was lonely and had even suggested that I get a job. It was the first time he'd brought it up since I'd had the twins, and although he pitched it as a chance for me to resume my career now that the children were older and would soon be starting school, I knew what he was really implying. He thought that life alone at home was getting to me and I needed a distraction.

He had caught me off guard when he first raised it and I'd looked at him, dumbfounded. 'You really think I should go back to work now? But what about my writing?'

'Simmy, I'm so proud that you got that article published in the magazine. But until things start to take off with your writing, maybe you'd benefit from a part-time job.'

'Do we need the money?' I left the finances to Jude, happy to live off the allowance he put into my current account every month and the joint credit card he paid off. I didn't ask questions because

I didn't need to know the answer, but I wondered if I should have paid more attention.

'No, it's not that. Look, you know I support your dream to be a writer, but when was the last time you actually wrote anything?'

It had been ages and we both knew it. I was preoccupied, my mind too all over the place to focus on words, to lose myself in fiction. 'I've got an idea for a story,' I'd said, and I'd hated how desperate I sounded, how feeble. I had never been a feeble person before, yet this is what I had become. I didn't know when it had happened, but this was who I was now.

'Maybe a change of scene would do you good,' he'd said gently. 'A bit of structure. You've been at home now for what? Three years? Four if you count maternity leave.'

'But who will take the kids to preschool if I get a job? Who will pick them up?'

'We can make it work. Lots of couples do. I just want you to be happy, Simone. Whatever you want, I'll support you.'

What Jude really wanted was for me to go back to how I was. Happy, confident Simone, grateful to be alive, content with our life and our family. Not this neurotic person who now saw the world as a threat, full of danger waiting to pounce. But I wasn't sure how to go back.

I had looked at his concerned face and taken the path of least resistance. 'You're right, I should get a job. I'll start looking for part-time roles.'

And I *did* look. In fact, it became another compulsion, one more task to add to my daily list of things I had to check before I could relax. I scoured job websites every morning and evening, yet I didn't apply for a single position because every time I saw a vacancy, I wondered how I would be able to fulfil it around looking after the twins. I wondered how I would be able to check in with Jude if I was in an open-plan office and going to meetings.

And I thought about having to commute and have appraisals and it all terrified me.

'Maybe I should wait until Ivy and Sam start school,' I'd told Jude after a few weeks. 'There'll be a lot of settling in sessions before they're in class full time.'

And he'd nodded and kissed me on the top of my head, just as he did with our children when they were tired or grumpy or being unreasonable. 'Sure, whatever you think is best.'

There was a time, not long ago, when I told my friends everything, when I would have relished sharing Jude's suggestion with the girls and getting their thoughts on the matter. But I hadn't breathed a word. I could imagine Shiv and Emily adding it to their dossier of evidence that Jude called the shots. *Oh yes, she can go back to work now*, I could almost hear them say. *Because* he *thinks it's the right time.* They were so wrong. Jude did not call the shots. He was not the one calling me three times a day just to check where I was. He was not the one constantly monitoring my every move. If anyone was being unreasonable, it was me. If anyone was trying to control our lives, the blame fell squarely at my feet. Yet I was powerless to stop myself.

So, this was our life now, for better or for worse. Jude and I had taken our vows and we were bound to one another in sickness and in health. Yet it was this bind that I feared the most. It was this connection that I knew would be our downfall, the thing that destroyed us.

Still, I tried to live my life. I got up every morning, I went through the motions. I pulled silly faces at the twins and had coffee with the other mums. I sent vacuous, humorous messages on the WhatsApp group between me, Helen, Emily and Shiv. I made noises about us going to visit Shiv in California, even though I knew there was no way we were getting on a plane this year.

Tick tock. The clock had become the soundtrack to my life. There were eight months left, and then the five-year mark would have passed. And if we were still standing, I could forget all about Mystic Maggie and finally look to the future again, or at least enjoy living in the present. I just had to get through the rest of this year and things would get better.

So, when my husband said to me, in a weary tone, 'Simmy, this has to stop,' I hung my head and nodded, even though he couldn't see me, even though he was miles away in his office.

'I know,' I said. 'I'm sorry. I love you.'

18

When Helen turned up on my doorstep unannounced, I was so delighted to see her that I didn't question why she was there on a weekday morning when she should be at work.

'What a lovely surprise,' I said, opening the front door wide to let her in. 'Coffee?'

'Yes please.'

Helen looked around at the toys strewn all over the floor and the unwashed dishes in the sink, but said nothing. I saw her expression though, and I knew what she was thinking.

'Sorry about the mess,' I said lightly, trying to hide my embarrassment given that the kids weren't even at home. 'When you have young children, your house turns into a warzone.'

'Of course it does.' Helen sat down and watched me as I boiled the kettle. 'How are you, Simmy?'

'Yeah, I'm fine.'

'It's been a while.'

'I know. I've been so busy with the twins. And what about you? I haven't heard from you in ages. Am I to assume there's someone new in your life?'

Helen shrugged. 'There is someone, yes. I wouldn't exactly say new.'

'It's not that young hippy girl again, is it?' I knew instantly from Helen's expression that it was. 'Blimey, Helen, you guys have been on and off for years now. Surely it's time to spill the beans?'

'I'm not here to talk about me, I'm here to talk about you.'

I carried two mugs of coffee over and passed one to her. 'What about me?'

'Jude called.'

My heart sank, as I realised that this was not an impromptu visit from my best friend wanting to have a long overdue catch up. This was an intervention. 'Okay.'

'He's worried about you.'

I shrugged, trying to remain impassive. 'There's nothing to worry about.'

'He said you're not sleeping. That you're calling him all the time, you're stressing about the twins' health too. He thinks you need help, Simmy. So do I.'

'I am tired,' I admitted. 'But it's not as bad as all that.'

'I disagree. It sounds like you've got yourself into a right state.'

Another friend might have eased me gently into a conversation like this, but not Helen. She always got straight to the point and it was what I loved about her, but not today. Today it was what I hated about her and I could feel my hackles rising defensively.

'That's a bit over the top, isn't it?'

'From what Jude's told me, I don't think it is, no.'

Her self-righteousness infuriated me. 'And what do you know about it? I haven't seen you in weeks, yet you waltz in here like you own the place and have a right to throw all this at me.'

'You're right.' Helen's impassivity only fuelled my rage. 'I've been a terrible friend and I'm sorry. But I love you, Simone. So please, talk to me. Tell me what's going on.'

'Nothing's going on. I'm fine.'

'No, you're not.'

'Yes, I am.'

We glared at each other, both reluctant to back down, but eventually Helen gave in first. 'Is this about what Shiv and Emily said at dinner a few months back? About you and Jude? Because I've talked to them about it since and they feel terrible for ambushing you.'

'It's not that.' I wasn't lying but it rankled that they'd all been talking about me.

'They realise that they overreacted and I don't think they'll be bringing it up again. And anyway, for what it's worth, I don't think they're right about Jude.'

'I said it's not about that.'

'So what is it? Is it Jude? Is everything okay between you?'

'Yes, it's fine.'

'Stop saying fine. It's me you're talking to here. And I'm not leaving until I get it out of you.'

I looked at her determined face, her mouth set in a straight line. I hadn't talked to anyone in so long, not properly. I'd chatted with lots of people but I hadn't *really* talked, not like I used to with the girls, before they'd turned on me at that dinner, before Shiv had moved to the US and Emily and Helen had got caught up in their own lives. I wanted to tell her everything, but I was afraid, of her reaction, her judgement, her mirth. I was afraid that she wouldn't understand.

'I feel like I'm waiting for something bad to happen,' I admitted tentatively.

'What thing? What do you think is going to happen?'

I wanted to tell her about the signs, I wanted to admit my deepest, darkest fear so desperately. But I couldn't stop thinking about her comments about Mystic Maggie, her disbelief when I told her that I was shaken by what the fortune teller had said. She would laugh at me, I knew it, she wouldn't understand and I would just feel worse about it. And so I couldn't bring myself to do it.

'I don't know,' I said. 'I'm just feeling a little overwhelmed at the moment.'

'Of course you are,' Helen said sympathetically. 'Raising children is hard work, let alone twins. You need to give yourself a break.'

'Yes,' I agreed, because it was easier to go with her narrative than mine.

'Have you ever considered that you might have PTSD?' Helen was enthusiastic, like she had just miraculously diagnosed my condition and solved all my problems. 'It happens to women, especially after a traumatic birth. And before you can recover, you're straight into raising babies and you have no time to sleep or think and eventually it all catches up with you, sometimes years later. It happened to a friend of mine, remember Iris?'

I nodded even though I didn't remember Iris.

'She had a breakdown when her son was three. She'd just been holding it all together for so long and she finally started to unravel. She had anxiety, she couldn't sleep, she was a mess.'

Did a fortune teller predict that her marriage was going to end in tragedy, though? Was she a ticking time bomb, waiting for the explosion? Tick tock, tick tock, seven months to go. I shook my head, trying to physically rid myself of my intrusive thoughts.

But Helen was on a roll now and didn't notice my discomfort. 'She started seeing a counsellor, had CBT, and now she's doing really well. Seriously, she's like a new woman.'

'Good for Iris.'

If Helen recognised my sarcasm, she didn't respond. 'Maybe

all you need is someone to talk to, Simmy. I mean a professional who can give you the support you need.'

It was not an unreasonable suggestion, yet part of me felt betrayed by Helen. Here was the person who was supposed to know me best, yet she hadn't pushed me, or prised the information out of me that deep down I craved to share with her. She had taken the easy route, made the most obvious assumption about my mental health. It wasn't her fault, I knew that. She was only trying to help and how was she supposed to know what was going on if I didn't tell her? And yet, I wanted her to guess. I wanted her to figure it out without me saying it.

And what if I went to see a counsellor? If I told them what was worrying me, they'd probably have me admitted to an institution or something. I knew my concerns were ludicrous but they had rooted themselves inside me, they were coursing through my veins and wrapping themselves around my limbs. They were real and terrifying but I was too ashamed to voice them aloud.

'Yeah, maybe I should see someone,' I said, to appease Helen.

'I'll get the counsellor's number from Iris,' Helen replied, already scrolling through her phone. 'Apparently this woman is the real deal.'

'Thanks.'

I watched Helen type out a message, presumably to Iris. How simple her life was, I thought. She could do her good deed for the day and then walk out of my house and get on with her easy existence, where she didn't constantly think about death and destruction and the end of everything. In that moment I resented her and wished that I *was* her in equal measures.

'What are you up to for the bank holiday weekend?' Helen asked me, once she'd put her phone down.

Going to a funfair to try and track down Mystic Maggie. Remember her? The woman who put a limit on my happiness. The woman who ruined my life. 'Oh, we haven't got many plans. How about you?'

'I'm going away for a few days actually, to the Lake District.'

'Oh lovely, who are you going with?'

I swear Helen blushed. 'Just a friend.'

'This girlfriend?'

'No.'

'Helen, what gives? You're so secretive about this woman.'

Helen looked pained. 'She's just a bit of a drifter, Simmy. She doesn't have a proper job, a proper home. She disappears for months on end then she turns up again and I can't seem to say no to her. It's like I can't resist her and this lack of control is totally messing with my head.'

'Do you love her?'

'I don't know. I'm infatuated by her. But there's no future between us and sometimes I wonder if I'm wasting my life, if I wouldn't do better to meet someone else and get on with things.'

'Well, she's going away with you, so maybe things are changing. People can't drift forever, eventually the nomadic lifestyle wears off and they want to settle down.'

'Maybe.' Helen didn't look convinced. 'Anyway, I'd better go, I need to get to the office. Promise me you'll get in touch with the counsellor when I send her details?'

I held my hand up in salute. 'Scout's honour.'

'And let's do dinner when I'm back from the Lake District.'

'I'd like that.'

Helen stood up and gave me a hug. 'Look after yourself, Simmy. I'm always here if you need to talk, okay?'

'I know, thanks. And enjoy your mini-break.'

After she left, I realised that I'd missed my first phone call of the day to Jude. I'd completely forgotten about it until that moment. I felt a strange sort of elation, of freedom. Perhaps Jude was right after all. All this festering around the house with nothing to fill my mind with but the constant fear of something bad happening wasn't good for me. I needed something to do, something else to fill up my time, and my mind. I should start looking for jobs again, I decided, and I stood up to put the kettle on, feeling a renewed sense of purpose.

But then I had another thought. What if something bad had happened while I'd been distracted with Helen? If it had, I'd never forgive myself. It would be my fault for not checking in, for not performing my daily duties. Panic surged though me and I grabbed my phone to check on Jude's location, waiting to see the little dot on the map so that I'd know he was at the office. But the dot wasn't at the office, it was a couple of miles away in Soho. What was he doing in Soho?

Don't do it, a voice inside my head said. *Don't call him. Let this be a turning point for you, when you can put all this behind you.* But I already knew that I was going to do it. I dialled his number and waited for it to connect, counting each ring. One. Two. Three. Four. Five.

By six my palms were clammy. Something was very, very wrong. And it was my fault.

On the seventh ring, he picked up. 'Simone, I'm in the middle of a client brunch, I told you about it this morning, you said you wouldn't call today.'

Everything came back into focus again and I exhaled. He had told me about it, I remembered now. 'I'm sorry, Jude, Helen came round and I completely forgot.'

I heard the noise in the background get quieter, as though Jude was walking away from the table, making his way to a quiet area or stairwell. 'Helen came? How did it go?'

'Yeah, good, it was nice to see her.'

'Did you two have a good talk?'

I knew exactly what he was asking me and, feeling guilty that I'd disturbed his client meeting, I gave him what he needed. 'We did, and she's going to send me the details of a counsellor that her friend recommended.'

'Oh that's great, Simmy, that's really great.'

'And I'm going to start looking for jobs again.'

'Oh wow, I'm so pleased.'

The joy in his voice almost broke my heart. I had to do better, for Jude and for the twins. 'I'll leave you to your brunch now, sorry to have disturbed you.'

'No problem, speak to you later. I love you, Simmy.'

'I love you too.'

He still said 'I love you', so it couldn't be too bad. There was still time to pull this back, to salvage things before they got out of hand. I wanted to do it, I wanted it more than anything. I looked at my phone, willing myself to resist. But I couldn't. I'd just check Jude's location one last time and then have a tiny little look to see what the twins were up to at preschool and then I would put my phone away. I would go for a walk, get some fresh air, buy some more milk and a nice meal for us to have for dinner. I would call my mum for a chat. I would send a message on the WhatsApp group to see how Shiv was and suggest some dates for Helen, Emily and me to go out for dinner. I would be a good, normal person.

But first, just a quick look.

19

The persistent April rain had finally departed, and the sun warmed my skin and soothed my soul. Ivy and Sam fidgeted in their buggy and I walked alongside them, looking down at their eager little faces and then back at Jude, who was pushing them. We looked so much like a happy, normal family having a day out that for a moment I forgot that we weren't.

Jude had no idea why we were going to the fair. He didn't know about my meticulous planning, my detailed spreadsheet. When I had told him that a fair was coming to our local park and suggested we take the children, he had agreed because it was a pleasant way to spend a Saturday afternoon and probably thought no more of it. I had thought a lot about it though, anticipation growing inside me as the weekend drew nearer. I had a growing, tingly feeling that this would be the one. Perhaps it was wishful thinking because the alternative, that Mystic Maggie was out of reach and gone forever, was impossible to bear. But I believed that I would find her.

As we entered the grounds, which were already filling up with people taking advantage of the spring sunshine, I cast my eye around, examining the attractions. The fair was larger than the one I'd taken the twins to the previous summer and there were some things about it which seemed familiar: the carousel with the painted horses, the helter-skelter. I felt a renewed surge of hope.

'Let's walk around the whole fair and get our bearings,' I suggested to Jude.

'Mummy, I want to go on that ride.' Sam was pointing at a small train.

'Me too! Me too!' Ivy had already taken off her buggy straps and was making a run for it.

Jude abandoned the buggy to run after her and I had no choice but to take his place and push Sam in the same direction. I hated the fact that in that moment, I resented my children for waylaying me and I forced a smile and tried to stay upbeat. Whatever the outcome, I decided, I would still be glad that we came. It was good for us to spend time together as a family, to enjoy each other's company, to do normal things like everyone else. Normal. It was a word I thought of a lot these days, as though it was an unobtainable goal just out of my reach.

Yet even then I still believed that I was in control, that I had a handle on my situation. My habits, as I called them, hadn't gone away. I still called Jude throughout the day, I checked his location constantly, I monitored the twins' preschool app and I furiously googled children's rare health conditions. But they hadn't got any worse either and that was something. Anyway, I wasn't doing any harm and if they made me feel better, then so be it.

The twins were growing up quickly, making friends. There was talk of play dates and meeting for picnics at adventure playgrounds. I politely declined all invitations from the other mums because I couldn't cope with the anxiety that each one caused, the list of things that could go wrong. What if one of the kids they spent time with was about to come down with chickenpox and they passed it on to Ivy or Sam? In rare cases, it could cause serious complications. Or what if I turned my back for a second and someone abducted one of my children from the playground? I'd read about it online and it had been known to happen, so I wasn't being irrational.

Yet I did know that this couldn't go on, not just because the mums were starting to give me a wide berth but because it wasn't fair on Ivy and Sam. By keeping them wrapped up in cotton wool, I wasn't giving them the childhood they deserved. But it wasn't forever. As soon as I found Mystic Maggie and cleared this up then it would all be okay. And that was exactly what I had come to do.

By the time I reached the train, Jude had paid the ride attendant and the twins quickly clambered on. It was too small for adults, so Jude came over to stand beside me and took his phone out of his pocket to take photos, waving at Ivy and Sam as the train started moving. I waved too but my eyes darted about, looking around for any signs of that little tent.

'You okay?' Jude asked.

'I'm fine.'

'You seem a little jumpy.'

'Actually, I really need the toilet. Is it okay if I head off and catch up with you in a few minutes?'

'Sure, we'll probably still be here.'

'Great.'

I breathed a sigh of relief as I left him, feeling free now that I was on my own. The twins were safe, that train was designed for young children and was moving at a snail's pace. But I couldn't take too long otherwise Jude would start to worry, so I hurried around the perimeter of the fair and scanned the field to see if I could find Mystic Maggie. As I was passing a dark-haired woman pushing a child in a buggy, my heart stopped for a second. I recognised her immediately and from the way she looked at me, I could tell that she recognised me too. For a brief, heady moment I thought it was the fortune teller, their characteristics were curiously similar, and I nearly reached out to stop her but then my brain caught up with my eyes. I had seen the woman before, but no matter how much I wanted her to be, she wasn't Mystic Maggie and I was too distracted to work out how I knew her. I looked away and continued my search.

After fifteen minutes, I still hadn't found any sign of Mystic Maggie and I knew that Jude would be wondering what had happened to me. I quickly bought a few drinks from a kiosk which would explain my longer absence and went to find him and the children, drowning in disappointment as I realised that this visit had been a bust. I'd wanted something so much that I had made myself believe it could happen, but reality was settling in now. Mystic Maggie wasn't here and I had no idea where to find her. Tears pricked at my eyes as my hope faded away.

I was startled by the sound of a child screaming and I turned to see a commotion going on behind me. People were rushing towards someone lying on the ground and I knew in an instant that while I had been distracted, something terrible had happened to Ivy or Sam. *No. No, no, no!* Why had I let them out of my sight in a chaotic place like this? Already I was imagining the ambulance arriving, the doctor at hospital shaking his head and telling me there was nothing they could do, Jude turning pale while I crumpled to the floor and convulsed with sobs. I started running, throwing my newly bought drinks onto the floor and pushing through the crowds, ignoring people's complaints as I elbowed them out of the way. Adrenaline was coursing through my body and my only goal was getting to that child on the floor. *Please tell me I'm not too late.* Finally, I reached the front of the huddle of people and saw a little boy wailing, his knee bloody and his mum and dad cuddling him. They looked up at me in alarm.

'Sorry,' I said breathlessly. 'I heard a scream and I wanted to make sure everything was okay.'

The mum smiled, although she was still looking at me curiously. 'He tripped up and cut his leg on a stone, but he'll be fine. Are you a doctor?'

'Oh, no, I'm not. I'm sorry. I'm glad he's okay.'

Red-faced with embarrassment, I lowered my head and weaved my way back through the crowds, ignoring the tuts of the passers-by I'd pushed in my haste. The funfair was closing in on me and the loud music, which had excited me when I first arrived, was making my head throb. I wanted to get out of this godforsaken place and return to the safe sanctuary of home.

'Simone?'

I spotted Jude a few metres away, holding Ivy in one arm and pushing the pram in the other.

'Where's Sam?' I demanded, looking around, panic already rising again. But then I saw him, behind Jude's legs and the last drop of adrenaline left my body.

'Where have you been? We've been looking everywhere for you.'

'I'm sorry, I stopped to get us some drinks.'

Jude looked at my empty hands and frowned. 'Where are they?'

'Oh, I...' I looked around, confused and disorientated. 'There was a commotion, a little boy got hurt and I must have lost them.'

When I looked at Jude again, he was watching me with an expression somewhere between concern, confusion and annoyance. 'The twins want to go on the helter-skelter,' he said.

'Oh I don't know, I think they're too young.'

'We can go on with them, take one each.'

But I looked up at the rickety old slide and all I saw was danger. 'I don't think so. It's not safe.'

'Why did we even come here, then, if you won't let them go on the rides?'

I ignored him and looked down at the children. 'Who wants a hot dog?'

'Me, me!' The twins' faces lit up and even Jude looked ready to concede.

'I'm pretty hungry,' he admitted.

'Great, let's get something to eat and then we'll scope out some more rides.'

I was desperate to leave but I knew I had to stay a little longer for Jude and the kids because it wasn't fair to ruin their day too and I didn't want to alarm my husband either. He was already worried about me, watching me like a hawk, and I had to at least try and act normal even if my nerves were in tatters. There was that word again. Normal.

But as we queued at the food stand, I was already checking my phone for the next funfair date. There was one opening at Hampstead on Friday afternoon. It was only a few miles away so if I arrived at the start, I could look for Mystic Maggie and still be back in time to pick the children up from preschool. It would be much easier on my own, I thought, my disappointment already beginning to ebb away. So, she hadn't been here today but there were plenty of fairs popping up over the coming months. I would find her. I would track her down and make her retract what she'd said if it was the last thing I did. I still had seven months to go. *Tick tock.*

* * *

Hey, just checking in. Have you contacted that counsellor yet? X

Not yet, been busy looking for jobs x

Found any decent ones yet?

No, still looking!

I reread the exchange between Helen and me and then put my phone down. I had no intention of calling the counsellor because I already knew what was wrong with me without needing professional help, and there was only one person who could get me out of this mess.

So, when the phone rang and I saw that it was Helen, I almost didn't answer because I wasn't in the mood for one of her pep talks. But if I ignored her, she'd probably keep ringing until I answered. I picked up my phone again with a sigh.

'Hey, Hels.'

'Hey. So I really think you should call this counsellor. It might even give you more confidence with those job applications.'

I closed my eyes. Life, to Helen, was so black and white. See a counsellor, get fixed, get on with your life. But most people's lives didn't work like that, they were complicated and messy.

'I'm going to call her, okay?'

'Fine. Talk me through these jobs you've been checking out.'

I knew she was trying to help but it felt like an interrogation. 'I'd much rather discuss it over a glass of wine.'

'Good plan. Shall we meet on Saturday night? The Usual Place?'

'I'd like that. I'll see if Emily's free too.'

'Great. Chat then.'

I hung up, glad the conversation was over, and opened my laptop. I'd had an idea for a story that had come to me, out of the blue, the previous day and I was keen to take advantage of my initial surge of enthusiasm to get writing. But after only a couple of hundred words I was already starting to lose steam and I gazed out of the window onto the street and watched the world go by. A snake of schoolchildren walked past, wearing little yellow tabards, and I recognised their uniform as being from the local primary school. The twins would be starting there in September, they had got their place the previous month. I wondered where the children were going; a school trip perhaps or a visit to the local playground. And I imagined Sam and Ivy going to school, being pulled even further away from me, and it was almost unthinkable.

When we got confirmation of the twins' primary school places, I had hesitantly suggested to Jude that we defer a year.

'Why would we do that?' he'd asked.

I had my argument ready to go because I'd rehearsed it several times. 'They were born in July so they'll be amongst the youngest in their year. And they were premature so their development might be delayed. I just wonder if they need another year before they're ready.'

It was a valid argument because plenty of parents of summer-born children deferred a year. But maybe Jude saw right through me or maybe he just disagreed. Either way, he said. 'We can't wrap them up in cotton wool forever. And we can't keep paying childcare costs either, you know how expensive it is.'

'I know that, but they're just so teeny tiny. One year can make a huge difference.'

'I know you're afraid of letting them go but that's not a good enough reason. They'll be perfectly happy and safe at primary school. It's where they should be.'

'Did you know that in some countries, children don't start school until they're seven?'

'But we don't live in some countries, Simone, we live in this one.'

He called me Simone now, not Simmy. Perhaps it was so subconscious he didn't even realise he was doing it or perhaps there was nothing to it. But I'd noticed it, and every time he didn't use my nickname it felt like we drifted apart a fraction more. He'd started going out more too, meeting friends for dinner in the evening or for a coffee on a Saturday afternoon. His sudden interest in a social life further fuelled my anxiety, not that I worried he'd met someone else, but because it increased the risk of something happening to him. My nerves were frayed from being on constant alert, from checking his movements every few minutes, but he wasn't a child, and as much as I wanted to, I couldn't forbid him from going out. He always came home, that was the important thing. He always came home to me.

'Can we at least think about the school thing?' I asked him.

'No.' His tone brooked no argument, like he was talking to Ivy when she asked for another chocolate. 'They're going to school in September and that's the end of it.'

Is this what we had become? Two people on different pages? Or had we always been like this and I'd only just realised? Shiv and Emily thought so. Helen didn't. I no longer knew what to think and I wasn't even sure I cared enough. I just wanted us all to be safe and alive, and everything else would sort itself out at some point. It wasn't too much to ask.

I still loved Jude, I loved him so much. But that was the problem. My behaviour was pushing him away but that was what I needed to do to keep him safe. At least that's what I told myself when I called him throughout the day, now four times instead of three. And he still answered, when he could, because he didn't want me to worry. Because he loved me too.

He may call me Simone, but he still said *I love you*.

So, all was not lost.

20

I'd just parked the car when I made my lunchtime call to Jude.

'Hey, how are you?' I asked, keeping my tone light.

'Yeah, fine, just about to grab a sandwich. How about you?'

'I'm in the car, heading to the supermarket. Do you want anything?'

'Will you get some beer? I think we're out.'

'Sure. I'll see you later.'

I lied to him now. I lied to my husband. But it was for his own good, so it was allowed. I wasn't on my way to the supermarket, I was sitting in a car park in Hampstead, waiting for the funfair to open. I was cutting it fine because if I got caught in any traffic, I might be late to pick up the twins but if I stayed focused, with my mind on the prize, I'd make it.

The rain had returned and when I trudged towards the entrance, there were very few people about. I pulled my hood up over my head, paid the £1 entry fee and walked into the empty fairground looking left and right. I could feel water seeping through my trainers and drenching my socks as I looked for Mystic Maggie's hand-painted sign. I weaved around bumper cars and hook a duck stalls, inhaling the smell of candyfloss, ignoring the calls of bored ride attendants offering three rides for a fiver, looking only for the tent. But after twenty minutes, I knew she wasn't there. Defeated, I plodded back to my car, checked Jude's location on my phone, opened the twins' preschool app and then finally looked at my spreadsheet for the next funfair. It was in South London the following weekend which would be more of a challenge to get to, but it was nothing I couldn't handle. I'd tell Jude I fancied a change of scene from North London, even suggest that I took the twins so he could have some time to himself. He'd like that.

Thinking of Jude reminded me that he'd asked me to pick up some beers. If I left now, I'd have time to call into the supermarket quickly on my way home. This simple act of buying him lager made me feel less duplicitous because it meant I *had* gone to the supermarket and when he got home and found them in the fridge, we could all pretend that everything was as it should be.

My phone rang, making me jump, and immediately worry started to kick in, as it always did these days when somebody called, especially when I saw it was from an unknown number.

'Hello?'

'Simone? It's Tom.'

'Oh, hi, Tom.' Relief flooded over me.

'Where are you?'

'I'm out and about, why?'

'Can we talk?'

'I haven't got long, I've got to pick up the kids soon.'

'It's really urgent.'

I looked at my watch. 'I'll be home in twenty-five minutes but I can't hang around.'

'Text me your address and I'll meet you there.'

'Okay.' I hung up and started the engine, wondering what

could be so urgent that it couldn't wait. I was sure it was nothing to do with Jude and the children, but I was still curious.

By the time I arrived, Tom was already waiting outside. His face was pale and I climbed out of the car and looked at him in concern. 'Are you okay? What's going on?'

'Can we go inside?' He was looking around nervously.

'Of course, come on.' I led him into the house and closed the door behind us, glad that Jude wasn't home because even though this meeting was entirely innocent, I was worried that it would trigger him. 'I would offer you a cup of tea but I'm afraid I haven't got time.'

'Don't worry about it. Look, I'm leaving and I'm taking Camille with me.'

My eyes widened. 'Okay. Where are you going?'

'I can't tell you, I can't tell anyone.'

'Right.' Why was he here then? Was it just to say goodbye? I felt sorry for him but I had enough problems in my own life without adding his to the mix.

'I just wanted to warn you to be careful.'

Fear never really left me these days. It was always waiting, ready to pounce. It came to me easily now as I digested his words, which sounded horribly threatening. 'What do you mean?'

'She knows about you, Simone. She knows that we dated and she knows that we met up recently.'

'Does she also know that I'm married with children and pose no threat to her?'

'It doesn't matter, not to her. The reason I'm leaving is, well, she did something, something bad, and let's just say it was the final straw.'

Oh my God. Jude, the children. Scenarios raced through my mind. If she'd hurt any of them, if she'd touched one hair on their heads, I would kill her with my bare hands. 'What has she done, Tom?'

'It's not you,' he said quickly, realising what I was thinking. 'It's nothing to do with you. There's this single mum at a toddler group that I take Camille to and occasionally sit next to. We ran into each other in the park once or twice and had a brief chat. I thought I'd been so careful, but I realise now that I underestimated her, even after all this time.'

Now that I knew it had nothing to do with me, I was morbidly intrigued. 'What did she do?'

'She must have followed this woman to the playground one afternoon and when she was distracted talking to some other mums, she took her child.'

My hand flew to my heart. 'She did what?'

'Not for long, only for half an hour or so. But this woman was terrified, she thought her son had been abducted. And then apparently the child appeared out of nowhere, completely unharmed.'

'So how do you know it was your girlfriend? The boy could easily have just wandered off.'

'It was her,' Tom said fiercely. 'I know it was her.'

'But surely they would have called the police? Searched the area? If she was hiding out with him, they would have found her.'

'I don't know how she did it but believe me, Simone, she did. She wanted to scare the crap out of this woman and she succeeded.'

It was like it had happened to me. I was imagining this poor woman's horror as she realised that she couldn't find her child, I was seeing myself in her shoes and my fear was very real.

'I don't think I'm safe around her any more,' Tom continued, 'and I don't think Camille is either.'

'But if you just disappear, won't that make things worse? She might report you, accuse you of taking Camille away from her. She may have problems but she's still Camille's mother. And you'll be on the run, Tom, what kind of life is that for you and Camille?'

'A safe one. And it's only temporary, once we're somewhere she can't find us, I'll call the police myself and tell them everything. I'll get a restraining order. I'll finally be free.'

I wasn't convinced that Tom had thought this through properly and I still suspected that as Camille's mother, his partner would have rights to contact. But I saw the look of determination on Tom's face and I had no desire to interfere. He was doing what he thought was right.

'And you have got somewhere to go? Somewhere safe?'

'Yes.'

'Well, I really hope that it works out for you. I'll be thinking of you, Tom, and if you need anything, just ask. I would say call me but I'm guessing you can't.'

'No. Listen, I have to go but I meant what I said, watch your back, okay? When she realises we've gone she'll be even more crazy and I don't know what she might do.'

My heart started pounding again. If Tom was right, if he wasn't being paranoid, then what did it mean for me? 'Am I in danger? Is my family in danger?'

He hung his head. 'I don't know, but I'm going to make this stop, I promise you.'

It occurred to me then that Tom was in my house, which meant that if this woman really was keeping tabs on him, she'd now know where I lived. 'Why did you come here?'

'I wanted to talk to you.'

'But why here, in my house?'

Tom was confused. 'Because this is where you said you'd be.'

'And now your girlfriend might know too.'

'No, don't worry about that, she's at work.'

'You've said that before, but she still saw us together, and she saw you talking to that other mum too. She's watching you, Tom, and now she might be watching me.'

Tom looked horrified. 'Oh shit, Simone, this is one big, awful mess.'

He looked devastated and I knew I should comfort him, but I was too furious. All this time I had been worrying about train crashes and childhood illnesses when perhaps my greatest threat all along had been Tom's ex, and soon she'd be on the rampage and looking for someone to blame. With the five-year mark rapidly approaching, this seemed like too much of a coincidence.

'You need to call the police now, Tom. You need to have her stopped.'

'I can't, not until Camille and I are safe.'

I glared at him. 'Do it now.'

'And what do I say? What if it's not enough to have her arrested? What if they don't believe me and then she finds out while we're still here?'

'Tell them everything. They have to believe you.'

'I will, Simone, just give me a couple of days.'

We stared at each other, neither backing down, both determined to protect our families. The phone ringing finally broke the silence. I looked down, saw the number for the twins' preschool on my screen and my world came crashing down. *She's got to them already. I'm too late.*

I almost dropped the phone in my haste to answer it. 'Hello?'

'Simone? This is Clara from Grey Oaks. Is everything okay? Ivy and Sam are still waiting to be collected.'

Shit, shit, shit. I'd been so preoccupied with Tom that I'd missed pick up. 'I'm so sorry,' I said. 'I got held up with something, I'm on my way now, I'll be there in five minutes.'

I put the phone back in my pocket and turned to Tom. 'I have to pick up the kids. I know you're scared, Tom, but you got me into this mess and you need to get me out of it.'

'I know,' he said. 'I will.'

There was no more time to press my point. I legged it out of the door without even saying goodbye to Tom and ran as fast as I could to the preschool, shame washing over me as I arrived and saw that Ivy and Sam were the last two children left. I'd never been late for pick up before.

'I'm so sorry,' I gushed.

The manager, Clara, smiled. 'No problem.'

'It'll never happen again.'

'Honestly, Simone, don't worry, it's fine. I know you're usually very prompt.'

I kissed Ivy and Sam, my shaking hands quivering as I stroked their heads.

'Is everything okay?' Clara was looking at me in concern.

I forced a smile. 'Yes. Rough day. But I'm fine.'

She looked sympathetic. 'Well, at least it's the weekend, I hope you have a good one.'

'You too.'

I took Ivy and Sam by the hand, and we began our slow amble back to the house. I had started leaving the buggy behind to get them used to walking in preparation for school and already I was wondering what I would do if I was ambushed by Tom's girlfriend, or ex, or whatever he called her, because I couldn't run fast with the twins. I was vulnerable and it scared me. We walked past the park and I scanned the crowds, looking to see if I was being watched.

'Where's my snack?' Sam demanded.

'Oh darling, I was in such a rush I forgot to pick one up. Tell you what, why don't we stop by the shops and get a treat? It is Friday, after all.'

Sam mulled this over. 'Chocolate?'

'Sure, why not.'

The children beamed and I marvelled at how something so small and simple could light up their entire world. And then I thought about Tom and my world clouded over again. I didn't want to go home, not if this woman knew where I lived. The one place that had been my safe sanctuary over the past few months now felt like the most dangerous location of all. I didn't know if I would be able to relax until I knew that she couldn't hurt us. But how would I find out if Tom disappeared and I never heard from him again? It felt like my life was in his hands and that wasn't good enough for me. I stopped abruptly in the street.

'Mummy, come on.' Sam was tugging at my hand, trying to drag me towards the shops.

'We need to make a stop first,' I said, turning around.

'No, Mummy! You said chocolate!'

'And we will get chocolate, I promise. But we need to do this first.'

I pulled the reluctant twins in the opposite direction, my feet moving before my mind had figured out a plan. I knew that at least one tantrum was brewing but I didn't care, and after a few minutes we reached the local police station and I walked in and strode up to the reception desk.

'How can I help you?' the man behind the desk asked.

'I might be in danger, someone might want to hurt me and my children.'

The man took my details and picked up the phone to make a call and I paced around the reception area, ignoring the children's complaints, until a female police officer appeared at the door a few minutes later, introduced herself and ushered me into a small room.

'Do you want someone to mind your children while we talk?' she asked but there was no way I was letting them out of my sight.

'No, they're fine, I'd rather keep them with me.'

She nodded. 'So, Simone – is it okay if I call you that? Can you tell me why you're here today?'

I looked over at the twins, who were bickering over an old, half-eaten packet of raisins they had found in Ivy's coat pocket and then I launched into my story. I think I knew, as I was talking, how vague and far-fetched it sounded but I kept going, willing the police officer to understand.

When I was finished, she looked at me. 'Do you know this woman's name?'

'No,' I admitted.

'Or where she lives?'

'In a flat on Raleigh Road, but I don't know the number.'

'What does she look like?'

I hung my head. 'I don't know.'

She asked me a few more questions, about myself, Tom, the girlfriend, but my answers were scant because I didn't have all that much to go on. So when she looked at me, I knew what she was going to say before she'd even opened her mouth. She was lovely about it, but the long and short of it was that she couldn't help me because there simply wasn't enough evidence. By this point the twins were kicking off and I was standing with one on each hip, which was no mean feat now that they were nearly four years old. I knew what I looked like to her, a neurotic, dishevelled mother with no grip on reality and I wanted to scream, shout, beg even to get her attention, to make her understand the danger we were in.

I made one last desperate plea. 'Can you just have someone watch my house for a while? It would make me feel much better.'

She had the good grace to look apologetic when she shook her head. 'I'm sorry, Simone, we can't do that. Is there anyone you could stay with for a few days, perhaps? A friend or relative? I could call someone for you if you'd like?'

'A detective? Someone who can keep me and my children safe?'

'What about your partner? Shall we give him a call and ask him to come and get you?'

'I'm not incapable,' I said, my voice rising to the point of hysteria. 'Is that what you think?'

'No, of course not, but I know you're worried and I want to help.'

By now I'd had enough, and I placed the twins on the floor, much to their disgust, picked up my bag and started making my way out. 'There's clearly nothing you can do.'

'Simone, wait...' the officer said, but I didn't want to hear what she had to say. I ordered the twins to follow me and bustled them out of the door, out of the stuffy police station and back out on to the street. As we walked, I felt tears streaming down my cheeks but I couldn't even wipe them away as I had a child clinging on to each hand, so I just let them fall, no longer caring what I looked like. Hot, salty tears dropped down onto my clothes, onto the floor, and I did nothing to stop them. There was nothing I could do to stop anything.

21

I called Jude on the way home from the police station and asked him to come home early. After establishing that no one was hurt, he said he'd leave in the next five minutes and hung up. I had considered asking my mum if we could stay with her but I had decided against it. I'd have to come home eventually because we couldn't camp out with Mum forever, so we might as well stay put. But I wanted Jude at home, with us, for our protection and his.

When we reached the front door, I put my key into the bottom lock and felt a jolt of alarm when I realised that it wasn't locked. I always double-locked the door when I went out. I pushed against the door but it was firmly shut which meant that no one could have broken in, could they? Visions of Tom's girlfriend waiting inside with a knife appeared in my mind, until I remembered that I'd left in such a hurry to get the twins that I had forgotten to double-lock it.

Still, I opened the door gingerly, stepping into the corridor and looking around to see if anything was different. It looked the same as I'd left it. We needed to get an alarm, I decided, already making a mental note to google local companies as soon as I'd got the twins settled. Ivy and Sam, who'd finally got the chocolate they'd been promised, were sugar-addled and had started jumping around on the sofa. I put the TV on for them and then grabbed a knife from the kitchen and walked around the house, checking every room, until I was satisfied that there was no one else there. I put the knife back in the drawer, got my laptop and sat down with the children to research home alarm systems, pausing every couple of minutes to look up Jude's location on the Find My app. He was still untraceable which meant that he was on the Tube. I knew I wouldn't relax until I saw that little dot appear, signalling that he was nearly home.

But as I waited for him, I began to wonder if I should tell him about what had happened. Would he be angry if he knew that I'd seen Tom again? Would he be furious that, by inviting Tom to our house, I had put the twins in danger? And my biggest fear of all was would he even believe me? It was clear that the police officer hadn't and Jude was already stressed about me. He thought my behaviour was irrational and this hardly did much to alleviate his concerns. But then if I didn't tell him, what if something happened and he wasn't prepared?

When the dot finally appeared, I watched it move all the way from the station to the house and I still hadn't decided what to do by the time he opened the front door.

'Is everything okay?' he asked, appearing in the doorway to the living room.

I made my decision. 'Yes, I'm sorry, I wasn't feeling well and I was worried about looking after the children, but I'm much better now.'

He came and sat down next to me. 'You still look a bit peaky. What was it?'

'I'm not sure, I thought I was going to be sick. Maybe it was something I ate. But it's passed now.'

'Good.' Jude turned his attention to Ivy and Sam. 'Come here you terrible two.'

The children launched themselves at him, rubbing chocolate-stained faces into his shirt and burrowing under his arms.

'Did you have a good day?' he asked them.

'We got chocolate on the way home!' Ivy declared.

'And we went to the police station!' Sam added.

My face fell as I saw Jude frown. 'You went where?'

'The police station. Nee naw, nee naw!'

Jude put the twins back down and looked at me. 'Why did you go to the police station?'

I tried to think on my feet but I couldn't come up with a reasonable explanation other than the truth. 'I'll explain when the kids have gone to bed,' I whispered.

'No, tell me now.' Jude stood up and gestured for me to follow him into the kitchen, which I did reluctantly. 'What's going on, Simone?'

'Tom called,' I began, watching Jude's face for any sign of suspicion but he just nodded at me to continue. 'He told me that he's leaving his girlfriend and taking their child with them. Apparently she's incredibly jealous and she's been doing some pretty scary stuff.'

'What kind of stuff?'

I told him about her abducting another woman's child, and some of the other things that Tom had told me in the past. 'Anyway, Tom warned me that she knew about me and that I might be in danger.'

If he hadn't looked suspicious before, he did now. 'What do you mean she knows about you? What's there to know?'

'Nothing,' I said, holding up my hands in surrender. 'Tom and I dated for a few months years ago, that's all there is to it. But then we bumped into each other a few months ago, as you already know, and apparently she may have seen us and got the wrong end of the stick.'

I didn't mention that she wasn't the only one to have done so. Jude may have been jealous but at least he'd confronted me at the time, and we'd dealt with it and moved on.

'So, what, he thinks she's coming for you?'

'He doesn't know, but he wanted to give me the heads-up.'

'And you told the police all of this?'

'Yes.'

'What did they say?'

'That there's nothing they can do. There's not enough information or evidence to go on.'

'Fuck.' Jude ran his hand through his hair. 'This is crazy, Simone.'

'I know.'

He frowned, and I could see the wheels turning in his head. 'You weren't going to tell me about this, were you? If Sam hadn't told me about the police, you'd have kept quiet.'

'I didn't know what to do,' I admitted. 'I wanted to tell you but I was worried about how you'd react.'

'What do you mean, how I'd react? You're my wife.'

'I know and I'm sorry. I'm all over the place, Jude.'

'Okay, so here's what we do.' He was pacing around the kitchen now, hatching a plan. 'We get in touch with this Tom guy and tell him he needs to contact the police himself. They're far more likely to believe the story if it comes from him.'

'I've tried that already. He says he will do but not for a couple of days.'

'Fine. Then we make sure the house is secure and you don't go anywhere by yourself for a while, okay? It's probably a fuss about nothing but it's better to be safe. Do you have Tom's number?'

'Yes.'

'Give it to me. I want to speak to him.'

'Jude, I'm not sure that's a good idea.'

'Give it to me, Simone.'

I nodded reluctantly and brought the number up on my phone, handing it to Jude. He immediately pressed dial and put the phone to his ear.

'It says it can't connect my call.'

'He must have turned his phone off or disconnected it.'

'This guy's an arsehole.'

'He's scared, Jude, he's trying to get away.'

'I need a drink.' Jude yanked open the fridge door and peered inside. 'Where are the beers?'

Until that moment, I'd completely forgotten about the damn beers. 'I'm sorry, I forgot.'

Jude was studying the fridge intently. 'What exactly did you get from the supermarket?'

I racked my brains, trying to think of something. 'Some toiletries,' I said.

He closed the door, slowly, in a way that made my hairs stand on end and then he turned and walked over to me. 'You're lying.'

'I'm not lying.'

'What's going on, Simone? Because something's not right here and I want to know what it is.'

I should have just told him the truth. Perhaps if I had, things might have turned out differently down the line. But I was too ashamed of lying in the first place and of admitting what I had been doing that afternoon. So instead, I stood firm to my alibi.

'I went to the supermarket, I bought tampons and toothpaste

and I forgot all about your beers because Tom called and told me his crazy girlfriend wanted to kill me.'

'He said that?'

'Well no, not exactly.'

'For Christ's sake, Simone, what the hell is going on here? Because I'm really confused.'

'I'm sorry,' I said, more placatingly. I'd already lost count of the amount of times I'd apologised in this conversation. 'I've told you everything. There's nothing more to this story, I promise.'

He looked at me for a long time and I tried not to wither under his gaze. I didn't blame him for being suspicious; after all, I had lied to him about my whereabouts that day and all this stuff about Tom was insane. But I needed him to have my back on this.

'Mummy.' Ivy had appeared in the door and was watching us. I didn't know how long she'd been there.

'What is it, sweetheart?'

'I'm hungry.'

I stood up from my chair. 'I'll start making dinner right now.'

Jude picked up his keys. 'I'm going to the shops to buy beer.'

'Jude...' I began. I wanted to tell him not to go, to stay at home with us, but I knew that it would annoy him even more. The shop was five minutes away, if that. He'd be back in ten.

But then he did something unexpected. He put the keys down and turned back to the fridge. 'On second thoughts, I think I saw a bottle of wine in here somewhere. I'll just have a glass of that, I can't be bothered to go out now.'

In that moment, Jude was my hero. He had known, without me asking, that I didn't want him to go out. 'Thank you,' I said, my voice barely above a whisper.

'I love you,' he said simply.

He still says he loves me. I closed my eyes for a second, letting relief flood my body.

I was going to fix this, I decided then. I was going to make things better. I'd get help, if that was what it took. I'd stop the constant phone calls to Jude and the incessant tracking. I'd stop ringing the preschool to check in on the twins. I'd delete the spreadsheet of funfair dates.

But first I had to make sure that we were safe. In some way, having a focus, a singular thing to concentrate my worry on soothed me. It gave me a valid reason for my fear, it justified some of my behaviour to Jude. A behaviour that was going to stop, I reminded myself.

And it would stop as soon as that psychopath was out of our lives for good.

* * *

That night I had a bad dream. It was a sunny day and I was having a barbecue in the garden. The twins were there, playing in the paddling pool, and Helen was there too. But then my phone rang and when I answered, it was the police, telling me there had been an accident and I knew immediately that it was Jude. I woke up dripping with sweat and turned to check that Jude was next to me. He was turned away from me, fast asleep, his breathing steady, and I put my hand on his back and felt the familiar warmth of his skin. Slowly, my pulse returned to normal.

Jude stirred slightly and I willed him to wake up so that I could talk to him, but then he shifted position and started snoring gently, so instead I lay on my back, staring up at the ceiling. We had double locked the door that night and put the chain on and I started to think about what we might do if there was a fire and we couldn't open the front door in time. I memorised the location of the keys so that I could grab them in an instant if I needed to. Then I thought about Tom and wondered where he was, which made me wonder where his girlfriend was too. What if she was outside right now, staring up at our bedroom window? I reached out and clutched Jude's hand. He grunted but remained fast asleep. Would he wake up if something bad happened? I wondered. He was such a deep sleeper and had often remained comatose when the twins were babies and they'd cried in the night. It had been a running joke at the time. I'd teased him about his incredible ability to sleep, but now it seemed like a curse not a blessing.

There was something niggling at me too, some iota of rationality in the back of my mind telling me how crazy Tom's story was. Could something so far-fetched really be true? But why would he lie to me? Why would he want to scare me for no reason? I racked my brains for an explanation and couldn't come up with a single one, which only left one conclusion. Tom's story was terrifying but real, and my family was in danger.

I got up and put my dressing gown on, creeping into the twins' rooms to check on them. They were both out for the count and I stayed awhile and then padded downstairs, put the kettle on and reached for my laptop. There was no way I was going back to sleep now and I needed something to do, to put my restless mind to work. The kettle clicked off and I made a decaf tea and took it with me to the kitchen table, opening up the spreadsheet.

Just hours earlier I'd promised myself that I would delete it but now, in the lonely, middle-of-the-night darkness, I decided to hold on to it for a little longer. Just until this business with Tom was sorted as that would mark the end of all of this. I looked at the next fair, the one in South London the following weekend. Hopefully by then Tom would have been in contact and I wouldn't have to go. I didn't want to think about what might happen if he didn't call.

I considered calling Helen, but it was two o'clock in the

morning and I knew that she wouldn't appreciate it. Instead, I picked up my phone and looked at the number that Tom had used to call me the previous day. He was the one who had got me into this mess, so he was the one who had to fix it. I dialled the number but, just as it had with Jude, it failed to connect. I tried a couple more times, even though I knew that it was pointless, and then threw my phone onto the table with frustration. The sound reverberated in the still, quiet air.

My ears pricked at the sound of a noise, adrenaline already starting to course through my body, but then the house fell silent again, and after a few minutes, I began to relax. But I craved the warm safety of Jude's body and so I closed my laptop and made my way back upstairs, checking on the twins one more time, before returning to our bedroom. Jude was exactly where I'd left him and I got into bed next to him and cuddled up as close to him as I could get. I was already dreading what would happen on Monday when he had to go back to work and I would be alone.

Perhaps I was going about this all wrong. Instead of waiting for Tom's ex to find me, maybe I should go and find her. Then we could have it out and when she realised that I wasn't a threat, hopefully she'd leave us alone and that would be the end of it. I tried to think of any snippets of information Tom had given me, but I hardly had anything to go off. He hadn't once mentioned his girlfriend's name, or what she did for a living, and he had never told me his full address. The only thing I knew was that their daughter was younger than the twins and was called Camille. Wasn't the fact that Tom had been so secretive strange? But then, I reasoned, if he was in a difficult relationship, he might not have wanted to talk about it at all. Still, at least I had something, I had a child's name. And Camille wasn't that common. Perhaps I could ask around at the preschool or park to see if anyone knew a child called Camille. There was a strong community around here and I was bound to find someone who had heard of her. And they might, with any luck, lead me to her mother.

Satisfied with my plan, I cocooned myself in the curve of Jude's back and felt my eyelids start to grow heavy. Against all odds, I could feel myself falling asleep and I let myself drift into the blissful oblivion of nothingness, for as long as I could get it.

22

When I woke up the following morning, Jude wasn't in bed. I craned my neck, listening for any noise of children playing, or the shower running, but there was nothing but silence. It was too quiet, too still. Something was wrong. I sprang out of bed and ran down the stairs, without even putting my dressing gown on, and discovered the living room door closed. I yanked it open and hurtled in, and three pairs of eyes turned away from the television and looked at me in surprise.

'Mummy, why are you naked?' Ivy asked.

'Well, I quite forgot to put my clothes on this morning,' I said with forced brightness, because the last thing I wanted to do was alarm the children. 'I'll go get my dressing gown.'

When I came down the stairs a second time, Jude was making coffee in the kitchen and he turned when he heard me enter. 'You were out for the count this morning and I wanted to let you have a lie-in, so I brought the kids downstairs and put the TV on low volume.'

'Thanks, I was up in the night, so I needed a bit of extra sleep.'

'Listen, I've been thinking about this whole Tom thing,' Jude said. 'I know you're stressing about it and I can understand why, but I really don't think you have anything to worry about. You dated him, what, five years ago? And you've hardly seen or spoken to him since, right?' He looked at me, almost like he was waiting for me to contradict him, but I nodded. 'Even if this woman is as crazy as Tom makes out, and there's always two sides to every story, I just can't see why she'd have any beef with you.'

'Apparently she has beef with every woman he has ever talked to.'

'Right,' he said slowly. 'And I was worried when you first told me too. The safety of you and the twins is the most important thing. But after giving it some thought, I think that even if this Tom guy is telling the truth, her priority will be finding him and their daughter, not you. Perhaps we're making a mountain out of a molehill.'

I knew Jude didn't like Tom so it was understandable that he was doubting his version of events, but I was having trouble doing the same. He hadn't seen the state that Tom was in the previous day, and he hadn't spent the last few months waiting for something terrible to happen either. He saw a molehill, I saw a giant, erupting volcano.

'I've got an idea,' I said, and I told him my plan to ask around about Camille. I expected him to tell me that I'd finally lost my marbles but to my surprise he seemed to be considering it.

'That's actually not a terrible idea. It might put your mind at ease a little if you know more about Camille's mum. But you'll need to tread carefully so that people don't think you're a mad stalker.'

I almost laughed. In this situation, it wasn't me who was the mad stalker.

'I'll just ask if anyone knows her, I could say I found a cardigan with her name on it in the park or something. Even if I do track down Camille's mum, I still might not approach her but if I know she's human at least, rather than a three-headed monster, she may seem less intimidating.'

Jude nodded. 'Tell you what, it's looking to be a lovely day, so why don't we take the kids to Priory Park today and you can ask a few people?'

I thought about that poor woman and her missing son. 'Okay. But eyes on the twins at all times.'

'Agreed.'

We smiled at each other and I felt so pleased that Jude was on my side about this. He may have been frustrated with me last night, but he seemed to have got over it. And in the bright morning light, with sun streaming through the windows, the world didn't seem as scary a place as it had done the previous night. We made breakfast together, treating the kids to toast and Marmite in front of the TV, and as we watched them giggling over their cartoons, Jude took my hand and squeezed it and I thought that, despite everything, it was going to be okay.

It took a while before we were all dressed and ready to go, and it was late morning by the time we left the house and started walking towards the park. Jude suggested we pick up a takeaway coffee on the way, and as we clutched our steaming cups and the twins chattered away, I felt, if not content, purposeful at least. I had a plan and maybe that was what I had needed.

The playground was already full of families and Ivy and Sam immediately ran off towards the swings. I looked at Jude, silently telling him to stick close to them, and he nodded his understanding and followed. Meanwhile, I scoped out the playground looking for parents who were with children around Camille's age. I spotted three mums standing by the sandpit while their young toddlers played together and I vaguely recognised one of them from a class I used to take the twins to. Before I could lose my nerve, I wandered over to them.

'Hi,' I said to the familiar-looking woman. 'I think I know you from Toddler Time?'

She frowned and then her face lit up with recognition. 'Yes! You've got twins, right?'

'That's right.'

'I used to take my eldest, Harry. He's over there with his dad.' The woman gestured to the other side of the playground. 'This is my youngest, Violet. How are the twins doing?'

We made polite conversation for a while, asking about preschools and primary school places and then I said, 'I don't suppose you know a child called Camille, do you? I found a cardigan here the other day with her name on and it's size 18 to 24 months so I thought she might be a similar age to Violet. It looks expensive and I'd like to get it back to whoever lost it if I can.'

'The name doesn't ring a bell.' The woman looked at her friends who also shook their heads.

I swallowed my disappointment. 'Never mind. It was nice to see you.'

I moved on, approaching another woman who was helping her child on the climbing frame and delivering my speech about the cardigan again, but she shook her head.

'No, sorry, I don't know a Camille.'

'It's okay, thanks anyway.'

I was walking away when she called out to me, 'You should ask Rebecca.' The woman pointed at someone who was over by the slide. 'I swear she knows everyone around here.'

'Ah great, I will, thanks.'

I made a beeline for Rebecca and introduced myself. As soon as I said the name Camille, her expression changed and I knew I'd hit the jackpot. I couldn't believe how easy it had been. Never mind MI5, if you wanted intelligence you only needed to head to the local playground.

'I do know a little girl called Camille actually, it might be hers.' Rebecca lowered her voice. 'Although I think a cardigan will be the last thing on her mum's mind.'

I feigned surprise and hoped that Rebecca was the type of person who liked to gossip. 'What do you mean?'

I was in luck. Rebecca looked around the playground as if she was checking to see if anyone was listening and then she leaned in conspiratorially. 'Her partner's just left her. He ran off with a mum from the toddler group we go to. I couldn't believe it when I heard.'

Given that Tom had only left the previous day, news had clearly travelled fast. But surely Rebecca's version of events was incorrect? When Tom had told me he was leaving, he hadn't mentioned anything about another woman. I could only assume that she'd got the wrong end of the stick, and I was a little outraged on Tom's behalf that he had been painted as the villain and not the victim in this mess. By this point the twins had come over to the slide and from the corner of my eye, I saw Jude approach and stand within earshot of us.

'How did you hear about it?' I asked.

'Someone from my daughter's nursery is close friends with Camille's mum, Lucy. She texted me this morning. Lucy is beside herself and she's such a sweet little thing. She wouldn't say boo to a goose. I feel so sorry for her.'

I suppressed a snort. From what I'd heard about Lucy, whose name I finally knew after years of hearing about her, she was anything but sweet. But I wanted intel and I couldn't reveal what I already knew, so I kept up the pretence of being clueless. 'I hope she's doing okay.'

'I'm just in shock. I mean, I went to that toddler group every week and didn't suspect a thing. I knew that they were friendly, Tom – that's his name – and this woman. They used to go to the park or for coffee together all the time, but I genuinely didn't think anything of it. And then the next thing I hear, they've headed off into the sunset together without a thought for anyone else.'

'Lucy must be missing Camille so much.'

I immediately realised my error. I had said too much, revealed my hand, and Rebecca looked at me in confusion. 'What do you mean?'

'Oh,' I stuttered. 'I assumed he'd taken Camille with him?'

'Of course not. Camille is with her mother. And to think, she went back to work full time to support them all after Tom was fired from his job. And now she's on her own, with a toddler.'

I stared at her, confused. 'He was fired?'

'Yes, some scandal where he worked, apparently. He's clearly a wrong 'un and she's probably better off without him, but you can't tell her that right now. It's too raw.'

History was being rewritten right in front of me again and I couldn't get my head around it. How could two versions of the same story be so different? I had known Tom for years and I had no reason to doubt what he'd told me. Why would he make it up? It made no sense. Perhaps this Lucy was so conniving that she'd convinced everyone she was a wallflower, but that didn't explain why Tom had left Camille behind. I was certain he would never have done that.

'And you're sure that he didn't take Camille with him?'

Rebecca looked at me suspiciously. 'I'm quite sure. Sorry, what did you say your name was?'

'Oh, it's Simone. I have three-year-old twins.' I pointed at Sam and Ivy who were taking it in turns to hurtle down the slide.

This seemed to placate Rebecca. The simple fact that I had

young children gave me instant membership to the inner circle of the motherhood clan. She leaned in and whispered, 'With all due respect, he wasn't thinking about his child, was he? He was thinking about his dick.'

This had to be a case of crossed wires or manipulation by Lucy. Tom had been trying to escape her clutches for years and he'd finally done it. I had seen genuine fear on his face, I was sure of it. But if what he had told me was true, why would he leave Camille behind? Had Jude been right to doubt Tom? Even I had briefly questioned his story. I felt disorientated, no longer sure what to believe. I was tempted to challenge Rebecca, to tell her that she must be wrong, but I didn't want to draw any more attention to myself than I already had.

Just then, Rebecca's daughter came running over and she picked the little girl up and looked at me. 'If you'd like to give me the cardigan, I can make sure she gets it.'

'Thanks, but I don't have it with me. Which toddler group did you say you go to? I might drop it there for her if I'm passing.'

'Friday mornings, ten o'clock, at the United Reformed Church, but Tom used to bring Camille most of the time, so I don't know if Lucy will take her.'

'Okay, well, I'll give it a go. It was nice to meet you.'

Rebecca wandered off and I headed towards Jude, knowing that he had heard most of the exchange.

'That was weird,' I whispered.

He didn't respond and when I looked at him more carefully, I was surprised to see that he seemed angry.

'Are you okay?' I asked him.

'You lied to me.'

I stared at him in shock. 'What? What are you talking about? I didn't lie.'

'All this stuff about Tom's girlfriend being crazy and you comforting him, it was all lies.'

'That's what he told me, Jude, I swear. I have no idea what's going on but as far as I knew, Tom and Camille left together yesterday.'

'Do you know what I think is really going on? You knew I was on to you and Tom and so you made up this whole, ridiculous story so that I'd feel sorry for you. Well, you know what? I don't.'

Jude and I had argued before but this was the first time his words had really stung, and my eyes filled with tears. 'Jude, how can you say that? Everything I told you is true.'

'Except it isn't, is it? This smug idiot, Tom, is clearly a philanderer who's run off with another woman. What happened? Did you say you wouldn't go so he found someone else?'

'No!' I was battling between fear that I was losing Jude and indignation. There were now three versions of this story and I only knew for sure that one of them was completely incorrect. A few people were looking over at us curiously now, attracted by our increasingly raised voices.

'I think we should leave,' I said quietly to Jude. 'We can talk about this at home.'

Jude looked over at the twins, who were still taking it in turns to hurtle down the slide, blissfully unaware of their parents' row. 'You can leave, I'm staying.'

'Jude, we need to talk about this.'

'I don't really want to talk to you right now.'

I realised I had no choice, unless I wanted to continue our argument in front of the local parenting community, who I already knew enjoyed a good gossip. With a last glance at the twins, I turned and walked away, wiping a tear away with my hand and hoping nobody noticed.

What had just happened? An hour ago, Jude and I were on the

same team, with a common goal between us. And now he was furious with me for a crime I hadn't even committed. How had I got caught up in the middle of all this, and what did it mean? Were Jude and I in trouble? And how had I managed to let Tom, a guy I had dated years ago, get between us?

Tom. This was all his fault. I had been convinced that Rebecca had got the story wrong but now my doubts were growing stronger. Had there not always been something about Tom that had set me on edge? Something I couldn't put my finger on exactly, but which made me wary of him? But why would he lie to me? I could think of a few reasons now: he was a compulsive liar, he wanted me to feel sorry for him, he was genuinely delusional.

I needed to find Lucy. It was the only way I could be sure. In the meantime, I had to sort out this rift between me and Jude before it got out of control. I only hoped that I wasn't too late.

23

I stood by the entrance to the church hall, clutching on to an old cardigan of Ivy's, and feeling like an imposter. I was certain I was about to be exposed for the fraudster I was. But I had no choice if I was going to put this whole Tom and Lucy thing to bed once and for all.

It had been a long week, made longer by Jude's stony silence, which had taken me two days to penetrate. He had been so angry with me that at first it had felt like nothing I could say would make a difference. We had maintained a united front for the children but in the evening, after they had gone to bed, his cold shoulder was enough to chill me to the bone. He had refused to talk to me, to interact with me or to listen to my side of the story and eventually I had given him some space, hoping that he would tell me when he was ready. I knew that this was bringing back memories of his parents' separation and his mum's betrayal and I wanted to show him that this was completely different, that I would never have an affair, but he had to be ready to listen first.

Finally, on Monday, after four missed calls to him which had sent me into a frantic spin, checking his location on my phone every two minutes and refreshing the news headlines for updates about a train crash or a bomb in Central London, he came home, kissed the children and gestured for me to follow him into the kitchen.

'Why didn't you answer your phone?' I demanded. 'I've been so worried about you.' I knew why he hadn't answered, he wanted to punish me and he'd succeeded, but I wanted to hear him say it.

He ignored my question, though. 'I met Helen for lunch today.'

'Okay.' I had been feeling sick all day, unable to do anything other than keep virtual tabs on Jude, and I wanted to rant at him for not answering my calls, but I knew I had to listen to him.

'Let's just say she talked me off the edge. I know you wouldn't lie to me and I know I flew off the handle. I'm sorry. Will you tell me what really happened?'

I exhaled slowly. 'I've told you everything. If Tom lied to me, I really have no idea why, but nothing happened between us. Nothing even came close to happening.'

'Okay.'

'Do you mean that?'

He looked straight at me. 'Yes. But you stay away from him, okay? He's one messed-up guy and I don't want you having anything to do with him.'

'Agreed.'

Jude came over then and gave me a hug and I breathed in and felt calm for the first time all day. I always felt safe in Jude's arms and I wanted to wrap them around me forever.

'You're too nice, Simone. Too trusting. People take advantage of that.'

'I still don't understand why he would lie, though.'

'Because he's a psychopath. But who cares, he's nothing to do with us.'

I had no doubt that someone was a psychopath in that relationship, but as to which one I still didn't know. And that was why I had decided to come to the toddler group today. I hadn't told Jude what I was planning to do because I didn't want to rock the boat any more than I already had, but I needed some closure on this situation, once and for all. I took a sip of my takeout coffee and watched the steady stream of parents starting to arrive with buggies and scooters.

When I saw Rebecca, my stomach lurched with fear, but she didn't look particularly surprised to see me. 'Hello again,' she said, unstrapping her daughter from the buggy and picking her up. 'You're in luck, apparently Lucy's coming today.'

I saw Rebecca's eyes fall to the cardigan in my shaking hand and I smiled, trying to sound more confident than I felt. 'That's great.'

Rebecca gave me another once-over and then headed into the room, along with a few other mums, until I was alone again. A few minutes later a woman with long, silky dark hair appeared with a fair-haired little girl, and I stared at her in shock, knowing instantly that it was Lucy and Camille. It wasn't just that I had seen Camille before but I had also seen the woman too and my pulse started racing as I realised exactly where. I put my hand out and touched the wall to steady myself, my thoughts and emotions all over the place.

Lucy stopped short when she saw me, her dark eyes widening in surprise, and I saw fear flash across her face.

'Hello, Lucy. I think we've met before.'

She visibly cowered. 'What do you want?'

'I could ask you the same thing.'

'I don't know what you're talking about.'

'Yes, you do. I know who you are. I remember you.'

Lucy's eyes darted around nervously. 'We can't do this here,' she said.

'I don't care where we do it, but we *are* doing it.' The conviction in my own voice surprised me. 'It's time you told me what's going on.'

Lucy peered into the church hall longingly, no doubt wishing that she was in there with her mum friends rather than out here with me. Then she turned back to me. 'Camille loves this class, I don't want her to miss it. Come back in half an hour and we'll talk, okay?'

'Fine.' I watched her lift Camille out of the buggy and walk into the hall and then I considered my options. I could go for a walk, but what if Lucy did a runner in my absence? No, this was my opportunity to finally learn the truth and I wasn't going to let Lucy slip through my fingers. I sat down resolutely on a chair where I had a good view of the toddler class and prepared to sit it out. Meeting Lucy had totally thrown me. I'd seen her before, but many years ago, and I wanted to know why she'd done what she did. She was not leaving my sight until I had answers.

While I waited, I watched Lucy intently, studying her features, trying to get a read on her. I could see Camille shaking a rattle and giggling, while Lucy held on to her to keep her balanced. I was almost captivated by them. A few years younger than me, Lucy was undeniably beautiful and although her daughter, with her fair hair and blue eyes, took after her father, she was as pretty as a picture. They looked like they belonged in a glossy magazine or upmarket clothing catalogue. I scrutinised Lucy's face, unsure what I was looking for. Hostility? Fear? Signs that she was a psycho? Given what I now knew about her, it put the odds of who was telling the truth more in Tom's favour, otherwise why would she have done what she did?

After thirty agonising minutes, the class finally finished and I waited for Lucy to come out. She saw me and nodded, resigned now to the conversation that had to happen. 'Let's go for a walk.'

I stood up and watched her as she strapped Camille back into the buggy and gave her a snack. Then we made our way out of the church together, heading down the street towards the park.

'How did you find me?' she asked.

'It's a long story.' I had no interest in divulging the details of my cardigan ruse.

'I assume you've heard about Tom? That's why you're here?'

'That's part of the reason, yes,' I admitted. 'But now I've seen you, there's more I want to know.'

Lucy looked around to check no one could hear our conversation. 'Go on.'

'Why were you following me?'

They say you never forget a pretty face. And Lucy's had been etched on my mind the day I'd seen her in the shops years ago and thought, for a moment, that she was the fortune teller. And I had seen her a few times since, but at that point I hadn't been suspicious enough to dwell on it. If she hadn't looked a little like Mystic Maggie, I probably wouldn't have even noticed her.

Lucy refused to meet my eye as she spoke. 'Tom and I were going through a rough patch back then and I suspected that he was cheating on me. So I followed him a couple of times and saw him with you. After that I followed you a few more times, too. I wanted to catch him out.'

So far, my allegiance was with Tom. Clearly Lucy was jealous, just like he'd told me, and the fact that she'd followed me proved that. 'Tom and I had a brief fling but it had ended well before then and nothing was going on between us any more.'

'Not with you, no.'

I looked at her. 'What does that mean?'

'Tom has been seeing other women behind my back for years.

He always denied it of course, he told me I was mad, that I was jealous, insane even. And in the end, he wore me down and I believed that he was right, that the problem was with me and not him.'

I frowned. 'Around that time, when you followed me, he told me you'd broken up.'

She shook her head. 'We never broke up. We've been together for ten years and throughout that time I've been nothing but loyal to him. Tom, on the other hand, has been manipulating me, making me feel like I was going crazy. I even caught him once, you know? He was hooking up with this girl he met on Instagram and I logged into his account and messaged her. She told me they'd been sleeping together for three months. And when I confronted him, he went mad. He told me this girl was a compulsive liar, that she was stalking him, and if I believed her over him then I was not the person he thought I was.'

The more she talked, the more I believed her. She spoke with a frank sincerity that I didn't think she would be able to fake. And anger began to rise inside me as I realised that, just like Lucy, I'd been taken in by Tom too. He'd wanted to get into my head and I'd let him.

'So yes, I did follow you and I'm sorry,' she continued. 'I can see why you think I'm crazy. I think I did go a bit crazy, to be honest. But Tom made me like that. And now I finally have the proof that he's a lowlife cheating scumbag, it's too late to confront him because he's gone.'

'What about Camille? Has he been in touch to arrange seeing her?'

'Of course not,' Lucy scoffed. 'The only person Tom thinks about is himself. He's got a new family now, this woman and her child. The only reason he'd get in touch with me now is if he thought he stood to gain from being the doting, conscientious father again.'

We looked at each other and I had no doubt whose side I was on. 'I'm so sorry, Lucy. If it helps, he fooled me too. I honestly thought he was the victim, not you. He told me all sorts of stories, like how you took a woman's child from the park.'

To my surprise, Lucy laughed. 'Oh, that's a good one. I've heard many stories about myself over the years. Did you hear the one about how I set fire to all his clothes? I think he read too many of those real-life magazines that my mum's obsessed with. He's a compulsive liar, Simone.'

'But you stayed with him,' I said quietly.

She shrugged. 'I loved him. And he made me doubt myself over and over again, he made me think that I had got it all wrong. It was easier to believe him than it was myself.'

'How do you feel now he's gone?'

'Honestly? Relieved. I wake up in the morning and I remember he's not there, and do you know what I do? I smile. Because I'm free now. It's just me and Camille and that's how I like it.'

'What if he comes back?'

'I doubt he will, but if he does, I'm not taking him back. I'm done with him and good riddance. I should have left him years ago and I'm furious with myself for being so pathetic.'

I put my hand on her arm. 'I don't think you're pathetic.'

Lucy smiled. 'Thank you. And I'm sorry for following you.'

'I'm sorry for thinking you were a psycho.'

We'd reached the playground by then and Lucy stopped. 'I'm going to take Camille on the swings. You're welcome to join us.'

But it was time for my next phone call to Jude. Anyway, I'd heard what I needed to hear. 'Thanks, but I have something to do. It was nice to meet you, Lucy.'

'You too.'

I watched as she opened the gate to the playground and pushed the buggy towards the swings, and then I turned and began walking away. I had the answers I'd come for and I was satisfied that I finally knew the truth. I was so furious with Tom that I wanted to hunt him down myself and have it out with him. What had been the point in contacting me again after all this time and getting me tangled up in his messy life? Had he been hoping to have one last fling with me before he left, or did he get a kick out of scaring me by making me think Lucy was dangerous? Perhaps he just wanted my sympathy to ease his own guilt. I'd never know the real reason but, whatever his motive, he'd been playing a game the whole time and I hadn't even realised. Helen's words from years earlier came back to me. *You're impressionable.* Who else had lied to me? Who else had I been taken in by, believing them to be honest and sincere? And if I couldn't trust Tom, and I wasn't even sure I could trust myself, then who was left? But I wasn't the only woman he'd fooled, I could console myself with that at least. He was a liar and a cheat, and Lucy was better off without him. So was I. The important thing was that he was gone and, hopefully, not coming back.

For a little while I felt so relieved that I even put off calling Jude so that I could enjoy the moment. My conversation with Lucy had given me the closure I needed and I now knew that I had nothing to fear from her. The sun was warming my face, I could hear children laughing and I still had a few hours to myself before I had to pick the twins up.

But then I realised something and my world clouded over again. Lucy was no threat to me or my family and I didn't think Tom was any more either. Which meant that the tragedy that the fortune teller had foretold had nothing to do with either of them.

So, what *had* she been talking about? What disaster lay ahead in my future, waiting to be discovered? With all this Tom and Lucy business, I'd dropped the ball on trying to track her down, my attention diverted elsewhere. And hadn't I promised myself just days ago that I would put a stop to it, delete my spreadsheet and move on? Hadn't I said that I'd get some help and try to forget all about Mystic Maggie? But suddenly I was more determined than ever to find her and get to the bottom of this curse she'd put on me. My children's lives depended on it. And Jude's.

Jude. I quickly reached for my phone and called him. But even though he answered, in a weary tone, even though he went through the motions of discussing what he was going to have for lunch, even though he ended the call by telling me that he loved me, I still didn't feel any better.

Would I ever feel better again? For a while, after I'd spoken to Lucy, I had felt hopeful that our troubles were behind us but now I was no longer sure. I didn't know where to turn or who to believe any more. Time was speeding up, accelerating me towards a future that I feared more than anything. There were just six months to go. *Tick tock.*

24

'Say cheese!'

We looked like the perfect family. Jude and I stood behind Ivy and Sam, our hands resting on their shoulders. Ivy was wearing a pink sundress with lemons printed on it, her long hair tied up, and Sam was sporting a polo shirt and shorts, a mini version of his father. The photo that Mum had just taken would probably be printed out, put in a frame and given pride of place on her mantelpiece, shown proudly to anyone who visited her. *Look at my daughter's beautiful family.* Yet, surrounded by my nearest and dearest, I had never felt more alone.

Jude no longer said *I love you*. He had stopped a few weeks ago, just as he had stopped answering his phone when I called. His patience had run out and perhaps I shouldn't blame him. But I did because each unanswered call sent me into an uncontrollable spin.

'It's getting out of hand,' he'd told me. 'People at work keep asking if everything's okay. They think you're unwell, and to be honest, so do I. You need to talk to someone, Simone. If you won't talk to me, speak to a professional. This has to stop.'

'So I'm not allowed to call my husband any more?' Even I knew my argument was weak.

'You know it's more than that. I want to help you, but you have to let me.'

I wanted to let him, of course I did. I wanted to get everything off my chest, to confide in my husband and feel the relief when he understood. But I knew that wouldn't happen. He would tell me that I was mad to be obsessing over this prophecy, that I was losing the plot. And deep down I think I knew that he was right, which made me even more ashamed of my behaviour.

So instead, I kept it all in, my thoughts and fears like a festering monster trapped inside my mind, becoming fiercer every day, taking over my life.

I no longer bothered attempting to write. I had stopped looking for jobs. I didn't socialise any more because it was too difficult, too stressful. I spent my time going round in circles, my compulsions dominating every aspect of my life. Call Jude. Check the twins' preschool app. Google health conditions. Search for funfairs. Call Jude. I could no longer cope with anything that took us out of our routine.

The only exception was fairs, which I had visited with increasing frequency as spring turned into summer. Most people went to the fair for a good time. I went because I had to. I tried to go during the week so that I didn't have to tell Jude about it, which restricted my search radius because I had to be back in time to pick up the kids. Sometimes, if I had no choice, I took them with me although I didn't let them go on any of the rides any more. But I bribed them with hook-a-duck stalls and candyfloss and they soon got over it. I had told them not to tell Jude about our visits, whispering in their ears that he loved fairs and would be so sad to know we'd been without him. Miraculously, neither of them had spilled the beans yet but I knew I was on borrowed time. I hated myself but I did it anyway. Every time I learned of a new funfair coming to town my heart soared with hope. Every time I went and didn't find Mystic Maggie it sank even lower. I had been to nine fairs so far and I still hadn't found her.

With all this going on, Jude had to convince me to throw a fourth birthday party for Ivy and Sam. I hadn't wanted to do it. I didn't want anyone in my house. I was nervous about seeing people again after becoming so reclusive. I felt guilty about coming face to face with Mum and my friends again because I knew I'd been negligent. And I was worried that they would confront me on my behaviour and I didn't know what to say to them.

But Jude had scowled when I told him that we should just stay at home, the four of us, and order pizza. 'Simone, it's our children's fourth birthday. They deserve a party.'

'But Jude, when they start school there'll be loads of parties. This is our last chance to do something small, just the four of us.'

'The kids are already talking about their party. It's downright mean to say no now.'

And I had nodded, reluctantly, because he was right. 'Just family and friends then.'

'Fine,' Jude conceded. 'I guess next year we'll probably have to invite the whole class.'

Since then I had been obsessing over the twin's fifth birthday party next summer. Would this be over by then? Would the tragedy have happened? Or would life have returned to normal again, all this madness put behind us? I prayed it was the latter; I feared the former.

But next summer seemed such a long way off now, as we smiled for the camera and tried to look happy. Our guests were sipping beers or fruit juice and chatting among themselves. Jude went outside to light the barbecue and I started chopping cucumber and carrot sticks in the kitchen, wishing I was invisible and hoping that no one came over to talk to me.

My heart sank when I saw Emily making a beeline for me. I hadn't seen her in months and she looked tanned and healthy, her slim figure a product of long weekend hikes and post-work gym sessions. In contrast, I looked like crap. I hadn't been to the hairdresser since February, so my grey, wispy roots had thrived and my hair was dry with split ends. I couldn't remember the last time I'd had a good night's sleep and my eyes were red and puffy, with dark circles underneath them. But putting on make-up seemed like too much of an effort and I generally wore the first thing I found in my wardrobe. I was the epitome of the phrase, *she's let herself go*. But who cared? Jude and I didn't even hold hands these days, let alone anything more adventurous. Our dwindling sex life had completely petered out around the time he'd stopped calling me Simmy. Or perhaps saying 'I love you'. I couldn't remember which one now.

'Long time no see, Simmy, how have you been?' Emily flicked her glossy blonde hair behind her back and perched on a bar stool.

'Oh, you know, just busy with the kids.'

'I can't believe they're four, where does the time go? Have you had a good summer? Did you go away anywhere?'

Jude had wanted to go to Spain or France. He'd sent me emails with links to all-inclusive hotels or small villas with pools. I'd deleted them all. None of us were getting on a plane or travelling to another country. The only place where I felt safe was at home and, increasingly, not even there.

'Not this year,' I'd told Jude, when he'd pushed the issue.

'Why not?'

'I just don't fancy it.' I'd sounded snappy but he had to know I wasn't going to change my mind.

He had looked at me, long and hard, as though trying to decide whether it was worth an argument. In the end, he'd turned around and walked away.

'We didn't go away,' I told Emily now. 'How about you?'

'Two weeks island-hopping in Greece,' Emily said. 'It was wonderful.'

'Wow, that sounds amazing, lucky you. How's the job going?'

'Busy,' Emily said, helping herself to a cucumber stick. 'But good.'

I continued chopping. Keeping this conversation going was so much effort. Emily and I had been friends for years, we'd never run out of things to talk about, but now I was struggling to think of a single thing to say to her.

'Listen, Simmy...' Emily said in a lowered voice. 'Is everything okay?'

'Yes, fine.' I didn't meet her eye.

'It's just you seem a little... oh, I don't know. Not yourself.'

I attempted a smile, which came out more like a grimace. 'Just tired, I guess, the twins aren't sleeping well at the moment. I think they're worried about starting school.'

'Ah I see.' Emily nodded, satisfied. How easy it was to fool people. Almost too easy. But I hadn't fooled Jude, I knew that. We were drifting apart, slowly but surely, and I wanted to stop it, I wanted to glue us back together but I didn't know how any more.

We were interrupted by Helen, who sat down next to Emily on a stool and propped her elbows on the kitchen island. 'What are you two talking about?'

'Summer holidays,' Emily said. 'I was telling Simmy about my trip to Greece.'

The way she said it made my ears prick up because it sounded like Helen already knew about it. I'd thought that the reason we didn't see each other as much any more was because we were all busy with our lives and somehow the absence of Shiv had broken us up, but now I wondered if I was wrong. Did Helen and Emily meet up without me? Paranoia crept in as I imagined them starting a new WhatsApp chat for just the two of them, going for dinners and coffees and deliberately not inviting me. I felt like a schoolgirl excluded from the gang.

But how could I blame them? Would I have even gone if they'd invited me? Probably not.

'Has anyone spoken to Shiv recently?' I asked.

I saw Helen and Emily exchange a glance. 'We're actually flying out to see her next month for a week,' Emily said. 'We just thought, with the twins and all, you wouldn't be able to come?'

They were right, I wouldn't have gone, but it still hurt that they were going without me. And more than that, I was jealous. Jealous that they were so carefree, that they hadn't lost their sense of self, their identity like I had, of how lovely their lives were.

But I said none of that. 'Oh, wow! Do send her my love.'

'You could do that yourself,' Helen said, and I detected a hint of disapproval in her voice. 'She says she hasn't heard from you in ages.'

'I've been busy,' I said dismissively.

'We should go for dinner,' Helen announced. 'We have a lot to catch up on. How about next Friday?'

'Sure,' I said vaguely, knowing full well that I had no intention of going. 'Sounds great. Hey, Helen, are you still seeing your mystery woman?'

'Not so much.' Helen shrugged. 'She's working, summer is her busiest season.'

'What does she do exactly?' Emily asked.

But our conversation was broken up by Ivy, who hurtled in from the garden, crying inconsolably.

'Ivy, what is it?' I asked.

'It's Daddy,' she wailed. 'Daddy's hurt.'

I dropped the plate I was holding with a clatter and ran outside, my heart pounding against my chest. Had Jude collapsed? Had someone hurt him? I thought of Tom, who I now knew was trouble, hiding in the bushes, waiting to pounce. Perhaps he had a knife, like the one I'd found in the flowers Jude had bought me all those years ago. It *had* been a sign. I knew for sure now.

'Jude,' I screamed, ignoring the stares of our family and friends as I nearly tripped running down the steps into the garden. I saw Mark and a couple of Jude's friends in a huddle and I raced towards them. 'What's happened?'

Mark turned to me and I swear he looked as terrified as I felt. 'It's Jude.'

'No!' I was in tears now, unable to stem the rising panic.

When I reached them, I saw Jude clutching his arm. He was alive, thank God he was alive. But he was clearly hurt and my eyes scanned the garden, looking for Tom.

'Simone.' Mark placed a hand on my arm and when I looked at him again, I realised that there was no terror on his face after all, just concern. And the realisation sank in that it was concern for me, not Jude. 'Jude's fine, he just burned himself on the barbecue.'

'Let me see.'

I wrestled Jude's arm away from him and saw the early signs of a burn, the reddening of his skin. I stroked it gently and it was hot to the touch.

'I'm fine,' Jude said, looking at me curiously, taking in my wild eyes and tear-streaked face. 'The barbecue exploded, but there's no harm done.'

'You scared the life out of me,' I said, still struggling to accept that everything was okay.

'Sorry. Ivy saw it happen and ran off before I could reassure her.'

Jude was still watching me and so, I realised, were the other guests outside. 'You'd better get it under some running water,' I said, trying to sound normal even though I didn't feel it.

'Yes, you're right.' Jude was speaking to me slowly and deliberately, as though I was crazy. But I wasn't crazy. My daughter had just come in shouting that her father was hurt, of course I was going to panic and jump to conclusions. Anyone would have done the same.

'Why did it explode?' I asked him.

'It's happened before,' he admitted. 'I think it's time for a new barbecue.'

Or someone wants to hurt you. But who? And was it even a person or was it just another of Mystic Maggie's signs, warning me that danger was imminent, that I couldn't control fate? As I came back down to reality, my anger changed direction, until it was pointing firmly at Jude. If he knew we had a dodgy barbecue, he should have replaced it. What if the twins had been playing near it when it happened, or he'd had his face over the flames? It could have been so much worse. Looking at the offending barbecue, which we'd had for years and had not bothered to maintain, the idea of Tom hiding in our garden seemed ridiculous. His interest had been in manipulating women into sleeping with him, not hurting other men. But I could no longer think straight any more, everyone and everything was a suspect in the plot to ruin my life.

'It was just an accident, Simone,' Jude said, as though he could read my thoughts. 'These things happen all the time.'

As I helped Jude back into the house, people were still looking at me. I wanted this party to be over. I wanted everyone out of my house so that I could lock the door and feel safe again.

But instead, I planted a smile on my face and reassured

everyone that Jude was fine and so was I. I had no choice, did I? I was going through the motions because I had to. Because I didn't want people to worry. Because I loved my children and I wanted them to have a good time. But all I wanted to do was hide from the world before it destroyed one of us.

The problem was that they didn't want to hide with me. The children wanted to play with their friends and run free and hurtle down slides. Jude wanted to go on weekend adventures and summer holidays and I was running out of excuses as to why we couldn't do that. And I knew now that we weren't even safe in our own back garden anyway, that danger lurked everywhere. I was running out of ways to protect everyone.

Everything was falling apart. Jude was increasingly distant these days, working longer hours, refusing to talk about his day, spending his evenings locked away in the spare room playing computer games. But at least he came home each day.

He no longer said 'I love you', but he still came back. So that was something.

* * *

After the party finally ended, I put on a Disney film for the twins and went into the kitchen to start clearing up. Jude appeared and helped himself to a bottle of beer from the fridge. His arm was bandaged but no serious damage had been done. Not this time at least.

'Helen said you're all going out for dinner next week.'

'Oh, I don't know. I said yes but I'll see how I feel.'

'You should go, Simone. It'll do you good to get out.'

'Yeah, maybe.'

It occurred to me again that they had been talking about me, that perhaps Jude had even asked Helen and Emily to arrange this dinner.

'Helen said that you still haven't contacted that counsellor.'

I looked at Jude crossly. 'She had no right to tell you that.'

'Why not? She's your best friend and I'm your husband and we're both worried about you. Why haven't you booked an appointment?'

'I don't need to see a counsellor.'

'I disagree. In fact, I insist that you do it.'

'You *insist*?'

'Yes.' He was unapologetic. 'You're depressed, you're anxious and you need help. I'm not sure I can take any more.'

He couldn't take any more? I almost laughed at him. 'I didn't realise you had a right to tell me what to do.'

'I do when our marriage depends on it.'

This shocked me. I knew that things weren't great between us, but I didn't realise they had got that bad. 'Are you serious?'

'Yes.' He took a deep drink of his beer, as if steeling himself. 'I know you're going through something and I want to be there for you, but I'm at the end of my tether. And it's not fair on the kids either. When was the last time we took them out somewhere?'

I didn't want to tell him about the funfairs we had been frequenting without him. 'They go to preschool every day. They play with their friends all the time.'

'But that's it. We should be taking them out, to museums, to shows. We should be socialising with friends, going on holiday. Instead, I feel like this house has become our prison.'

'Jude, you go to work every day. You go out with your friends after work. I'm hardly holding you captive. I'm the one at home all day, every day.'

'By choice!' I could hear the frustration in his voice. 'What's happened to you, Simone?'

This was my moment, perhaps my last chance to tell him everything. He might not understand but at least he'd know. My deep, dark secret would finally be out in the open and we could deal with it. Maybe he'd even be sympathetic and agree to keep things low-key for a while, just until the end of the year. Or maybe he'd be angry and we'd argue. But at least I would have said it.

But I couldn't say it. The words were lodged too deep inside me now, too used to being concealed. So instead, I looked away. 'I'll call the counsellor on Monday.'

I heard him exhale. 'Thank you,' he said simply.

I knew I wouldn't call but it had bought me some more time. My reprieve was temporary but it was better than nothing. At some point Jude would ask if I'd done it and he'd be furious when he knew that I hadn't, but I'd deal with that when we came to it.

And after all, there wasn't that much longer to go. Five months and it would all be over.

25

Without the crowds, noise and bright lights, the atmosphere on the fairground was completely different. Workers were beginning to pack up, stalls were being dismantled and rides loaded onto lorries and the grass beneath my feet was muddy and trampled.

I had planned to visit the fair at the weekend but then Ivy had caught a virus and had been sent home from school on Friday with a fever. She had been clammy and irritable and although I had tried not to show my fear for Ivy's sake, visions of meningitis or a rare complication from strep A invaded my mind and the horrible thing was that these weren't irrational thoughts, they were very real possibilities, as I kept telling Jude over and over again while he tried to calm me down. By Saturday evening her temperature was nearly forty degrees and, in a blind panic, I had rushed her to A&E, clutching my little girl to me and praying for her to be okay. I had been certain that the tragedy was finally happening and I was petrified and furious with the world for being so cruel. *Take me instead*, I had said repeatedly in my head, *just please don't hurt my daughter.*

By the time we saw the paediatrician though, Ivy's temperature had dropped and she was showing off in front of the nurses and demanding a snack. To me, her transformation from sickly patient to boisterous four-year-old was nothing short of a miracle, but of course the doctor had seen it all before and she sent us home advising Calpol, rest and fluids.

'Children get viruses all the time when they start school,' she had told me, as if I didn't know that already. 'Try not to worry.'

So, I could add the doctor to the list of people who thought that I was neurotic. I wanted to scream at her, to tell her that if she'd seen Ivy just a couple of hours previously then she would have brought her to hospital too. I wished that I'd taken a photo of the thermometer showing her high temperature as proof that I hadn't overreacted. But of course I did neither of these things, I simply thanked her for her time and left.

On the way home from the hospital, Ivy dozed off in the back and I drove like a pensioner, as I always did now, slowly and steadily. But inside, although I knew I should have been relieved that Ivy was okay, I was fuming. With the doctor for being so flippant, with the fortune teller for ruining my life, and with Jude too. He had made me send the children to school when I hadn't wanted them to go this year and look what had happened?

'But nothing has happened,' Jude had said, when we got back. 'The doctor told you, kids get ill all the time. It's natural. You can't stop them from going to school just in case they get sick.'

Why couldn't I do that? Sure, Ivy was fine on this occasion but what about the next time? Or the time after that? What was wrong with wanting to keep my children safe, to prevent them from hurt or suffering? Surely it was only what any mother wanted? But Jude didn't see that any more, he considered my feelings unreasonable, my thoughts irrational, and he had given up trying to understand or help me. That's what hurt the most.

I could feel him slipping away from me with each day that

passed. And I was standing by and letting him go. Not physically – physically I needed him near me – but emotionally. He may not have been fighting in my corner any more, but I was no longer fighting for him either because I didn't care if he loved me, I didn't care if he called me Simmy. I only cared that he was alive.

Jude had been so proud on Ivy and Sam's first day at school. He had taken the morning off work and come to school with us, taking a hundred photos of them in their uniforms, standing outside the gates, or with their preschool friends who were starting with them. He had chatted with the other parents, shaken hands with the Reception teacher, laughed and made jokes. And I had hidden in the shadows, hating every damn second of it.

Ivy and Sam had been thrilled to start lessons. I had expected tears and for at least one of them to cling on to my leg and tell me they didn't want to go in. I had hoped for it because then I could declare that it was too soon and they weren't ready yet. And I could take them home and hold them to me and no one could hurt them. But the twins had marched into their new classroom without even a backward glance, as if Jude and I didn't even exist, and my heart had broken. They were ready, I knew they were. But I wasn't and I didn't think I'd ever be.

Just a week later, Ivy had caught this horrid virus and I had never known such fear. On the first night she was sick I had stayed by her bedside all night, holding her hand, making sure she was breathing. I had been too afraid to fall asleep, even for an hour, in case I missed something. Jude who, from the start, had told me there was nothing to worry about, had given up trying to persuade me to come back to bed. But forty-eight hours later Ivy was as bright as a button again and by Monday she was well enough to go back to school, much to my disappointment.

The only good thing about her being at school was that I could visit the funfair before it was gone. It was September, the season was winding up and soon there would be no more fairs to visit. I hadn't found Mystic Maggie. I hadn't even come close to finding her. I hadn't met a single fortune teller all summer but this only added to the air of mystery surrounding her, further fuelling my fear that she was not a fairground novelty but was unique and special.

This fair, in Hertfordshire, was the last on my list. Hopelessness lay in wait as I moved closer towards the inevitable conclusion that I would never be able track down Mystic Maggie. I was on my own in this nightmare that I now lived in and I had nowhere to turn, nowhere to hide. Even as I walked around the desolate fairground, I knew that I was fighting a losing battle.

'Can I help you?'

I looked up to see a man observing me and I walked over to him. 'I'm sorry to bother you, I'm trying to find a fortune teller.'

The man chortled. 'Want your money back 'cos you didn't meet a tall, dark, handsome stranger?'

'No, nothing like that. I met her a few years ago at a funfair and she was great, so I'd just really like to see her again. For a paid reading.'

The man gazed at me and then he pointed at a caravan. 'Over there.'

I was so surprised by his words that it took me a few seconds to digest them. After months of searching for her, visiting a dozen fairs, it hardly seemed possible that I'd finally found her. I looked over at the small caravan, its curtains drawn tightly across the windows and then back at the man, trying to gather my wits about me so that he didn't become suspicious.

'Great, thanks,' I said, as I began walking towards the caravan. I could feel the man's eyes on my back and with each step I took, nerves and anticipation grew inside me until I felt sick. I should be excited but instead I was scared. I had no plan for this moment, no script of what I was going to say to Mystic Maggie. My focus all these months had only been on finding her.

I took a deep breath and knocked on the door, taking a step back and glancing over at the man, who was still watching me. Suddenly it all felt too much, my legs were wobbly, I was light-headed and dizzy with nerves. But then the door opened and as I stared into the eyes of a dishevelled-looking woman, I hurtled back to grim reality again.

'What do you want?' the woman asked irritably, and I realised I'd woken her up.

'I'm so sorry, I made a mistake.'

The disappointment was so acute. The woman standing in front of me may have been a fortune teller but that was the only thing she had in common with Mystic Maggie. She was significantly older, her hair was short and grey and she wore a furious scowl on her face. I looked into her narrowed eyes and something inside me gave way. Before I knew it, tears were running down my face and I was bent over double, crying away some of the disappointment, fear and agony I felt.

The woman said nothing, but she didn't close the door either. She just stood and watched me and gradually my tears began to subside and I looked up at her to see that her expression had softened a touch. 'Do you want a cup of tea, love?' she asked, and I nodded gratefully.

The woman disappeared into the caravan, leaving the door open, but I didn't want to invade her privacy, so I hovered outside and waited for her to return, which she did a few minutes later with two steaming mugs of tea. She handed one to me and then sat down on the step.

'I'm guessing you were hoping I was someone else?' she asked.

'Yes,' I said quietly.

'Who?'

She seemed genuinely curious and I don't know why but I decided to tell her the truth. Perhaps it was easier to explain it to a stranger than to the people I loved.

'I went to see a fortune teller at a fair a few years ago and she gave me a terrible prediction. It's taking over my life and I thought if I saw her again, she could somehow make it go away.'

'What did she tell you?'

The woman raised her eyebrows as I explained what Mystic Maggie had said to me. 'In a couple of months, it will be five years since I got married and I keep waiting for something terrible to happen,' I said.

'Who was this woman?'

'The name she used was Mystic Maggie. She was young, in her twenties. Long dark hair. I've been trying to track her down all year, but I haven't been able to find her.' I suddenly had an idea. 'Hey, would you be able to read my fortune? Maybe you can tell me if what she said was correct?'

The woman looked thoughtful. 'No, love, I don't think so.'

I couldn't hide my disappointment. 'Why not?'

She shrugged. 'Sure, I could read your fortune but I'm not sure it would be the right thing to do. Look, love, I do this for entertainment purposes, you get me? I tell people what they want to hear and then they go about their day. It's just a bit of fun.'

'Would you ever tell people what Mystic Maggie told me?'

'Absolutely not.'

'So why do you think she said it?'

'I don't know. But my advice would be not to read anything into it. Sure, there are things in life that we can't control but no one can predict your future with that much accuracy.'

I knew she was trying to reassure me, but her words felt hollow. 'So you think she was lying?'

'I think she had no right to say what she did. As to whether she was lying, I can't say. She must have had her reasons but only she knows what they are.' The woman looked thoughtful. 'You know, funfair fortune tellers are a dying breed, there aren't many of us left. But I did hear of a young woman travelling with another fair. It could be your Mystic Maggie.'

I felt a surge of hope. 'Do you know the name of the fair?'

The woman pulled her mobile phone out of her pocket and started fiddling with it. 'Here we go. Bingham's Fairs. They're currently just outside of Birmingham.'

I stared at her. 'Right now?'

'Right now, although the fair ended last night so I imagine they'll be packing up today.'

'Where are they going next?'

'This is their last event of the year, love. The season's over.'

'And then where do all the people who work on the fair go?'

The woman shrugged. 'It depends. Some go off and find other jobs for the winter, others travel. Some people have homes they go back to.'

'So are you saying that if I don't go now, she might disappear for the winter?'

'Probably.'

I stood up, handing over my half-drunk tea. 'Thank you for your help.'

The woman took my mug. 'Good luck, love. I hope you find your Mystic Maggie.'

As I dashed across the empty fairground, I considered my options. Birmingham was at least two hours' drive away, so even if I left now there was no way I'd be back in time to pick Ivy and Sam up from school. If I waited until after school, I feared I'd be too late and the fair would be gone. But there was no one I could ask to pick them up for me. I'd made no effort to socialise with my fellow school mums and I'd ignored birthday party invitations and offers of play dates and Friday evening drinks. I knew the other parents thought I was rude but I hadn't cared at the time. Only now, my antisocial behaviour was coming back to haunt me.

I could only think of one viable option, and without pausing to consider the ramifications of my actions, I pulled my phone out of my pocket and called the school office.

'Hi, this is Simone, mum to Ivy and Sam in Reception. I'm afraid we've had a family emergency and I need to pick the twins up right now... Yes, I'm on my way.'

I hung up and ran towards the car. The children missing a few hours of school when they would probably only be playing anyway seemed a small price to pay for tracking down the woman who was destroying my life, so I ignored the seed of doubt in my mind. I was doing the right thing.

* * *

'Mummy, are we nearly there yet?'

It was the fifteenth time Sam had asked that question. Or maybe the sixteenth. I'd lost count about forty minutes ago. I'd picked the children up from the school office and ushered them out before the staff could ask me any probing questions about my so-called family emergency. They had been excited by my sudden appearance and even more so when I told them that we were going on a great adventure. But now, after two hours in the car, the novelty had worn off.

I looked at the satnav. 'Not long, Sam, another ten minutes or so.'

In my hurry to collect the children and get on the road, I'd committed the cardinal sin of forgetting snacks and it had been a long journey, with near-constant complaints from the back seat. But as we got closer to the fair, I could feel my excitement growing. I finally had a lead, a solid one, and I felt more hopeful than ever that I was going to find Mystic Maggie.

'Mummy, I need a wee-wee.'

I glanced down at the satnav again. 'We'll be there in seven minutes, Ivy. Can you hold it until then?'

'I don't think so.'

I tried, unsuccessfully, to hide my impatience. I was desperate to get to the fair, fearing that even a few minutes' delay could jeopardise my mission. 'Look, Ivy, you're just going to have to hold on, okay?' I snapped. 'We're nearly there.'

There was silence from the back, followed by quiet snuffling which quickly developed into loud, noisy wails. I felt terrible, but I was more focused on getting to the fair than I was on calming down my daughter so, ignoring my pangs of guilt, I kept driving. *This is it. This is finally it.*

As we approached the park, I saw signs for the fair and butterflies danced around in my stomach. Even the spatters on my windscreen as the first drops of rain began to fall didn't dampen my spirits. We parked up and I turned to the children with a smile. 'We're here!'

It was then that I realised Ivy had wet herself. She looked at me, her cheeks red, her eyes both afraid and defiant, and I realised that I didn't have a change of clothes with me. I was so stressed by this unexpected disruption that I had to use every ounce of strength I had not to lose my temper with Ivy. What kind of a mother was I? I was a monster, that was what I was. But the clock was ticking and finding Mystic Maggie was more important than anything else.

'Right,' I said purposefully. 'Take everything off except your T-shirt and jumper. Then we'll put your coat on over and you'll be grand.' I looked out at the drizzle. 'It's not that cold.'

I jumped out of the car and helped Ivy change out of her wet clothes, and then I zipped her coat up and looked down at her bare, tight-less legs. She'd be fine, I decided. 'Come on, kids.'

Grabbing them by the hand, we crossed the road and entered the park. The drizzle was fast turning into driving rain and I pulled the children along, walking as quickly as I could around the perimeter of the park, my eyes constantly searching the grounds for a funfair.

'Mummy, I'm cold,' Ivy complained.

'I'm hungry,' Samuel added. 'Where are we going? Is this our adventure?'

'You'll see soon,' I lied, knowing that a long drive followed by a trawl around a closed funfair was hardly an adventure.

After ten minutes we were soaking wet and still hadn't found the fair. I was practically dragging Ivy and Sam around, and Ivy was complaining that her shoes were rubbing her bare ankles. My impatience and frustration with them, myself and the situation was at risk of falling off the chart.

'Please be patient,' I begged. 'We're nearly there.'

Another ten minutes later, we reached the top of a slope and as I looked down, I stopped short. Beneath us I could see a large clearing, the perfect site for a funfair. But there was no carousel or helter-skelter, no caravans or lorries. All I saw was trampled grass, some empty plastic cups scattered around on the ground and tyre tracks leading to a gate on the far side.

It was gone. I was too late.

I stood there, looking down, clutching on to the twins' hands, tears mingling with raindrops, and I knew that it was over. I was never going to find Mystic Maggie and there was no way to put this right. I fell onto my knees, defeated.

'Mummy?' Sam was looking down at me, shivering. 'Why are we here?'

I couldn't meet his eye as I said, 'I don't know. I just don't know.'

26

By the time we got home, the children were both fast asleep and I parked the car and looked up in surprise as Jude hurtled out of the house and yanked the car door open.

'Where the hell have you been?' he demanded, his face furious.

'I...' I was momentarily stunned. Jude wasn't due home from work for another hour. 'What are you doing here?'

'Never mind that, where have you been?' His raised voice woke both the children up and they took one look at him and simultaneously burst into exhausted, confused tears.

Jude sprang into action, opening one of the back doors and pulling Ivy out first. 'Why is her car seat wet? Why isn't she wearing any bottoms?'

'I did wee-wee in the car,' Ivy wailed. 'Mummy wouldn't stop.'

I could tell Jude was apoplectic, but he maintained a veneer of calm so that he didn't upset the children any more. 'Poor little sweetheart,' he said soothingly, holding Ivy close to him as he walked around the car and unstrapped Sam from his car seat. 'Let's get you both inside.'

He hurried in, as though he couldn't get away from me fast enough, but I remained in the driver's seat. I didn't want to go inside. I didn't want to face Jude, or the reality of what my life had become. I was afraid, I was ashamed. And I was broken.

As I sat there, alone, I just wanted it all to be over. There was no way forward but there was no point in wishing I could go back in time and never see the fortune teller either. All I could do was wait helplessly in the present, powerless to change my fate.

I was still sitting in the car when Jude came back out, half an hour later. He sat down in the front passenger seat and sighed. 'The kids have had a bath and are eating toast and watching TV.'

I said nothing, just stared straight ahead. But I could feel his gaze on me.

'What's going on, Simone? The school said you picked them up early because of a family emergency and I was beside myself when you wouldn't answer your phone. Then Ivy said you travelled in the car for hours just to walk around a park in the rain? What the fuck?'

Finally, I turned to look at him. 'Why did you come home early?'

He ran his hand through his greying hair. 'When you didn't make your usual phone calls to me I got concerned. I sent you a message and you didn't reply so I decided to come home and meet you at the school at pick-up. But then the teacher told me what had happened.'

It was almost funny. Those incessant phone calls to Jude, which he loathed, had been the thing that had alerted him to my deception. In the chaos of the day, the excitement of finding Mystic Maggie, the need to get to Birmingham, I'd forgotten to call him and that had been my undoing. Or perhaps he would have found out anyway. The twins couldn't keep my secrets forever.

'Are you going to answer me?' Jude was still staring at me.

But I had no words, nothing to explain what I had done, no way of rationalising my behaviour that day. I turned my head away from him and looked out of the car window.

I heard Jude sigh again. 'I'm going back inside now. Are you coming?' When I didn't respond, he turned away from me and opened the door, getting out without saying another word.

I don't know how long I stayed in the car but it was dark by the time I finally got out. My back was stiff, I was freezing cold and I knew that I couldn't hide from Jude forever. By the time I went inside the twins were in bed and Jude was sitting at the kitchen table. I went and sat down opposite him, wrapping my cardigan, which was still damp from the rain, around me.

'I can't do this any more, Simone.'

I looked at him, my face pale, and waited for him to continue.

'These past few months have been a nightmare and I've tried to understand, I really have. I told myself, she's going through something, but she'll come back to me. The most important thing is that she's a wonderful mother to our children. But now I'm not sure I think that.'

If I'd thought I was broken before, I was now. I wanted to argue, to say I was behaving in this way *because* I was a good mother, because I wanted to keep our children safe. But I didn't have any fight left in me.

'What you did today makes no sense and that terrifies me. To take the kids out of school, to drive them two and a half hours up the motorway for no reason. To let poor Ivy have an accident in the car because you wouldn't stop for her. Do you have any idea how upset she was?'

I was filled with shame but still I said nothing.

'And it's not just that. You don't let them play with their friends, you don't let them go to parties. It's like you're keeping them prisoner, like you're afraid to let them out of your sight. It's not healthy and it's not fair. So I'm asking you one last time, Simone. What's going on?'

I looked down at the table surface, studying the intricate lines in the wood, tracing one of them with my finger. After a minute of silence, Jude put his head in his hands. 'I feel like we've lost you and I just don't know how to get you back.'

What could I say? I didn't know how to come back either. I was lost in the darkness, unable to feel my way out. The dimming light was finally extinguished. And all I could hear was the doomsday clock, ticking loudly in my mind. *Three months to go. Tick tock.*

'I'm going to take some time off work,' Jude continued. 'I don't think you should be looking after the children right now.'

'Okay.'

His words were a relief. With Jude at home, I wouldn't have to worry about him as much.

Jude stood up. 'I'm going to check on the kids.'

I heard him leave but I didn't look up. I continued tracing the line of the table. How had it come to this? I had everything I had ever wanted but I couldn't enjoy any of it. It was tainted now and all I saw was the end, getting nearer and growing larger as it appeared over the horizon.

* * *

With Jude taking over childcare duties, it became even less necessary to leave the house, or even get dressed. And now that my regular check-in phone calls to him no longer dictated my day, because he was at home most of the time, I quickly slipped out of my usual routine. I stayed in bed for hours, not sleeping, not reading, just lying there. Jude had made me call the doctor but they didn't have an appointment for two weeks. I'd booked it, satisfied that I'd done all I could, and then gone back to bed, retreating from the world as it continued to turn in my absence.

Then Helen appeared, presumably summoned by Jude. She sat down on the edge of my bed and looked down at me. 'Talk to me, Simone.'

Her kindness brought tears to my eyes and she held my hand tightly as I cried. But when I was done, I still couldn't find the words to explain it to her.

'There's this place,' Helen said, 'where you can go and spend some time, talking to people, recharging your batteries. Apparently, it's amazing.'

It was obvious that she was talking about some kind of rehab centre. But there was absolutely no way I was leaving my family now. I needed them near me, as close as possible. 'I'm not going.'

'I think it might be just what you need.'

'I said I'm not going.'

'Simone.' Helen lowered her voice. 'Jude's in bits. He doesn't know what to do. He said something about the children not being safe with you? I really think you need to do this.'

All I wanted to do was keep the children safe, why did no one understand this? But of course they didn't understand, because I hadn't told them.

And then it came out, with no warning, no premeditation or long anticipated build-up. 'Did you know that in a few weeks it'll be mine and Jude's fifth wedding anniversary?'

Helen stroked my hand. 'Oh yes, I guess it will.'

'That's when it's going to happen.'

'What's going to happen?'

'The tragedy.'

Helen was looking completely confused. 'What are you talking about, Simmy?'

'That's what she said. Mystic Maggie.'

I saw realisation dawn on Helen's face. 'Oh my God, is that what this is all about?'

'She said I'd have five years of happiness, but it would end in tragedy.'

'And you seriously believe that? You're honestly letting this stupid woman get into your head?'

'She's ruined my life, Helen. My life and my marriage.'

Helen opened her mouth and closed it again. She seemed to be grappling with what to say to me, torn between amusement, disapproval and concern. 'Simmy, I love you so I'm going to be frank with you. The only one ruining your marriage right now is you.'

I don't know what I had expected from her when I finally revealed my darkest, most terrifying secret. I'd always known that she wouldn't understand, which was why I'd hidden it from her in the first place, Jude as well. But I hadn't imagined she would place the blame at my door.

'If that fortune teller hadn't said what she said, none of this would have happened,' I said.

'True,' Helen conceded. 'But they were just words. Reckless, false words. You're the one who is letting them destroy you. And it has to stop, now, before it's too late.'

'Too late for what?'

'For you, Simone! For your marriage!'

I turned away. 'I knew you wouldn't understand.'

'I'm trying, I really am. Why haven't you told Jude about this?'

'Because he'll react the same way you are now. No one gets it. You all think I'm mad but it's easy for you to say, isn't it? You're not the ones who were told that their marriage will end in tragedy. So you can all go and laugh it off at my expense but you don't really know how it feels.'

'My God.' Helen still looked a bit stunned. 'Well, there's only one thing for it. We're going to find this bloody woman and expose her for the fraud that she is.'

'You won't find her,' I said bleakly. 'I've been trying. Over the past few months I've been to a dozen funfairs. I almost thought I'd found her a few days ago but I was too late.'

'That's why you went to Birmingham.' Helen's eyes were wide with realisation. 'You were looking for her, weren't you?'

'Yes. I got some good intel that she might be there but by the time we arrived, the fair had gone.'

'No one is untraceable. We'll find her.'

'You won't. She's vanished.'

'So that's it, is it? You've given up? Checked out on life?'

I refused to answer, turning away instead.

Helen stood up and started pacing around the room agitatedly. 'This whole thing is one big mess. There's got to be a way to put it right. But you need to tell Jude what's going on.'

'No.'

'If you don't, I will.'

For the first time in days, I felt a fire in my belly. 'Helen, you have no right to do that.'

'Yes I do, if I think it's for your own good.'

'He already thinks I'm insane, if you tell him that, he'll have me committed.'

'Right now, I'm not sure that's a bad thing.'

'Helen!'

'Look.' Helen came and sat back down. 'I'm begging you, with every inch of my being, do not let the thoughtless words of a fraudster mess up your life any more than they already have. Forget about fate, or prophecies written in the stars, or whatever, it's bullshit. I promise you.'

'You say that, Helen, but do you know how many stories I've

read online about people whose fortunes came true? Dozens. Hundreds. It's not bullshit.'

'Yes, it is! Okay, so occasionally they may get something right by the power of probability or sheer luck but none of it's real. They don't make your future, Simone, you do.'

Helen's phone pinged and although she ignored it, I knew she was itching to check her messages.

'You'd better go,' I told her. 'Shouldn't you be in work?'

'Yes,' she admitted. 'I've got a meeting in an hour.'

'So, you should go.'

Helen looked reluctant to leave but eventually she nodded. 'I'll be back at the weekend, okay? I love you, Simone. We're going to fix this.' She kissed the top of my head and then she left. A minute later I heard her talking quietly to Jude downstairs and I wondered what she was saying to him, but when he appeared shortly afterwards I could tell from his expression that she had kept my secret. For now at least.

'Helen says she'll be back again in a few days.' He said it like a doctor talking to a patient. Any affection he'd shown towards me had gone. 'I'm going out to the shops. Do you want anything?'

'No.' He turned to walk away and I shouted after him. 'Jude! Take your phone, okay?'

He nodded wearily. 'Of course.'

I heard him walk downstairs and waited for the sound of the front door closing. Then I reached for my phone so that I could track his journey to the shops. But as I opened the Find My app and saw Jude's name and photograph, I frowned. Underneath were the words 'not available'. They usually only appeared if he was somewhere without reception, like on the Tube. The only other possible explanation was that he'd turned either his phone or his location settings off because he didn't want me to know his whereabouts. But why would he do that?

My heart started racing as I refreshed the app over and over again, just to make sure it wasn't a temporary glitch. But each time I got the same result. Not available. I called him and the phone rang, confirming that it was switched on, which only left one option. He'd turned his location settings off. Why would he do that to go to the shops?

'Simone, I've literally just left the house.' He couldn't be bothered to hide his annoyance.

'Why have you turned your location settings off?'

There was a pause. 'Have I? I didn't realise.'

'Yes, they're off.'

'I didn't do it intentionally. Maybe one of the twins did it by mistake when they were playing around with my phone.'

I closed my eyes and exhaled. The twins messed around with our phones all the time. 'Will you turn it back on?'

'Sure, I'll do it later.'

'Will you do it now, Jude?'

Another pause. And then, 'I'll do it when I get back, Simone. I won't be long.'

And then he hung up. It was the first time he'd ever hung up on me. For the first time that day, I got out of bed and dashed to the window to see if I could still see him, but he was out of sight. I considered running after him, but I was still in my pyjamas. I wanted to call him again but I knew it was too soon so instead I set a fifteen minute timer for my phone and told myself I wouldn't try again until then. With any luck he'd be back.

When fifteen minutes came and went, I called him but he didn't answer. I tried again but it rang out. By forty-five minutes I was in bits. He should be back by now, the shops were only a short walk away. An hour and six missed calls later, I was about to call the police.

Then I heard the front door opening and I rushed downstairs. 'Where have you been?'

Jude wasn't holding a shopping bag and he wouldn't meet my eye either.

'Where have you been, Jude?'

'I went to view a flat,' he said simply.

'You what? Are we moving?'

'You're not. I am. Well, me and the twins.'

I staggered backwards and fell onto the bottom step. 'What are you talking about?'

'I need some space, Simone, I can't cope any more. I'm sorry.'

'Are you leaving me?'

'No,' he said, finally looking me in the eye. 'I just think we both need a break.'

'Jude, no, don't do this.'

'I'm sorry, Simone. It's done. I've already booked the flat on Airbnb. It's just a short-term let, for a month. It doesn't have to be permanent. Let's just take it a day at a time, okay?'

But the thought of Jude being away from me, somewhere where I couldn't watch over him, was unbearable. And then I digested what else he'd said.

'You're taking the twins?'

'Yes. You can see them any time, Simone, I'm not going to keep them from you, but you're not well enough to look after them at the moment.'

'Jude, come on, it's not that bad.'

'Yes, it is.'

'I'll get help,' I pleaded. 'I'll do anything. But please don't do this. Don't take my children away from me.'

'I'm not taking them away from you. You can see them any time, okay? We'll only be round the corner. I think it's for the best.'

'The best for who?'

He looked away and I saw shame on his face. 'For me and the twins.'

How dare he, I thought angrily. Trying to make out like I was a liability or, even worse, dangerous. That I couldn't be trusted to look after our children. He knew that wasn't true and he was using my well-meaning protectiveness over our family as ammunition against me. This wasn't about me, it was about him. It was gaslighting, that was what it was.

'You're a bastard,' I spat.

But he didn't take the bait. His mind was made up and he clearly had no appetite for a row. I already suspected that whatever I threw at him would make little difference. 'I'm going to pack up a few things for me and the kids and take them to the flat after school.'

'What? You're leaving today?'

'Yes.'

'How could you do this to me?'

Jude looked at me then and I saw real pain in his eyes. 'I'm sorry.'

Was this the start of it? The beginning of the end? Jude was going and taking the twins with him. I would no longer know where they were, what they were doing. I would no longer be able to protect them because they weren't under my careful watch. Earlier, I had told Helen that I wouldn't leave my family, but I hadn't considered that they would leave me. And, I realised as my darkened world went completely black, there was nothing I could do about it.

27

Jude and the twins had been gone for six days. He brought them round every day, letting them stay as long as they wanted to, but he hadn't left me alone with them and he hadn't invited me round to the flat, either. If the twins were confused by this sudden change to their routine, they didn't appear to be showing it. If anything, they seemed to be treating it as one big adventure, far more exciting than the bogus one I had taken them to in Birmingham.

I hadn't slept since they left. I lay awake at night, imagining worst-case scenarios, picturing Jude falling ill in his sleep and no one being there to save him or one of the twins stumbling and falling in the unfamiliar flat and breaking their neck. But I no longer called Jude. I had made the transition from active to passive, with no energy left to fight fate. I had given up on trying to defuse the ticking time bomb and I was just waiting for the worst to happen.

Helen hadn't visited like she had promised, and I hadn't heard from her. I was alone, living for when Jude brought the twins over and dreading when they were out of my reach. I hadn't left the house once. There was nowhere I wanted to go, no one I wanted to see.

On the afternoon of the sixth day, Jude sent me a message to say he was popping over to pick up his raincoat. I decided to get it out for him and as I was taking it off the hook, I slipped my arms into it, closing my eyes and inhaling the familiar scent of the coat, and my husband. I missed him so much, and the twins even more and yet I still didn't fight for them. I slipped my hands into the coat pockets, touching a used tissue and some paper. Pulling the detritus out to throw it in the bin, I found a receipt, dated from four weeks previously, for a restaurant in town. I remembered that Jude had said he was going to a colleague's leaving do that night and as I read the receipt, I wondered why he had paid for two meals, not one.

I was still holding the receipt in my hand when Jude let himself in a few minutes later and stopped short when he saw me wearing his coat.

'What's this?' I asked, proffering the crumpled receipt at him.

He took it from my hand, frowning, and then I saw a flash of recognition on his face before he quickly screwed it up into a ball. 'It's nothing.'

'Who did you go to dinner with?'

He looked down at the paper ball in his hand and then at me. 'Okay, fine, I have nothing to hide. I went for dinner with a friend. We've been meeting up a bit over the last few months, just a quick lunch during the week or the odd dinner. I needed someone to talk to, Simone.'

'To talk to about me, you mean?'

He nodded. 'Yes, you. Me. Our marriage. How I am, which isn't great, by the way.'

'And this friend, they've been supporting you?'

'Yes. To be honest, I don't know what I'd have done without them.'

I mulled this over. I hated the fact that Jude had been dissecting our relationship with someone else, someone I didn't know. Unless it was someone I did know?

'Is it Helen?'

He looked away. 'No.'

I frowned. 'Who is it, Jude?'

'It doesn't matter.'

'If it doesn't matter, then just tell me.'

His answer was so quiet that at first I thought I'd misheard.

'Did you just say *Emily*?'

'Yes.'

'But... since when were you and Emily such good friends?' I knew they had worked at the same company for a while, but as far as I was aware they rarely crossed paths and in our nearly five years of marriage they'd always been polite but they hadn't been close. If anything, I thought that Emily didn't like him. After all, she'd tried to warn me off him.

'It was a few months ago,' Jude said. For someone who claimed that he had nothing to hide, he looked remarkably shifty. As for Emily, I couldn't believe she'd kept this from me either.

'Go on,' I prompted him.

'We bumped into each other in town. I'd just got off the phone to you, it was like the third or fourth time you'd called, and I was feeling pretty stressed out. I think she caught me at a vulnerable moment and when she realised I was upset, she suggested we go get a coffee. So we did, and I told her a bit about what was going on. Anyway, she was great, really understanding and I just appreciated a listening ear, you know?'

Oh, I knew, but I still couldn't get my head around it. My

husband had confided in Emily months ago and she hadn't breathed a word about it to me? Where did her priorities lie? Or Jude's, for that matter?

'After that we got together every so often for a catch-up. She's never said anything bad about you, Simone, okay? That's not what this is about. If anything, she tried to help me understand what was going on. We talked about how lots of new mothers struggle, and postnatal depression and so on. And I told her how I was feeling, you know, about how our lives had changed.'

Oh, I'm so happy you had someone to talk to, I thought uncharitably, still seething at Emily as well as my husband. Perhaps I didn't have the right to be angry that he'd confided in someone but I was angry about who it was because it felt like a betrayal of my friendship and my trust. I'd known Emily for over fifteen years and I'd always thought her loyalty was to me.

'So does she know you've left me?'

'Yes,' Jude said. 'Actually, she's been a great support over the past week. She helped me find the Airbnb and came over to make it nice and homely for the kids.'

I think he realised he'd said too much as soon the words came out, but by then it was too late to take them back.

I glared at him. 'She's been to the flat? I'm not allowed to go but *Emily* has been?'

'Yes, I didn't mean... Shit. Look, Simone, it's not what you think. There's nothing going on between me and Emily, okay? She's a good person, she just wants to help.'

'Ha!' My laugh, when it came, was shrill. 'She just wants to help!' I knew I sounded hysterical, but I was fast hurtling towards a conclusion that my naive husband hadn't yet reached. *Women don't behave like this towards a married man unless they have an agenda.*

I thought about the Emily I knew, or at least thought I knew.

She'd been with Mark for almost as long as I could remember. They seemed happy, although I knew she'd always wanted children and although she'd never spoken about it, I assumed they'd tried but it hadn't happened for them. She was a funny, kind and thoughtful person. So yes, perhaps Jude was right, perhaps she was just being considerate, helping a man when he was down. But something was nagging at me and I couldn't help but think there was more to it than that. And the more I thought about it, the more certain I became. Mum used to say, 'It's always the quiet ones you need to watch.'

Jude was looking agitated. 'Seriously, Simone, don't fly off the handle, okay? Emily's done nothing wrong, I don't want you giving her a hard time.'

'Has she spent time with our children, Jude?'

'What?'

'Has she spent time with our children?'

'Yes. She's been round a few times.'

'Does Mark know?'

Jude frowned. 'I don't know.'

'Oh, Jude.'

It was strange, though. I was being kicked when I was already down and I should be falling to pieces, but instead I felt more alive than I had done in months. It was like I'd just woken up from a bad dream, my senses rapidly returning to me. The world, which had been blurring at the edges for so long, was coming back into focus. All this time I'd been looking for danger, something had been happening right under my nose and I'd been too lost in my own head to pay attention. But I was paying attention now, as I absorbed Jude's conflicted expression, like a child who knew he'd done wrong but wasn't sure what it was yet. Something wasn't right here and I was going to find out what it was. The fire in my belly was growing stronger by the minute, as I thought of Emily making my children's rooms pretty, sharing a bottle of wine with Jude.

Emily was trying to muscle in on my husband, and my life, and I wanted to know why. I was almost excited as I turned away from Jude and headed upstairs to get in the shower. Christ, I was angry. Not just angry, I was raging. And after days of bleak nothingness, it felt good.

* * *

Emily answered the door in a tracksuit, her painted toenails glistening on her bare, tanned feet and her fair hair tied up in a messy, yet stylish bun. Perversely, my first thought when I saw her wasn't, *What's your business with my husband?* It was, *Christ, I wish I looked that good in a tracksuit.*

'Simmy, what a surprise! I wasn't expecting you!'

I had to hand it to her, she seemed genuinely pleased to see me.

'Is Mark around?' I asked.

'No, he's out tonight.'

'Great, we can have some girl talk.'

'Sounds fabulous,' Emily enthused, opening the door wider to let me in. I followed her into the kitchen where she reached for a bottle of wine from the fridge and two glasses.

We walked over to the large corner sofa in the living room, which was infuriatingly neat and uncluttered, and I sank down onto the soft grey cushion and took a glass of wine from her.

'I spoke to Shiv today,' Emily said. 'She's coming back for Christmas. Won't that be lovely?'

'Lovely,' I said vaguely.

'I was thinking we could have a New Year's party, all of us together, the kids too of course. What do you think?'

'Yeah, sounds good.'

'Are you okay, Simmy? You seem a little distracted.'

I studied Emily, like a scientist might study a specimen under the microscope. I was strangely calm, but I knew that my temper was lying in wait for its opportunity to pounce and that the smallest thing would set it off. I'd been in Emily's house for less than five minutes but I already knew what I needed to. Emily was fully aware that Jude had left me, she would realise that I must be in bits, but she was acting like everything was perfectly normal. She was lying to me.

'So, I hear you've been hanging out with my husband.'

Emily's perfect mouth made a little O. 'I didn't realise he'd told you.'

'Yes, he's told me everything.'

Emily's expression was the epitome of contrite. 'Oh, Simmy, I'm so sorry. I've wanted to talk to you about it so many times, but Jude begged me not to. I've felt so caught in the middle.'

Oh poor, poor Emily. How hard it must have been for you. 'Mmm, yes, I understand,' I said. 'But I guess my question is, why are you so interested in Jude?'

'What?' Emily laughed incredulously. 'I'm not interested in him. I'm just being a friend.'

'To Jude.'

'Yes.'

'But not to me.'

'I want to be a good friend to you too, I really do. I'm always here for you.'

'Except for when you're hanging out with my husband. And my children.'

Emily's expression changed in an instant, like I'd said the trigger word. 'Your children are beautiful. You have no idea how lucky you are, Simone.'

'I do, actually. Or at least I did. Until they all left me. Was that anything to do with you?'

'Look.' I could see Emily taking deep breaths, trying to keep control of this situation. 'I don't want to fall out with you, okay? I'm sorry if I overstepped the mark.'

'I'd say you took a giant flying leap over the mark, Emily.'

'Well, with all due respect, what did you expect? You've been acting like a control freak, keeping Jude and the children on such a tight leash. They were bound to want to escape from you.'

It seemed that Emily couldn't keep her temper, or her opinion, under control after all.

'And that's your business because?'

'Because Jude made it my business. When he confided in me. When he told me how you'd been acting and how it made him feel. When he came to me for support.'

'Which you provided willingly, I'm assuming.'

'Yes, I did. Jude's a wonderful man, one of the best. He deserves to be happy.'

'My goodness,' I said, realisation dawning. 'You're in love with him, aren't you?'

'Don't be ridiculous.'

'You are. You're in love with him. How long have you been in love with him?'

Emily was quiet, as though considering her next move in what was fast becoming a mental game of chess. Would she deny it and claim I was losing my mind, as everyone else seemed to think? Would she confess and beg for forgiveness? But her response, when it came, was unexpected.

'I had him first.'

I stared at her in disbelief. 'What do you mean, you had him first?'

She looked at me with an expression so smug that I wanted to punch her beautiful face. 'He was mine before he was yours. You never knew that, did you?'

Was she lying again? Was she delusional? Or was it possible that she was telling the truth? Emily had worked in the same office as Jude, so it wasn't beyond the realms of possibility, but if it was true then why didn't I know about it?

'Jude and I were a thing.' Emily's eyes had become misty. 'It was brief, but it was amazing.'

'If that's true then why didn't any of us know about it?'

'No one knew but me and him. I was with Mark, you see, so it had to remain hush-hush. It was our little secret, which only made it more exciting.'

Instinct told me that she was telling the truth, about this at least. 'So, what happened?'

Emily's face clouded over. 'He ended it, is what happened. Told me he didn't want to have an affair. I said I'd finish it with Mark, but he told me not to.'

'Why did he tell you that?'

'Because he met you.' Emily almost spat the words out. 'At that bloody house party. And then it was all, Simone this and Simone that.'

I couldn't believe it was the first time I was hearing this, that Emily had kept this secret for so long, or that Jude had either. He should have told me. Emily should have told me. Someone, at least, should have bloody told me. And what about poor Mark, the man who Emily went on to marry? Now I knew that he'd been second best in Emily's eyes, but he had no idea.

'If I'd known that you and Jude had history, I wouldn't have gone out with him. You should have just told me!'

'How could I?' Emily threw her hands up in the air. 'If I'd told you, then you'd know that I cheated on Mark. Every time we met up, you'd be looking at him and thinking, *Poor Mark*.'

It was so close to what I'd just thought that I didn't answer.

'Of course, I thought you'd just go out a few times and that would be that,' Emily continued. 'But then you had to go and marry him. I tried to put you off him, but you weren't having it.'

I thought back to those early months with Jude, Emily warning me to be careful, telling me that she thought he was controlling. She'd even got Shiv onside. But all this time, she'd been trying to get me to break up with him because she couldn't stand the sight of us together. My temper was flaring now, reminding me that it was ready to go at any given moment.

'And then you had to go and have children with him. Two beautiful, wonderful little children and I've stood by and watched you wreck it all. Well, I'm not standing by any longer.'

That must have been the final straw for Emily. Not only had she lost Jude but she'd also had to stand by and watch us having children, wishing she was in my shoes. But they weren't her shoes.

'They're my children, Emily, they're not yours.'

'They should be mine,' she snapped. 'I'd be a much better mother than you. I'd be a much better wife too, come to think of it.'

'So, that's it, is it? You want to take my place? Steal my husband and children from me?'

'I'm not stealing, Simone, you threw them away.'

Any polite pretence between us was completely gone, Emily's cards were on the table for all to see. She must be desperate, I thought. 'And what about Mark?'

'He'll get over it. Life's too short, Simmy, you have to grasp your chance of happiness when you have the opportunity. You can't let it get away from you.'

I'd grasped happiness when I met Jude. And I'd let it get away from me, in my obsession over Mystic Maggie. I'd let Jude walk straight into the firm, slender arms of my so-called friend.

Except that he hadn't walked into her arms, had he? She hadn't won this, not yet. 'Jude thinks you're just friends,' I told her. 'There's nothing romantic in it for him.'

Emily laughed. 'Yeah, you keep telling yourself that.'

'He says nothing has happened between you and I believe him.'

'Oh, it's only a matter of time. So you go back to your nervous breakdown, or whatever it is, and leave your man to me, I'll take care of him. I'll take care of your kids too.'

Fifteen years of friendship and this was what it had come down to. How could I have been so wrong about a person? Maybe Emily hadn't started out like this, though. Maybe fifteen years of heartache and disappointment had done it to her. Either way, the result was the same.

It came to me then. Was this my tragedy? My husband and children being stolen by one of my closest friends? The pain would be acute, there was no doubt about it. The idea of Emily tucking my children into bed, kissing their little heads and then going down to snuggle up with Jude on the sofa sickened me to the core. I'd never survive it, it would kill me. But, I realised, if this really was the foretold prediction, then it hadn't happened yet. There was still time to change this course of events, I just had to take back control and I was now determined to do it.

'You're not getting my husband or my children, Emily. They're mine and they always will be.'

'That's where you're wrong. You've lost them, just accept it.'

'I'll never accept it. I'm going to fight for my marriage and I'm going to win. I'm not giving up.'

'And you think you can beat me?' Emily's fists were clenching, her mouth forming a thin line. This was not the Emily I thought I knew, this was a stranger, someone I didn't like and didn't trust. But I wasn't sure if I trusted myself either. Rage was building inside me, bubbling up and spilling over. I'd been dormant for months and now I was ready to explode, all my suppressed fears and worries coming to the surface, ret hot and uncontrollable. How dare Emily try to take advantage of me being vulnerable to move in on my husband and children? Who the hell did she think she was? I moved my gaze from her fists to her eyes.

'This is not a competition, Emily. It's not a game. This is my family we're talking about.'

'Actually, you're wrong, it is a game, Simone. And you've lost.'

I don't know who moved first. All I know is that in an instant we were on each other, adrenaline sparking like electricity between us, all our hurt and anger being taken out on the other. It was horrific for us to be behaving like this, but it was also the physical release I had perhaps craved. I was fighting for myself, yes, but also for my husband and children. This wasn't the way to do it, this wasn't how I was going to win them back, but I was in too deep to stop now.

Neither of us knew how to fight and if anyone had been watching us, they might have even laughed. We were frantic and out of control, rolling around on the sofa, scratching and pulling each other's hair, attempting to throw punches, and making a ridiculous spectacle of ourselves. But then, and to Emily's credit I still don't think she meant it to happen, I fell off the sofa and crashed to the ground, hitting my head on the corner of the coffee table on my way down.

It had been an impulsive decision to fight with Emily. I had no plan, no agenda, and no idea how it was going to end. I wasn't thinking, I was simply lashing out and I don't think it even occurred to me for a second that I wanted Emily to get seriously hurt. But the moment that she climbed on top of me so that I was wedged between the sofa and the coffee table, I began to wonder if it was different for Emily. My head was throbbing and I felt dizzy, but even through my blurred vision, the way she was looking at me scared me. Her eyes were wild, almost inhuman, and her fists were still clenched. Suddenly I felt less like Emily's opponent and more like her prey. I tried to move my arms, but Emily had pinned them to my side with her legs and days of inactivity and lack of sleep combined with the knock to my head had left me weak.

'Get off me,' I shouted, wriggling my body and trying to loosen her grip on me. But she just sat there, on top of me, looking down, holding firm. 'Get off,' I screamed again.

When Emily finally spoke her voice was cold, calculating. 'You're weak and pathetic, Simone. No wonder Jude doesn't want you any more. No wonder your children prefer me to you.'

Her words enraged me but no matter how hard I tried to get her off me, she was too strong, her legs firm from regular gym sessions and spinning and whatever else she did to maintain the figure that I had always admired. 'You're wrong,' I spat.

'No, I'm not. You know, just last night, as I was reading the children a bedtime story, Ivy looked up at me with her gorgeous, round little eyes and asked me if I was having a sleepover. She really wanted me to stay. It was very touching. So, I told her, "Not tonight, but maybe one day soon." And do you know what she said? She said, "I can't wait."'

'Fuck you!' I was exhausted from the effort of trying to free myself, but I still kept trying, I wasn't giving up. I managed to move my wrist a fraction so that I could dig my nails into her leg but it only made her grip my body tighter.

'So, you have two choices now, Simone. Either you accept that you've lost and walk away or you carry on living in your ridiculous state of denial. Either way, this ends tonight.'

'You're deluded, Emily do you know that? You're completely deluded and when Jude and Mark find out about this, they'll realise what a complete psycho you are. You will never see my children again.'

Emily's expression hardened. 'You're not taking them away from me.'

Did she even know what she was saying? 'They were never yours to begin with, Emily. Why can't you see that?'

'Liar!' Emily was beyond reason, I realised that now. She was lost somewhere in the fantasy she had concocted for herself, one where she slipped seamlessly into my place. It didn't matter what I said to her, all that mattered was that I managed to get her off me and escaped from this house. I had to speak to Jude and tell him what had happened, and then this would all be over.

I turned my head to look at the coffee table. There was a marble pyramid sculpture on it, its layers of black, pink and white leading up to a sharp point at the top. I'd always admired that sculpture and had even considered getting one myself. Now, as I stared at it, all I was thinking about was somehow freeing one arm so that I could grab it and use it as a weapon to get Emily off me. Just one bash so she loosened her grip and I'd be able to escape. Emily followed my gaze to the sculpture and I took advantage of her momentary distraction. Using every ounce of strength I had, I squeezed her leg tightly with my left hand and when she cried out in pain, I finally managed to free it. In a second my hand was reaching for the sculpture. I was almost there, just centimetres to go but, sitting on top of me, Emily had the advantage. She reached out and grabbed it and with horror I saw her hold it above my head.

'Emily,' I said, almost pleadingly. 'Just let me go.'

She looked down at me and her grip on the sculpture was firm. 'You had your chance, Simone.'

The last thing I remember was a flash of pink as the pyramid came crashing down towards me. And then everything went black.

28

I had spent so long fearing death. Jude's death, Ivy or Sam's death. In all the many scenarios I'd pictured over the last year, I was the one left in the fallout, the survivor who had to come to terms with whatever tragedy had befallen my family, wondering how I would ever be able to recover from it. I had been so preoccupied with worrying about the people around me, that somewhere along the way I'd forgotten to consider that I might be the victim.

It had only occurred to me in the split second before Emily sent the pyramid plummeting into my skull that I was the one who had been destined to die all along. It was four weeks before Jude and I would celebrate our fifth wedding anniversary when the clock finally stopped ticking. And, oddly, I had not been afraid in that brief, fleeting moment. I'd been relieved that it was me. I was prepared to die if it meant that the rest of my family would be saved.

I think Emily would have succeeded in killing me, too, if Helen hadn't arrived when she did. Helen, who I thought had given up on me after I finally revealed my obsession with the fortune teller's prediction. Helen, who, when she didn't come to see me as promised at the weekend, I assumed had left me to my paranoid delusions because she just didn't get it.

I realise now that Helen didn't have to get it. She didn't have to understand my fears, or even attempt to untangle how I'd got myself into such a state over something she perceived to be so trivial. All she had to do was care. To love me and to want to help.

Helen had a secret too, one which she'd somehow managed to keep from us all for five years. On the night of that ill-fated trip to the funfair, she'd caught the eye of a young woman, the daughter of a travelling family. And, unable to stop thinking about her, Helen had gone back on her own to see her the following night.

It was only ever meant to be a one-off. Their lives were incompatible, their personalities couldn't have been more different. Yet Helen hadn't been able to forget about her. So, they had kept in touch, meeting up every so often, neither making promises to the other that they couldn't keep. There could be no commitment, they both agreed, this was not a conventional relationship. And yet, five years later, they were still in touch and Helen had not found love with anyone else.

It was this woman who she had called the minute she left my house after hearing how terrified I was of Mystic Maggie's prediction. This woman was the reason why she hadn't come to see me at the weekend because she had taken Helen to meet Mystic Maggie so that she could finally uncover the truth that would set me free.

She was almost too late. If she'd arrived even a couple of minutes later, Emily might have delivered the fateful blow. If she hadn't come at all, I doubt I'd be still here today.

After finally tracking down Mystic Maggie, Helen had tried to call me numerous times, but I'd put my phone on silent when I went to see Emily, not wanting to be disturbed. Worried about my welfare,

Helen had called Jude to ask if he knew where I was and when he'd heard the panic in her voice, he hadn't hesitated to act. It's quite funny, if you think about it. For months I had been tracking Jude via the Find My app, hoping that it might somehow save his life, even though that was nonsensical. But in the end, it had saved my life, not his.

As soon as Jude traced my location to Emily's house, he had told Helen about our conversation earlier that day and how upset I'd been to hear that he'd been spending time with Emily. Helen, the only one who had all the pieces of the puzzle, had immediately hung up and rushed to Emily's house, letting herself in with a spare key she'd been given to water the plants when Emily and Mark were on holiday and hurrying into the living room to find Emily on top of me.

She told me all of this as she sat on the edge my hospital bed, holding my hand.

'Emily slipped Mystic Maggie twenty quid to warn you off Jude,' she said. 'I'd told her that he fancied you and she was desperate to make you say no when he asked you out. She hoped that if the fortune teller warned you off a future love interest you might give him a wide berth. It was just a spur-of-the-moment idea she came up with on the night, Simmy, I don't think she planned it.'

I don't think she planned to attack me, either. That had been another opportunity seized in the moment. She had stood by quietly and watched Jude and I fall in love, get married and have children. And the whole time she had been silently seething about it, imagining how different her life would have been if he'd chosen her and not me. Resentment and jealously does terrible things to a person over time. Slowly it turns into hate. And I know now that she hated me.

When she saw her opportunity to claim Jude for herself, she

hadn't hesitated. And when I threatened to stand in her way, she had wanted me out of the picture, pure and simple.

But I don't think it was premeditated. I said that to the police when they came to see me, not because I wanted to protect Emily but because I wanted to tell the truth. I was sick of lies, sick of secrets. I also told them that I didn't know who started the fight, that it could have been me. We were both angry, both irrational, and we both wanted to lash out at the other.

But it was Emily they arrested, Emily they charged with attempted murder. Emily who was now in custody while the rest of us tried to pick up the pieces of what was left behind.

'I can't stop thinking that if I hadn't said anything to Emily about Jude fancying you, none of this would have happened,' Helen said, gripping on to my hand tightly and fighting back tears.

'It wasn't your fault,' I told her, because it was true. I wasn't sure whose fault it was. Emily was the obvious culprit of course, but Mystic Maggie had taken the bribe and spoken the words that sent me into an eventual spiral. Yet I was the one who had allowed it take over my life, and to this day, I still don't know why my paranoia managed to override my reasoning.

But it had happened, there was nothing I could do to change the past. Now I had to find a way to move forward, towards a future which I finally realised wasn't written in the stars.

'I wish you'd told me,' Helen said. 'We could have sorted this out years ago.'

'I wish I'd told you too. And Jude.'

Jude was a mess. He blamed himself for not realising Emily's intentions. For not telling me about her in the first place because he had thought their fleeting relationship irrelevant. For letting her come between us like she had. Masquerading as a well-meaning friend, she had been slowly planting seeds of doubt in his mind about me and he had let her do it because he was struggling to rationalise my increasingly erratic and controlling behaviour. And, he admitted later, he had allowed his own insecurities to fester, convincing himself that I was lying about Tom, which Emily had seized upon and used as ammunition against me. Emily had failed in her attempts to warn me off Jude, but she had almost succeeded in warning him off me.

'I'm sorry,' he kept saying, over again. 'I'm just so sorry, Simmy.'

He had started calling me Simmy again. It made me smile to hear it, despite everything that had happened. Perhaps I should be angry with him, and maybe that anger would come at some point in the future as I processed what had happened to us and how he had failed to stand by me when I needed him the most. But I had pushed him away too, I had lied to him about what was going on, and I accepted my part of the blame. We were both sorry and we both wanted to fix this. For better or for worse, we'd said to each other on our wedding day. We'd certainly been through the worst now and I hoped that we'd come out the other side stronger. We had to at least try, for the sake of the children as well as us.

My mother had been minding the twins while Jude visited me in the hospital. She had come to see me, though, a bouquet of flowers in one hand and a stash of magazines in the other.

'Oh, Simmy,' she'd said. 'I'm so sorry.'

Everyone was sorry. Everyone blamed themselves. Mum felt that she should have known something was wrong and tried to help me. But I'd kept her at arm's length for months, making excuses as to why we couldn't visit her, or she couldn't come and stay. I had known that I wouldn't be able to hide my breakdown from her and so I had pushed her away too.

But they had all come together for me now. Helen, Jude, Mum. Shiv was flying over from the States that evening. Even some of the new school mums that I'd avoided had sent cards and flowers, sending their best wishes and offering to help with childcare if we needed it. Everyone wanted me to get better, but the most important thing was that I did too.

Emily had fractured my skull, so I had to stay in hospital for observation. But in all those long, boring hours I spent in bed, I didn't once check Find My, I didn't call Jude, I didn't search for funfairs, and I didn't doom-scroll childhood illnesses either. In fact, I avoided the internet completely because I didn't want to read about Emily in the news. I looked at photos of the children on my phone, I read the magazines that Mum had brought and I spoke with a psychologist. 'I need some help,' I told her. If only I'd said those four words sooner.

When I was finally discharged, Jude drove me home and the twins were waiting for me at the front door with Mum. In my absence, Jude had moved them all back in.

'Remember you've got to take it easy,' he warned me. 'No acrobatics with the twins.'

'I know. I'm just happy to be home.'

Conversely, despite what had happened and my narrow escape with death, I was no longer afraid of the world. It was like someone had flicked a switch in my head and I finally understood that life wasn't full of danger, it was full of possibilities. I wanted to make the most of it, to live it again, because I'd already lost too much time. I'd suggested to Jude that we book a holiday for the February half-term, talked about repainting the twins' bedroom, and I wanted to write again.

'Woah, steady on, Simmy, let's just take one day at a time,' he'd replied.

He was right, of course. My first step had been coming home. My next would be recovering, both physically and mentally. After that, who knew? But I was ready to find out.

I spent the first few days resting and getting my strength back.

But I got showered and dressed every morning because I knew it was important to have structure in my day and for the twins to see me up and about. I greeted them with open arms as soon as they got home from school and I made their dinner and sat with them as they ate, asking about their days.

On my third day home from hospital, I had an unexpected visitor. Lucy, Tom's ex, came to see me. She appeared on my doorstep with two coffees and a smile, and while she didn't know the whole story, the North London mum rumour-mill had given her some of the basics.

'How are you doing?' she'd asked.

'I'm okay,' I said truthfully. 'A little bruised and battered, but okay.'

We talked for a while. She told me that Tom had been in touch, wanting to see Camille. She'd agreed, because he was her father, but that she refused to let him back in her life.

'And how do you feel?' I asked her.

She had smiled at me then, her young, pretty face open and happy. 'I feel free.'

That was how I felt too. Free from the burden of the horror story I'd been living in. Free to see clearly again for the first time in ages. I was still afraid of what had happened to me, what I had allowed myself to become, and I was fearful that it might happen again. Sometimes I had nightmares where Emily was on top of me, but in my dreams, Helen didn't appear to save me and Emily kept pummelling me until I woke up, in a cold sweat, convinced I was dead. The moment I came to, I always felt Jude's arms around me, holding me close, and slowly I remembered that I was safe again. Emily couldn't hurt me any more and nor could my own invasive thoughts, because I wasn't going to let them. Mystic Maggie was a fraud, a woman who had ruined my life for twenty pounds, and I had let her. Never again would I be so gullible.

On the fifth day, Mark appeared, his eyes red-rimmed, his face gaunt. He was clutching a box of chocolates and he looked like a rabbit caught in the headlights.

'How are you?' I asked him, giving him a hug.

'I'm so sorry, Simone.' I could feel his shoulders shaking in my arms.

'Me too, Mark.'

We were both victims in this, but in some ways it was harder for Mark than it was for me. We had both been betrayed, but I still had my family to go back to.

'Have you been to see Emily?' I asked.

He shook his head. 'No. I can't bring myself to do it. Maybe one day, but not yet.'

'I understand.'

'I just don't get how she could do this. Any of it. All these years we were together and I never suspected a thing. I must be so stupid.'

'It was the same for all of us, Mark. We all saw Emily the way you did. You mustn't beat yourself up about it.' I winced at my careless choice of words. 'What I mean is, Emily is responsible for what she did, not you. And now you have to rebuild your life again.'

'Is that what you're going to do?'

I smiled as I looked at him. 'Yes, Mark. That's exactly what I'm going to do.'

I didn't know what would happen next because no one's life can be seen through a crystal ball. There are too many twists, too many surprises. Life is unpredictable and sometimes that can be terrifying, but other times it's wonderful because you can make it your own. You can't control everything that happens to you, but you do have a say in how you respond, which path you take.

The trees on our street and in the park were bare now, the

frosty ground hard beneath our feet. Our surroundings had transformed into the grey palette of winter, and it would be months before the flowers started to bloom again. But to me, the world had never seemed so full of colour. Soon it would be Christmas and we would decorate our tree and wrap presents for Ivy and Sam. We would wake up together and I would be grateful for the family I had almost lost.

After that it would be a new year, our sixth year of marriage, and I no longer needed to look for danger. I would make friends with the school mums, I would take the twins to parties and play dates. I would talk more to Jude and write again. I would embrace the life that I had been given.

I had nearly died, and yet I was no longer afraid.

EPILOGUE

The twins raced around the garden, squealing as they were chased by their school friends. I watched them from the kitchen window and smiled when I saw the innocent joy on their faces, which were shiny and flushed from the cold fresh air.

It was late February, too cold to linger outside for long, but it was a sunny Saturday afternoon and we'd decided at the last minute to invite some people round. Jude and Helen had gone out to stock up on beer and snacks while I stayed at home to greet the first arrivals. There were a couple of families I'd met through the school and Mum was there too, chatting with a new friend of mine whose daughter had become close with Ivy. Mark was hovering in the corner with an orange juice in his hand, looking awkward, and I looked over my shoulder and gave him a reassuring smile. I'd made an effort to keep in touch with Mark and although I knew that Jude struggled to understand why I would want a reminder of Emily in our lives, he'd accepted it without question because he didn't have to get it, he just had to know that it was important to me.

Emily. I tried not to dwell on her too much. I'd talked it over with my counsellor, who I went to see every week. She had helped me to understand that my intrusive thoughts didn't need to dictate my life. I still thought of Mystic Maggie and sometimes, when I was feeling anxious, I called Jude just to check in on him. He always answered within two rings. But it didn't happen four times a day and these were habits which would take time to break. I had to be patient.

Feeling sorry for Mark, who was on his own, I wandered over to him. 'How's it going?'

'Yeah, okay. I've found someone to rent the house, so I'll be moving out in a couple of weeks.'

Until Mark finalised his divorce with Emily, he couldn't sell the house, but he didn't want to live there any more, not after what had happened in it. He was moving to Manchester, to be closer to his parents, and I hoped the distance would bring him peace.

'I went to see Emily,' he began hesitatingly.

I felt a familiar lurch in my stomach. 'How did it go?'

'It was weird to be honest, but I felt like I had to see her one last time, for closure I guess.'

'How was she?' I was genuinely curious.

'She didn't say much at first. But then she suddenly started talking nonsense and I couldn't make neither head nor tail of it. In the end, I didn't stay very long.'

I frowned. 'What was she saying?'

Mark looked uncertain. 'Are you sure you want to talk about this?'

I nodded, even though I wasn't sure. 'Yes.'

'She kept banging on about that fortune teller, about how she'd lied.'

But I already knew that. She'd lied because Emily had paid her to, which Helen had explained to the police when she went to the station to give her statement.

Mark wasn't finished though. 'She was saying something like how she'd only paid her to tell you that a man was going to ask you out, but that you should say no. She claimed that she didn't have anything to do with the rest of her prediction.'

I could feel my hands beginning to shake, my senses becoming overloaded, but I closed my eyes and breathed steadily, remembering what the counsellor had said. *They're just thoughts, just feelings, they can't hurt you. They can't control you.* Then I opened my eyes again and looked at Mark.

'Maybe she's confused.'

'Yes, I think she was,' Mark said quickly. 'I don't think she really remembers the events as they happened. Perhaps it's some sort of emotional trauma or self-defence mechanism.'

Mum had drifted over and was listening in to our conversation. I turned to her and I could tell that she understood how I was feeling.

'Let it go,' she said quietly. 'Let it go, Simmy.'

Mark looked stricken. 'I'm sorry, I shouldn't have said anything.'

But I smiled at him. 'It's okay, Mark, don't worry.'

I walked away from him then and Mum followed me. 'You okay?'

'I'm fine.'

'It's me you're talking to, Simmy.'

I looked her straight in the eye. 'I'm fine, Mum, really I am.'

And I was. Mental illness didn't just disappear overnight, it took time to heal, but I *was* healing, I was becoming stronger and more resilient every day and I wasn't going to let Emily, or the crazy ramblings of a fortune teller, derail my recovery. I wasn't going back into the tunnel again.

The children had come inside now and were hovering by the table, looking for snacks. I hoped that Jude wouldn't be too much longer or we'd have a mutiny on our hands. Things between the two of us were much better. We would never go back to how we were before, when our lives were easy and uncomplicated, but we were finding new ground, learning to trust each other again and to be honest about how we were feeling. I knew Jude still felt terrible about what had happened, but I didn't blame him. I didn't blame myself any more either. All I wanted was for us to be a team again and with every day that passed, it felt more like we were.

The kids had started singing a song they'd learned for a school assembly and as their group bravado grew, so did the volume, until they were all yelling at the tops of their voices. I watched them and laughed, enjoying the sight of Ivy and Sam surrounded by their friends, living the life they deserved, being the happy, carefree children they should be.

A school mum friend came over to chat. 'I'm so pleased that Ivy and Sam can make Mary's party next weekend.'

'Oh, they wouldn't miss it for the world. It's all they can talk about.'

'Well, if we're lucky, we might get another rendition of this delightful song.'

We laughed together, enjoying the shared moment of pride as our horrendously out-of-tune offspring lived their best lives. I was still laughing when the doorbell rang and I went to answer it, wiping my hands on a tea towel, ready to chastise Jude for forgetting his keys. Even when I saw two uniformed police officers standing on the doorstep, the smile didn't leave my face.

'Can I help you?'

'Mrs Pearce?'

'Yes, that's me.' I could still hear the children in the background and I wondered if our grumpy neighbour had made a complaint about the noise. But at the back of my mind a thought was developing and quickly becoming stronger and overpowering.

That's not why they're here. Old habits take time to get rid of. Compulsions can return as quick as a flash.

'May we come in, Mrs Pearce?'

I ushered them into the hallway, the smile frozen on my face, my heart beginning to pound. I saw Mum appear, her eyes widening when she spotted the two officers. When I saw the concern on her face, I think it was then that I really began to unravel. *Deep breaths, deep breaths.*

'Is this about Emily?' I asked.

I saw the perplexed look on the officers' faces and knew in an instant that it wasn't. Jude should have been back by now and yet he wasn't. I hadn't thought to call or check on him, I'd been too busy having fun. I'd let myself get distracted. I fell back against the staircase, my legs threatening to give way beneath me, and Mum rushed to my side, gripping my hand tightly. 'What is it? What's happened?' she asked the officers.

But I already knew. I'd always known, hadn't I? You can run but you can't hide. It didn't matter what I did, what I said, how many times I visited a counsellor and dissected my darkest fears. How much I convinced myself that my thoughts weren't real, that they couldn't harm anyone. It didn't matter how many times I googled health conditions, called Jude or checked his location. Some things are just out of your control and there's nothing you can do about it.

The officer looked at me solemnly. 'I'm so sorry, Mrs Pearce. There's been a car accident.'

'It's Jude,' I said. 'He's dead.'

'No!' Mum gasped.

I looked at the officer, waiting for her to confirm what I already knew. Waiting for her to utter the words that would destroy my life forever. But then I frowned. Something about her expression told me that I was wrong. Hope soared inside me as I realised that Jude was still alive, that I had, yet again, jumped to the wrong conclusion. But if Jude was okay, then why were they here? The police didn't just turn up on your doorstep for no good reason.

And then it finally hit me, as though Emily had struck me with the pyramid all over again. I'd got this wrong from the very beginning. It was so clear to me now that I almost laughed, not with triumph at my realisation but with horror because I'd worked out how this ended.

'You're my person.' She had said it to me so many times. I was the one she could rely on, the closest thing she had to family, her named next of kin. But I'd let her down. And I knew that whatever people told me later, no matter how much they tried to convince me that it was a tragic accident and that it wasn't anyone's fault, they were wrong. When I chose to marry Jude, I had sealed her fate. Because if I hadn't, she would never have been in the car with him.

'Your husband is okay,' the officer said. 'It's your friend, Helen.'

ACKNOWLEDGEMENTS

Every novel I write takes me on a new journey, but this one has definitely been the biggest road trip so far. It took over my life but in the best possible way, and I've met so many wonderful people en route who have helped me to reach my destination.

This is my first novel with Boldwood Books and I'm so proud to be one of their authors. Thank you to my editor, Isobel Akenhead, for believing in my writing and for making me part of Team Boldwood. Your support, expertise and advice, which you generously gave before I'd even started writing this book, undoubtedly made it what it is. And to the rest of the Boldwood team for your wonderfully warm welcome, I'm so excited to be working with you all.

To my fabulous fellow author and friend, Keri Beevis, who gave me words of encouragement when I needed them the most and has been a fount of knowledge, advice and support over the past year.

Thank you to my sister Zoe who reads all my manuscripts and always gives me such brilliant feedback. And to Barry Clark, who I have a terrible habit of accosting at family gatherings to ask him about police procedure. I love how you always answer my questions with wisdom and humour! And a big shout-out to my family, Jon, Rose and Alice. Writing a novel is a rollercoaster and you've had to ride it with me. Thank you for your love and support, and I'm sorry for what I said when I was grumpy/hungry/out on submission. Oh, and also for that holiday to Norfolk when I basically ignored you for five days because I was head down in the first draft.

To my incredible friends, who buy, read and share all of my books. You know who you are and I love you. This is my fifth novel and yet your enthusiasm is as strong, and even more appreciated by me, as much now as it was when I released my debut.

And finally, to all my readers. I hope you enjoyed reading this as much as I enjoyed writing it. By reading my books, you've given me the opportunity to keep writing and I am eternally grateful.

ABOUT THE AUTHOR

Natasha Boydell writes internationally bestselling psychological suspense stories. Her debut, The Missing Husband, was an Amazon Kindle UK top 100 bestseller in 2021. She previously worked as a journalist and in communications in the charity and education sectors before pursuing her lifelong dream of writing novels. She lives in North London, with her husband, two daughters and two rescue cats.

Sign up to Natasha Boydell's mailing list for news, competitions and updates on future books.

Follow Natasha on social media:

- facebook.com/NatashaBoydellAuthor
- x.com/tashboydell
- bookbub.com/authors/natasha-boydell
- instagram.com/tashy_boydell
- tiktok.com/@natasha_boydell

Milton Keynes UK
Ingram Content Group UK Ltd.
UKHW041625310724
446328UK00001B/13

9 781835 333020